FALLING FOR A FRENCH DREAM

JENNIFER BOHNET

Boldwood

First published in Great Britain in 2021 by Boldwood Books Ltd.

Copyright © Jennifer Bohnet, 2021

Cover Design by Debbie Clement Design

Cover Photography: Shutterstock

A CIP catalogue record for this book is available from the British Library.

Paperback ISBN 978-1-80162-266-0

Large Print ISBN 978-1-80162-261-5

Hardback ISBN 978-1-80162-260-8

Ebook ISBN 978-1-80162-258-5

Kindle ISBN 978-1-80162-259-2

Audio CD ISBN 978-1-80162-264-6

MP3 CD ISBN 978-1-80162-263-9

Digital audio download ISBN 978-1-80162-257-8

Boldwood Books Ltd
23 Bowerdean Street
London SW6 3TN
www.boldwoodbooks.com

For Richard with love. (JOACHIM)

1

The letter landed on the doormat the first Saturday after New Year, sandwiched between the final telephone demand and the usual junk mail. Bending down to pick it all up, Nicola Jacques saw the French stamps on the envelope and frowned. She threw the junk mail in the bin, put the telephone bill on the kitchen table to deal with later and thoughtfully studied the envelope. Written in Henri Jacques' distinctive handwriting, it was addressed to '*Mme Nicola Jacques*' and not to Oliver, her son and Henri's grandson, which was unusual. Her limited communications with the French family had always been between her, Aunt Odette or Aunt Josephine, Henri's unmarried twin sisters. An unexpected letter from Henri himself could only mean one thing: bad news. Slowly, Nicola opened the envelope and took the letter out. Hadn't the world thrown enough trouble at her in recent years?

Chère Nicola,
Tu will come to La Prouveresse immédiatement. We have

matters d'urgence to discuss. Marc's things to settle. Tu will
bring Olivier.
Regards, Henri.

The letter with its clipped English sentences and ad-hoc
French words conjured up an immediate picture of her ex-father-
in-law. Old-fashioned almost to the point of eccentricity, she
knew he'd never change his view of the way the world should be.
He wrote English the same way as he spoke it – short and sharp
with no regard for grammar. And with little regard for other
people's feelings either. Whatever lay behind this order to visit,
Henri would have disregarded both her thoughts and Oliver's as
being of no concern of his and of no consequence. He'd simply
decided their presence was needed in France so the command
had been issued.

Nicola placed a coffee pod in the machine, pressed the button
and stood gazing thoughtfully out of the kitchen window as the
machine squirted coffee into the cup. What lay behind this unexpected demand? Was Henri feeling guilty about his treatment of
her and Oliver over the past years? Did he want to make amends
somehow? Whatever it was, it made no difference. There was no
way she was going to France simply because Henri commanded
it. She and Oliver would go together one day, when Oliver was
older and could understand why things were the way they were.
For now she had to protect Oliver and lead her own life as best
she could. Albeit a different life to the one she'd known during
the years when she'd been married to Marc Jacques, Henri's
only son.

'Morning, Mum,' Oliver's voice jolted her out of her thoughts.

Oliver rubbed the sleep from his eyes before moving across
and kissing her on both cheeks. Before it had all gone wrong,
Marc had always greeted her like that every morning and as a

small boy Oliver had determinedly copied his daddy. These days, it was still a natural part of thirteen-year-old Oliver's morning routine. One that Nicola cherished and hoped would continue forever.

'Want some toast?' Oliver asked, slotting two slices of bread into the machine.

'Not right now, thanks.'

'Who's the letter from?'

'Papa Henri.' Nicola hesitated before pushing the letter across the table to him and waiting silently while he read it.

'Any idea why he wants us to go?' Oliver asked, looking up at her.

Nicola shook her head. 'No.'

'Are we going?'

'No, we are not. Papa Henri has no right to make a demand like that.' Her words fell into a tense silence as Oliver looked at her.

'Actually, Mum...' Oliver hesitated. 'I wouldn't mind going. Not because Papa Henri has demanded it, but...' he gazed at Nicola sadly. 'Before he... he died, Dad was talking of taking me later this year, when he was between jobs, and I'd like to see where he grew up. Maybe get to know Papa Henri a little bit better.'

Nicola was silent, looking at Oliver in surprise. In the thirteen years since Oliver had been born, because of the feud between father and son, they'd been to visit Marc's family just twice. Once, when Oliver was a new baby to show him off to his French family and again just before his fifth birthday. Had Marc been beginning to perhaps regret the ongoing feud that had caused the estrangement from his family? If he had, he'd certainly not mentioned it to her. As for the possibility of taking Oliver to France to get to know his relatives, that again was something never talked about.

'I didn't know Dad was planning to take you – he never mentioned it to me.'

'I asked him if he'd take me and he said, maybe.'

Nicola gave a wry smile. A 'maybe' to Oliver meant that if he kept asking he'd eventually get a 'yes' to whatever it was he wanted.

The toast popped up out of the toaster at that moment and Oliver grabbed both slices and started to butter them, while Nicola watched him, lost in her thoughts. Had Marc been planning on taking Oliver to the family farm this year? She smothered a sigh. There was no way of knowing the answer to that question. Marc's tragic death three months ago had left both Oliver and her reeling. Perhaps a visit would be good. Allow Oliver to grieve and accept the loss of his father in the place where Marc had been born and spent his early life.

'Mum, are you okay? You were miles away.'

'I'm fine, just thinking.' Nicola pinched a piece of toast from the plate. Playfully, Oliver smacked her hand before putting another two pieces of bread in the machine. 'So you'd like to visit Papa Henri?'

'Yep. Half-term in France would be cool.'

Nicola looked at her son and sighed. 'I know he's always remembered your birthday and sends you a present at Christmas, but don't expect him to be a storybook grandfather, will you? If he was, he wouldn't have shut your dad or you out of his life for so long. I have a feeling that there is more to this sudden demand to visit than a simple desire to be reconciled with us.' She remembered the two occasions she'd travelled to France with Marc, hoping for a reconciliation between father and son, only to be disappointed. Whilst she understood Marc's need to live his life away from a domineering father she'd always secretly hoped that time and absence from the family would have softened both men's attitude and they would be reunited.

Oliver shrugged. 'So what. It's only a visit. I know I probably won't be the grandson he wants. Besides, it's not just him, is it? There's the aunts as well.'

Mention of the aunts made Nicola smile. They'd all had fun together on the couple of occasions they'd met. And both the women on that first visit had cuddled baby Oliver at every opportunity.

'Okay,' she said. 'I'll write and tell Papa Henri we can't come "immédiatement" as he demands, but we will go to France at February half-term.'

A car horn tooted outside.

'Your lift to football practice is here,' Nicola said. 'You got everything?'

'Kit's in the hall.' Oliver grabbed a final piece of toast. 'See you later.'

Nicola winced as the front door banged behind him.

Crossing over to the machine she made herself another coffee. Thankfully, she wasn't due back at the garden centre where she worked until next Monday, she needed time to assimilate this sudden, disturbing appearance of the past into their lives. Returning to France, spending time with Marc's family without him would, Nicola knew, feel strange. The aunts were sure to welcome Oliver and her with hugs and cries of delight, but Henri? Henri had always been polite but reserved with her, behaving like a distant relative who didn't know her quite well enough to treat her with familiarity. How would he treat her now that, technically at least, she was no longer a member of the Jacques family?

2

Wandering into the sitting room to sit and drink her coffee, Nicola paused by the small table with its table lamp and three silver framed photos. One was a family photo of the three of them taken a year ago that had turned out to be the last Christmas with Marc. Another photograph was of Marc and Oliver in wetsuits holding windsurfing boards and both of them were smiling broadly. Taken at Easter last year when Marc had signed the two of them up for a three-day course. Nicola bit her lip as she looked at it – nine months ago nobody had any idea of the tragedy about to engulf them. The third photograph was a windswept one of her and Marc taken by friends as they climbed a Dartmoor tor during the early days of their marriage.

Marc was already living and working in the UK when they met. Nicola, who loved browsing in any charity shop she came across, had wandered into her local Oxfam in search of a summer skirt, not expecting to find her future husband among the bric-a-brac and second-hand goods. Audrey, the volunteer behind the till, recognised her as a regular and smiled her welcome as Nicola walked in but didn't break off listening to the tall man at her side who was patiently explaining some process of the shiny new till on the counter.

Registering the man's attractive foreign accent as she walked past, Nicola guessed that with his olive skin he came from the Mediterranean area – France or maybe Italy. Probably France, she decided, trying to listen discreetly. His accent, while lovely to listen to, didn't have that animated note to it that native Italians tended to have whatever language they were speaking. Ten minutes later, when she approached the desk with not only a skirt but also a top, it was the man who stepped forward to serve her, glancing at the volunteer as he did.

'Audrey, she has something she like to say to you,' he said as he put Nicola's purchases in a bag and rang the money into the till.

Nicola looked at Audrey who was trying not to laugh.

'Nicola, may I introduce you to Marc Jacques, the newly appointed Facilitator for Oxfam in the West Country.'

'Pleased to meet you,' Nicola said, wondering what was going on between the two of them. 'So what exactly is it you facilitate?'

'Basically, I look after all the branches in the West Country and make sure they are operating as efficiently as possible.' The shrug he gave was definitely a Gallic one. 'It means wearing a lot of different hats.'

'He's very good at it all too,' Audrey said.

'I am about to take a short break for a coffee in the café across the road,' Marc said. 'And as we have now been formally intro-duced, I'm hoping you will join me.'

A burst of laughter escaped from Nicola.

'He's a very nice man,' Audrey whispered. 'Do go.'

'I'd love to,' Nicola said.

And that was how it all began.

The one thing Nicola had difficulty coming to terms with, was

Marc's estrangement from his family. Her own parents had died
when she was a teenager, leaving a huge gap in her life and she
couldn't understand Marc's continued acceptance of the family
rift. When she mentioned sending a wedding invitation to Henri,
Marc's reaction was a swift, 'No. He won't come.' It was only after
Oliver's birth that Marc finally took her to meet his family.

She'd realised early on in their relationship though, that Marc
was a man with boundless energy and a deep desire to help
people and make a difference to their lives if he could. He was
also a man who craved excitement and abhorred the dull day-to-
day routine of ordinary life. He was always urging Nicola to be
more spontaneous, wanting her to drop everything and join him.
He'd suggest a day at the seaside when they should both be
working or suddenly start to paint the kitchen sunshine yellow
one evening without warning because it was too dull.

One amazing night, he persuaded her to join him skinny
dipping at midnight at a secluded pond in a local park. The
memory of that long-ago event would live on forever in Nicola's
heart. The fact that Marc was one of the kindest people she'd ever
met, was fun to be with and she loved him more than she'd ever
thought possible, made the early years of their marriage when it
was just the two of them a delight. From time to time, though,
Nicola would protest about the lack of routine in Marc's life. Her
words 'It's routine that pays the bills' were always met with that
Gallic shrug and a smile.

But then Oliver was born and Nicola's own hard-won spontaneity was buried by necessity under the responsibility of moth-
erhood. Fatherhood changed Marc too. Oh, he still railed against
the boredom of a routine, but he was devoted to Oliver and
helped look after him. As Oliver grew older and went to
playschool and then into reception for primary school, Nicola
sensed that Marc was becoming increasingly disenchanted with

the way his life had developed a routine. He'd escaped from what he regarded as a rut on the family farm in France, only to settle in England and become frustrated with the life he found himself living.

Sitting there, she let her thoughts drift back to that last visit the three of them had made to 'La Prouveresse', the olive farm nestling in the hills behind Nice that had been in Marc's family for generations. At the time of the visit, Nicola had hoped grievances would be put aside and that family visits would finally become a regular feature in their lives, that Marc would be reconciled with his father, their differences forgotten.

But nothing had changed by the time their short holiday was over; if anything, things had worsened. As the aunts kissed them all goodbye, Henri had stayed firmly down in the vineyard, too busy apparently to stop and wish them 'Bon voyage' with his sisters. It wasn't until they were home that Nicola was told about the decision Marc had made and realised why.

It was a decision that changed the course of his life again – all their lives – and put the final seal on the rift with his father. She'd been totally unprepared for the bombshell he dropped after they arrived home from that last visit to France eight years ago...

They'd arrived home tired after a day travelling and Nicola had quickly sorted some food for them all and organised bedtime for Oliver. After reading him a bedtime story and tucking him up in bed, she went downstairs hoping that Marc had opened one of the bottles of red wine they'd brought home with them, and looking forward to spending a quiet evening together.

Marc was sat at the kitchen table sorting through the post that had arrived while they were away, a glass of wine already in front of him, one waiting for Nicola.

'I need to tell you something,' Marc said as he handed her the glass. 'You'd better sit down.'

Something in the tone of his voice alerted her to the fact that this 'something' was serious. She sat, took a sip of her wine and waited.

'I've applied for and been accepted as an organiser for another charity.' He held up his hand as Nicola smiled and went to speak. 'Wait. It's a position with Médecins Sans Frontières, which means I can expect to be sent anywhere there is a humanitarian need at a moment's notice to organise the relief aid needed on the ground. My contract starts on the first of next month.'

'It sounds like the kind of thing you've always wanted to do,' Nicola said slowly, desperately trying to get her head around this bombshell and wondering where she and Oliver fitted in to it. 'A real hands-on important job. But the first is only a few days away – what about working your notice at Oxfam?'

'I've been working my notice out for the last month,' Marc said quietly. 'They've been very supportive. The holiday in France was time I was due and I'm no longer an employee.'

Nicola stared at him as her anger started to rise. 'Marc, you're way out of order with this. Why the hell didn't you discuss these plans with me before? Surely it's a decision we should have made together?'

'Because I didn't want you to try to stop me. Selfish, I know, but this is something I want... *need* to do for me. I know your life will change when I'm not around all the time.' Marc looked at her steadily, his eyes sad. 'But it won't necessarily be all bad. I'll be home on leave every few months.'

'Is this why Henri didn't come and say goodbye properly? You told him what you were doing and, once again, he didn't approve.' Something she had in common with Henri then.

'He reacted as I expected him to,' Marc said, shrugging.

'What about Oliver? You're going to miss so much of him growing up. How do I tell him why you're not here for weeks on end?'

'You tell him the truth, that Daddy has gone to help some other less fortunate people and little children.'

'And me? How am I expected to cope with you being away?' Marc knew how much she missed him when he was away even for a few days but here he was, expecting her to cope for weeks, months, on end.

'You're a strong woman, Nicola, I know you'll cope.'

'You're not giving me any choice.' Nicola remembered rubbing her face with a trembling hand, before pushing her chair back and standing up. 'I do understand what is driving you to do this, but I wish with all my heart that you'd discussed this with me before simply going ahead,' she'd said, turning and leaving the kitchen before Marc could see the tears that were beginning to course down her cheeks.

She hadn't known it at the time, but Marc's decision to join Médecins Sans Frontières was the beginning of the crack in their marriage that would widen and widen until everything fell apart.

3

Taking a sip of her now almost cold coffee, Nicola thought about those first months after Marc had left to start his new life away from them eight years ago. A young Oliver had coped well with the new dynamic of their lives. After a nightly bedtime, 'I wish Daddy was here,' for a few weeks, he'd settled down into their new routine. Nicola had tried to make everyday life as normal as possible for Oliver as she struggled to adapt to coping with the strangeness of being alone. Together they looked forward to the times when Marc came home on leave and they were a family again.

Nicola did grow accustomed to her strange lifestyle – a single mum for several months and then Marc would return home and become the head of the family again for a few weeks.

The next devastating shock came a year or two later.

Marc, arriving home for a few weeks, elected to sleep in the spare bedroom – and told Nicola he wanted a divorce.

In vain, Nicola had protested. 'I don't want a divorce. Why can't we just let things stay as they are? Okay, it's not ideal, but it's worked for us since you joined Médecins Sans Frontières.'

Marc had shaken his head sadly. 'Nicola, you are a great mother to Oliver and I know you would like more children, but I'm no use as a father or a husband, living the way I do. It isn't fair on either of you. I love you, so it is better I let you go. Let you be free to meet someone else.'

Nicola had stared at him in disbelief. She'd thought they were happy. Their lifestyle was a little strange, but it worked. She still loved Marc, but now he was telling her that because he loved her, he wanted a divorce. Nicola couldn't see the logic in his argument at all, but Marc was adamant and the divorce went ahead.

Afterwards, Nicola struggled sometimes to remember they weren't still married. Outwardly, everything carried on as it had before. Marc continued to work wherever in the world he was needed and at home she and Oliver got on with their daily lives – Oliver at school, Nicola at the garden centre. Whenever Marc was in the UK, he stayed with them, using the spare room as his base, so he could spend the time with Oliver.

It took Nicola a long time to recover from the hurt and the pain of the divorce. She didn't, as Marc had hoped, meet someone new and remarry. Her main concern was giving Oliver as stable a family life as she could manage under the circumstances. When Oliver was older, more independent, perhaps then she'd give some thought to her own feelings.

It was hard to believe now that so many years had passed whilst they'd lived that kind of separate, yet together, existence, since Marc had changed the pattern of their lives. How long it would have continued in the same manner if three months ago the accident hadn't happened, Nicola had no way of knowing.

Marc had been in Umbria, Italy, for just thirty-six hours, helping rescuers in the aftermath of the 6.6 magnitude earthquake that had destroyed villages and killed hundreds of people. The colleague who broke the awful news to her said that Marc had died a hero, pulling a small child out of a partially collapsed house. He'd barely handed the child over when there was a loud crack and a rumble and, before he could move, the rest of the house started to give way, a large stone falling and hitting Marc unconscious before the rest of the building buried him in debris. He died before they could get him out.

Sighing, Nicola stood up, took her coffee cup into the kitchen and began to clear the breakfast things away. Marc's absence from everyday involvement in her life for so long had certainly cushioned the initial impact of his death for her, but she still felt bereft and sad for Oliver's loss. It hadn't helped that, as Marc was a French citizen and because of the divorce, she was no longer shown as next of kin. His body had been flown back to France for Henri to deal with.

When Nicola had telephoned the farm to ask about the funeral arrangements so she could book flights for herself and Oliver, a tearful Odette had answered. Within twenty-four hours of Marc's body arriving back on French soil he'd been cremated.

'Henri's decision,' Odette had said. 'He wanted it all dealt with tout suite. Claimed it made no sense to extend the misery.'

Nicola remembered sighing at Odette's words. So neither she nor Oliver had been given the chance to say that final, important goodbye.

As she stood there deep in her thoughts, she noticed that the sunlight pouring in through the window was highlighting the dust particles floating in the air above the cooker. The place could do with decorating, she realised, the paintwork was faded, the kitchen units old-fashioned. The large map of the world that Marc had pinned on the back of the larder door before his very first contract in Japan so that Oliver could see which part of the world he was in was curling around the edges, still with numerous pins dotted over its surface. In the beginning, Nicola had hated looking at it, but Oliver had asked her to leave it.

'I still like to look at it. See all the places where Dad had been helping people. Besides, the kitchen wouldn't be the same without it,' he'd said.

Nicola sighed. For the last few years, the need to keep the kitchen, the house itself updated, had been the least of her worries. Now she had another worry – what exactly lay behind Henri's invitation to visit? Only one way to find out. She'd phone the farm and ask the aunts before she wrote to Henri.

Her fingers were crossed as she listened to the ringing tone. Hopefully Henri would be busy outside with farm work.

To Nicola's relief, it was Aunt Josephine who answered the phone and was thrilled to hear from her. After the usual pleasantries, Nicola took a deep breath.

'Henri's written to me demanding I bring Oliver over immediately. D'you know why?'

'Trust my brother not to tell you the reason he wants you both here.' There was a short pause. 'Henri, he feels it's time to scatter Marc's ashes on the farm. Odette and I tell him you and Oliver should be here, he is Marc's son after all, and you were Marc's wife.'

Nicola was silent. She hadn't anticipated that. There was no way she could refuse to go and turn down the unexpected opportunity of saying a final goodbye to Marc. Oliver, especially, needed closure.

'Will you come?' Josephine asked quietly.

'Yes. But I can't come until the February half-term because of school and work commitments. Henri probably wants it to happen before then.'

'Half-term week it is,' Josephine said. 'I will tell Henri that it is arranged. He will have to wait.' Pressing the disconnect button, Nicola couldn't help wondering how Henri would react to his plans being put on hold. One thing was certain, he was sure to blame her for the delay.

4

Josephine Jacques smoothed the quilt over the freshly made-up bed. She'd used the best linen for Nicola. Linen that she'd washed and dried the old-fashioned way across a bed of wild herbs before folding it carefully and placing it in the old armoire. Now, as the smell of lavender and rosemary wafted through the room, she could scarcely believe this longed-for visit was about to happen.

Glancing out through the small window set high in the eaves, Josephine could see Henri walking slowly along the old olive grove terrace at the back of the farm. Twenty hectares of olive trees to the south of the house now grew La Prouveresse's commercial crop, but Henri maintained that this small terrace planted by their great-great-grandfather still bore the best olives. Only oil from those particular olives was ever used in their kitchen.

Josephine watched her brother for a few moments. He'd visibly aged in the last year. The shock and grief of losing Marc had hit them all hard, but it had hit Henri the hardest. Yet at sixty-six, there was still something lingering in the set of his shoulders,

the way he walked, that reminded her of the large-hearted boy
he'd been when they were all growing up. He'd been a great practical joker and had delighted in catching out his younger twin
sisters, but never in a malicious way. He was always the first to
shoulder the responsibility when things went wrong and protect
his sisters.

She remembered too, how ambitious Henri had been in those
far-off days. Henri Jacques was going to be someone and something when he grew up. The most famous saxophone player in
the world was top of the list. But when his father insisted that, as
the only son, it was his duty to take over the farm and look after
his sisters, Henri had had to give up all his dreams of pursuing a
life away from the farm. Years later, he'd never understood, or
come to terms with, his own son's refusal to even contemplate a
life on the farm. Josephine remembered the family rows as Marc
grew older and Henri expected him to take on some of the
responsibility.

'The farm is your birthright. I had to stay. What's so different
for you?'

'I am sorry, but it's not the life I want. You, of all people,
should understand that.'

In vain, Henri had told him, 'Only lucky people or fools get to
live the life they want. The rest of us compromise.'

Bernadette, Marc's mother, had been the peacemaker
between them, telling Henri he couldn't keep Marc a prisoner.
That things had altered during the last century, changing the
world in the twenty-first century into a different place, with more
opportunities for those who wanted to see the world. Once he'd
seen some of it, Marc might well be back. Reluctantly, Henri had
finally agreed to Marc spending a year travelling, on the condition that when the twelve months were up he would return to
work on the farm.

When Bernadette died shortly after Marc's nineteenth birthday and he returned for her funeral, Henri insisted that Marc stayed.

Within six months, Marc had said he couldn't take any more. The strict boundaries of his life were smothering him.

The last bitter row escalated into a slanging match, with Henri finally shouting, 'If you don't stay and do your duty, I'll cut you off.'

Marc had sighed. 'Papa, I'm truly sorry and that is your decision to make, which I must respect, as you must respect mine – I can't stay.' The next day he'd gone.

It had been ten years before he returned, bringing Nicola and baby Oliver to La Prouveresse to meet them all for the first time. A short holiday that had soothed some of the old hurts away but failed to heal the rift.

Josephine knew that for over twenty years Henri had been living with the hope that Marc would one day regret leaving the farm and return for good. Then a catastrophe in a foreign country had finally killed Henri's dream.

Watching as Henri reached the end of the olive terrace and half jumped, half slithered down the jutting-out rocks that served as steps back to level ground, Josephine prayed Nicola and Oliver's visit would be the beginning of a new chapter in all their lives. A time when she, Odette, and hopefully Henri, could put the past behind them and create a proper family bond between the five of them,

Making a mental note to place a fresh vase of flowers on the dressing table the day Nicola and Oliver arrived, she closed the bedroom shutters before she hurried downstairs to make Henri's morning coffee.

'Ça va?' she asked automatically as he opened the kitchen door.

'Oui,' Henri answered, wiping the mud off his boots on the old olive oil filter that served as a back doormat.

Josephine poured his coffee before saying, 'Just think, one more day and Nicola and Oliver will be here. I find it hard to believe they are coming.'

Henri looked at her, irritated. 'Taken them long enough. Can't for the life of me see why they didn't come when they got my letter.'

Josephine gave an exasperated sigh. 'Why do you always have to be so belligerent, Henri? You know why they couldn't come before. Nicola works and Oliver has school. It had to be this half-term. Besides, you should think yourself lucky they're coming at all. I wish it wasn't for the sad reason it is, but...' Josephine shrugged. 'Personally, I wouldn't have been surprised if Nicola had refused. She must be wondering what sort of reception she's likely to get after all this time.'

Henri shrugged his shoulders but didn't answer his sister.

'Please, for all our sakes, be gentle with Nicola and Oliver when they get here. They have both been through so much and have always stood by Marc and his pursuit of happiness.' Josephine paused. 'I've made up the bed in Marc's old room for Oliver. And before you say anything, it's about time that room was used again.'

Henri looked at Josephine, his face expressionless as she continued.

'When Nicola and Oliver leave, I'm thinking of turning it into a sewing room.'

'We'll see about that,' Henri said and he opened his *Nice Matin* newspaper to the sports page, effectively shutting out his sister and daring her to disturb him.

Josephine sighed and fetched her workbox from the dresser.

Ten minutes with the crochet hook as she drank her coffee would serve to calm her down.

They both glanced up as Odette opened the kitchen door, Josephine with a smile of welcome on her face for her sister and Henri in irritation as the draught rustled his paper.

'Busy down in the market this morning?' Josephine asked, getting up to pour her sister a coffee.

'Normal crowd, although there were a few strangers, early tourists I think.' Odette glanced in Henri's direction as she started to put the shopping away. 'Sylvie says you haven't forgotten you're taking her out tonight, have you?'

'Non,' Henri answered irritably as he stood up. 'Although why I need another woman bossing me around when I've got you two is beyond me. I'm off to the barn to check the sheep,' and the door banged behind him.

Josephine and Odette looked at each and smiled. They'd both agreed years ago that their friend Sylvie Traille, widow, mother and grandmother, was good for Henri. It was to Sylvie that Henri had turned when the news about Marc had arrived. The twins had done their best to comfort him, but it had been Sylvie who'd stopped him drowning his sorrows in pastis every evening. Sylvie had joined with them too in persuading Henri to write and invite Nicola and Oliver to come for the scattering of Marc's ashes, even if he had failed to mention what was behind the invitation. Family unity was important to Sylvie and she'd always told Henri he was wrong not to accept Marc's decision to live a different life.

'Sylvie have anything else to say?' Josephine asked.

'Raoul's in trouble with the villagers. You know the land below us he inherited from his father's brother, Dominic, last year? Well, he's decided he wants to sell it and the village is up in arms about it. Accusing him of selling his heritage and giving newcomers and foreigners the opportunity to buy "their" inheritance. One or two are even moaning about the fact they can't get their vegetables there any more.'

Josephine laughed. 'Nobody bought any stuff from there regularly once the supermarché was built, what, five, six years ago?'

Once, the smallholding had been a thriving pépinière, the main source of plants, vegetables and fruit for the village, but now its land lay overgrown and neglected. The small cottage, empty for over a year, was in urgent need of some loving care and attention.

'I know,' Odette agreed. 'Raoul's been looking for a tenant but nobody wants to take it on. Eight hectares is too big for most people to garden, but it's not really big enough for commercial purposes. He says he's got no option but to sell. Besides, he needs the money for something else.'

'Any idea what?' Josephine asked curiously.

Odette shook her head. 'Hasn't even told his mother. Some investment he wants to make is all he's told Sylvie. He's asked her to mention the pépinière to Henri. Although why he should think Henri needs any more land is beyond me. Enough work up here for the three of us, without taking on more hectares half a kilometre down the road.'

'True,' Josephine said. 'There used to be a couple of good olive trees on that land though. And some citrus. Vines too, if I remember. Shame if it's all grubbed up and built on.'

Odette glanced at her. 'Sounds as if you'd like to save it.'

Josephine shook her head. 'Too late for me to take on something like that,' she paused. 'But I do wonder sometimes, if Henri and Sylvie were ever to get married, where you and I would go?'

5

Nicola folded Oliver's freshly ironed favourite T-shirt, unplugged the iron and carried the pile of ironing upstairs to finish packing for their holiday. Refusing to use a suitcase, Oliver had dragged one of Marc's old rucksacks out of the attic and its pockets and pouches were already filled with the essentials of Oliver's life – his iPod, a travel game, the baseball cap Marc had brought him back from Mexico after one of his missions and his camera. One of the smaller pockets held a notebook and Nicola could see the edge of a black and white photo sticking out between its pages. Nicola knew without looking it was the photo of Marc that had been on Oliver's bedside table for the last few months.

When, after her phone call with Josephine, she'd gently told Oliver the reason behind Henri's invitation to La Prouveresse and confirmed they were going at half-term, she'd seen the way he struggled to hold back the tears. He hadn't protested when she'd taken him in her arms.

'It won't be an easy occasion for either of us,' she'd said. 'But we'll get through it. We'll also try to make some happier memories for you to bring back while we're there as well.'

Oliver had sniffed. 'I wish Dad hadn't died. I miss him so much. Going to France without him seems wrong.'

Nicola, fighting back her own tears, had given him a tight hug before murmuring, 'I know, I know.'

Now, as she placed Oliver's clean T-shirts on the bed, she prayed that their visit to Marc's family home wouldn't be too traumatic an experience for his son.

Nicola heard the front door slam and called out, 'I'm upstairs in your room.'

'What's for tea?' Oliver demanded as he threw his school bag and then himself onto the bed. 'I'm starving.'

'Nothing new there then,' Nicola teased. 'Andrew's coming for supper, so I'm making spaghetti Bolognese.'

'That'll be ages,' Oliver moaned. 'Can I make a cheese sandwich NOW?'

'Finish your packing while I go downstairs and make you one.'

An hour later, as she zipped her own suitcase closed and checked the buckles on Oliver's rucksack were tight enough, Andrew arrived.

Originally Marc's friend, he'd become more and more entwined in their lives as the years went by, so much so that Nicola knew Oliver regarded him more like a big brother rather than as a friend of his father. Marc had often teased Andrew about finding himself a wife and settling down, but Andrew had simply shrugged, saying he was happy as he was. With Marc away for months at a time, he had quietly become an indispensable part of Nicola's support system, never hesitating when she asked for help, especially in those early days after Marc's death when she'd barely been able to function.

Recently though, she'd sensed a subtle difference in him. Something in his gaze when he looked at her made her suspect that his feelings towards her were changing. That he was beginning to think of her as more than a friend, which was something she knew she could never be. He was a kind, good-looking man and she was fond of him as a friend, but that was all he would ever be to her, a friend. She simply didn't see him in any other way.

Her suspicions had been aroused when the half-term visit to France had first been mooted and Andrew had offered – wanted – to go with them.

'For moral support,' he'd said. 'I don't like to think of you facing Henri alone. Marc told me how controlling he was.'

Gently, Nicola had dissuaded him. Going to France this first time with just Oliver was something she had to do alone. The thought of turning up there with another man in tow was a complication she didn't need. She was grateful when Andrew had insisted instead that he'd move in while they were away to keep an eye on the place and to look after Frisby, the cat. When she returned from this holiday in France, she would have to carefully explain and make sure that Andrew understood she would only ever like him as a friend, nothing more.

While Nicola finished organising supper, Andrew challenged Oliver to a game of computer chess.

She poured them both a glass of wine.

'You all set for tomorrow?' Andrew asked, as Nicola handed him his glass.

Nicola nodded. 'You sure you don't mind taking us to the airport early tomorrow morning? I can order a taxi.'

'Don't be silly. Of course I'm taking you. Still wish I was going with you to France.'

'I explained this was something Oliver and I had to face alone,' Nicola said, giving him a smile before he turned his attention back to the game on the computer.

* * *

Later, after supper and with Oliver in his room, Andrew pulled out the put-you-up and Nicola fetched the bedding. As they companionably made up the bed, Andrew glanced at her.

'It's going to be strange living here for a week without you and Oliver being around.' He pushed a pillow into its case and threw it onto the bed. 'Years ago, when Marc asked me to keep an eye on you while he was away, make sure you were all right and coping, I was happy to do so,' he said, hesitating. 'I didn't realise how much I would come to care for you both. Now Marc is no longer with us, I was wondering whether you could ever see me as anything other than a good friend?'

Nicola's heart sank. Damn, leaving things until she was back from France was clearly no longer an option. She concentrated on shaking the duvet into position for a moment before looking directly at Andrew and smiling.

'You're the big brother I never had, as well as my best friend. I honestly don't know how I'd have got through the past months, years, without your help.' Did her gentle words convey enough meaning for him to realise the truth? That there could never be more than a good friendship between them? She took a deep breath. 'They do say men and women can never truly have a platonic friendship, but you and I are the example that breaks the rule, aren't we?'

As the silence between them deepened, she realised Andrew was struggling to contain his words.

He looked at her sadly for several seconds before taking a deep breath and giving a resigned nod. 'You'd better get to bed and get some sleep, you and Oliver have a long day tomorrow.'

Nicola swallowed a sigh of relief. Hopefully Andrew had accepted her decision and a crisis in their friendship had been averted. When they returned from France, she'd make a determined effort to step back a little and try to keep their friendship on the even, platonic, keel it had always been for her. Andrew was a good, kind man, and there was no way she wanted to hurt him, but she had to somehow make sure that he realised that he would never replace Marc in her affections. She wasn't sure there was anybody who could do that, even after the way Marc had treated her.

6

As the plane swooped down low over the Mediterranean on its approach to land at Nice Côte d'Azur airport, Nicola caught her breath. She'd forgotten how scary the landing was here, with the sea in such close proximity to the runway. The two-hour flight from Bristol had passed pleasantly enough. Oliver, once he'd got over the excitement of take-off, had plugged his earphones in and listened to his music, while she read the inflight magazine in an effort to keep her mind off the forthcoming meeting with Henri.

This visit, however difficult it proved to be, was a way of giving both herself and Oliver closure over the death of the man they'd both loved and lost. Finding closure and moving on after the loss of a loved one was hard enough, Nicola knew from bitter experience. But without a funeral, and that final chance to say goodbye to Marc, accepting his demise was proving to be harder than Nicola had anticipated. It was also a chance for Oliver to get to know his grandfather and his great-aunts. To give him the opportunity to try to build some sort of relationship with them. Whatever happened during the course of the next few days, she must remember she was here purely for Oliver's sake. She was determined to be civil to Henri at all costs and put all feelings of resentment about the way Henri had treated Marc and her over the years out of her mind.

It wasn't until they were waiting for their luggage to show up on the baggage carousel that Nicola began to worry about the journey from Nice out into the back country. Stupidly, she'd been so concerned with actually getting them to France that she'd forgotten La Prouveresse was an hour's car drive inland from Nice. She could only hope that Henri, knowing the time their flight arrived, would be there to meet them, even if that would mean a difficult journey back to the farm. If Henri hadn't arranged for them to be met, she'd have to hire a car and drive them there herself, which was not something she wanted to do.

As she and Oliver walked through to the arrivals lounge, she saw the back of a man who seemed familiar. When the man turned, smiled and held up a small placard with 'Jacques family' written on it, she recognised Raoul Traille, Marc's old school friend, immediately. She and Marc had never visited France long enough for her to get to know Raoul well and once she'd heard about a dreadful incident in his past, she admitted to taking a step back and not wanting to get too close to him.

'Nicola. Welcome back.' As Raoul kissed her cheeks, Nicola tensed before remembering this was the normal French greeting, nothing more. 'It's been a long time,' Raoul said, looking at her. 'But you haven't changed a bit. I knew I wouldn't need this, but I thought you might not remember me.' He threw the placard into a bin. Smiling, he turned and gravely shook the hand Oliver had shyly extended. 'Welcome to France, Oliver. I was your father's best friend at school. So I'm the one to talk to if you want to hear about the mischief he got up to.' As Oliver laughed at Raoul's words, Nicola began to relax. That was the kind of thing that Oliver needed to help lessen his grief.

As Raoul took her suitcase and led them outside to his car, Nicola asked, 'Is Henri all right? To be honest, I'd forgotten about having to get from here to the farm. I suppose I'd expected him to meet us.'

'You know Henri,' Raoul answered. 'Not much of a traveller. Nice is just that bit too far from the farm for him and the old heap he calls a car. When he heard I was going to be down here today, he assumed I'd have no objection to meeting you. He was right, of course.' He smiled.

The road out of Nice into the back country was busy, but this didn't stop Raoul from talking and pointing out places of interest to Oliver. Nicola, sitting in the front seat, closed her eyes. She'd forgotten how maniacal French drivers could be and there were a few stretches on the N202 where she wished that Raoul would give all his attention to the road rather than turning to show Oliver something out of the window.

Oliver was fascinated by the medieval villages he glimpsed perched way up in the mountains but not so keen on the horse-shoe bends on the minor road leading to La Prouveresse.

'Scary,' was his verdict, as Raoul stopped for him to look over a particularly deep abyss with nothing between them and the edge.

The village was quiet as they drove through. Initially, it still seemed to Nicola to be a typical sleepy French village, unaltered from her memories of eight years ago. Bougainvillaea still climbed rampant over the castle ruins that had once stood guard above the narrow streets. Oleander bushes alternating with tall plane trees lined the pavements. The smell of strong coffee still wafted out from the café. Opposite the station, the old men of the village were gathering for their daily game of boules.

It wasn't until Raoul pointed out the new bridge crossing the river that she realised the village had suffered and changed in recent years. Torrential rains five years ago had swept away the gently curved fifteenth-century bridge, Raoul explained, eroded the banks of the river and left tons of stones in the riverbed. Now, a modern suspension bridge carried the road out of the village across the river. Ancient houses on the banks on either side had been demolished and huge boulders were now in place to keep the river at bay.

The village fountain, though, stood unscathed in the midst of the square. The square itself, with its restaurant tables and bright parasols, hadn't changed. Nicola even thought she recognised the brown dog from eight years ago, still sleeping in front of the entrance to L'Olivieraie restaurant and hotel.

Driving out through the village, Nicola could feel herself tensing. Two more minutes and they would reach the farm. She glanced at the derelict Le Jardin de Dominic pépinière as they passed it, remembering how different it had looked on her last visit.

'That place looks sad. Such a waste.'

'I know. The whole village is on at me about it,' Raoul said.

'It's yours?' Nicola said, surprised. Raoul nodded.

'When Uncle Dom left it to me, I decided I didn't want to live there, but I can't find anyone to rent it. So I've said I'm going to sell it and invest the money in something. But, according to the village, I should keep it. I had hoped Henri might buy it, but he's not interested.'

Raoul changed down a gear and negotiated the entrance onto the track leading to La Prouveresse carefully.

'About time Henri did something about the track,' he grumbled, trying to avoid potholes. 'No wonder they don't get many visitors up here.' He stopped the car in front of the farmhouse and turned to face Nicola. 'Voila. We've arrived. If you want, I can come in with you,' he offered. 'Help ease things along.'

Nicola shook her head. 'Thanks for the offer, Raoul, but we'll be fine. Henri has invited us, so it's not as if we're unwelcome. Come on, Oliver. Let's introduce you to your grandfather and your aunts.' And the two of them got out of the car, Oliver grabbing his rucksack while Raoul lifted Nicola's suitcase out of the boot.

As Raoul disappeared back down the lane with a sharp toot of the horn, the sisters ran down the steps at the side of the house and they were both enveloped in tight hugs. There was no sign of Henri, something which failed to surprise Nicola.

'Bonjour, Nicola and my petit Oliver,' Josephine said.

'Petit' Oliver dwarfed both Josephine and Odette when they hugged him, by at least five inches, but he smiled good-naturedly at them.

'Come on in.'

The farmhouse kitchen was warm and inviting, the kettle whistling on the range, cakes and biscuits ready on the table.

'Coffee or tea? We have some tea especially for you.'

'A cup of tea would be lovely,' Nicola said. 'Henri working on the farm?'

'Tsh,' Odette said, shrugging her shoulders. 'One minute he is here waiting and the next, he disappears.' She looked at Oliver. 'I think he'll be in the barn. Go and ask him if he wants a cup of tea and a slice of gâteau. The sheep barn is just across the back yard,' and she pointed out through the kitchen window towards a large stone building.

Oliver looked at Nicola uncertainly.

'Do you want me to come with you?' she asked.

Before Oliver could answer, Josephine gently touched Nicola's arm.

'Non, Nicola. It's better they meet alone, I think,' Josephine said quietly.

'It's okay, Mum,' and taking a deep breath, Oliver opened the back door and went in search of his grandfather.

* * *

A sharp draught of air blew into the barn as Oliver pushed open the door, snatching at wisps of straw bedding and lifting them haphazardly towards the rafters, before letting them drift back down and settle onto the backs of the barn's occupants. Carefully he closed the old wooden door behind him and stood for a few seconds listening to the frenzied bleating of the sheep wanting their food, and absorbing the warm animal smell that hung in the air.

He could see Henri in the far corner, his back towards him, carefully measuring food into buckets, ready to be poured into the various hoppers inside the sheep enclosure. Meg, his old collie dog, sleeping on a pile of discarded oil filter mats under the work bench, thumped her tail in welcome before getting up and ambling towards Oliver.

'Bonjour, Oliver,' Henri said, without turning.

'Bonjour, Papa Henri. Comment vas-tu grand-père?' Oliver answered shyly.

Henri put one last scoop of food into a bucket, straightened up and slowly turned to face Oliver.

'Tu parles français, Oliver?'

Oliver shook his head. 'Not really. Dad taught me a bit, but I'm not very good at it. You speak English though, so that's okay,' and Oliver smiled at his grandfather. 'Can I help you feed the sheep?'

Silently, Henri handed him a bucket and indicated he should pour its contents into one of the hoppers. Together they moved around the enclosure until all the hoppers were filled.

'Your dad ever talk to you about La Prouveresse?' Henri asked, bending down to secure a food sack.

Oliver nodded. 'Dad used to tell me about growing up on the farm. Reckoned it was brilliant. Said there was always stuff to do but mostly it was good fun.'

'I didn't know that,' Henri said slowly. 'He never told me. I thought he couldn't wait to get away.'

Oliver shrugged. 'He just didn't want to be tied to one place all his life, he wanted to see what the world had to offer.' As he put the last empty bucket down near the food sacks, Oliver said, 'The aunts sent me to tell you tea and gâteau are ready in the kitchen. Mum's waiting there too,' he added, looking at Henri.

'Come on then. We'd better get back or I'll be in trouble for keeping you out here,' Henri replied.

* * *

Nicola looked up as they entered the kitchen together and felt some of the tension leave her body. Oliver had got over the first hurdle of meeting Papa Henri safely.

Josephine poured the tea as Henri greeted Nicola. Tentatively, she responded to the unexpected hug that accompanied the customary cheek kissing.

'You look well. Thank you for inviting us, Henri. Oliver has been really looking forward to it.'

Henri shrugged but sent an affectionate glance in Oliver's direction.

'Which day have you organised for... for saying a final goodbye to Marc?' Nicola asked quietly, looking across at Oliver, who was eating cake and chatting to the aunts. 'Will there be lots of people attending?'

'Midday tomorrow, here on the farm. Best to get it done with,' Henri said matter-of-factly. 'Just the family, plus Sylvie and Raoul.'

Nicola nodded. 'Okay.' A small gathering would be perfect. She didn't want Oliver feeling overwhelmed with the sadness of the occasion and too many people.

'Afterwards I will begin to show Oliver, La Prouveresse. This week he needs to learn about where he comes from. I will teach him about the heritage Marc threw away when he left.'

Nicola frowned, but before she could say anything, Henri had moved across to sit at the table and help himself to a piece of cake. If Henri upset Oliver with double-edged remarks like that Nicola knew she'd have no choice but to tell him to stop. To her ears, it sounded as if Henri intended to try to make Oliver feel guilty by pushing a 'sins of the father' card on to him. There was no way she'd allow him to do that.

Besides, as far as she was concerned, Henri himself had played a large part in Marc leaving the family farm. And she, for one, wouldn't hesitate to hand the 'sins of the father' card straight back to Henri, pointing that out.

7

That evening after supper when Henri had taken Oliver over to check on the sheep before closing the barn for the night, Nicola had asked the sisters for a little more detail as to what would happen in the morning. 'Just so I can be ready if Oliver gets upset. I know Henri said just family earlier, but is there going to be a celebrant present?'

'No, it's just the family welcoming Marc home and setting him free for the final time,' Josephine said, a catch in her voice. 'Henri will probably say a few words. You can too, if you want?' She gave Nicola a questioning look.

Nicola shook her head. 'No. I'd rather not. Where is it going to take place?'

'The field that edges the terrace of the old olive grove,' Odette said. 'It's where Bernadette was scattered and Henri has had a small memorial stone placed there.'

Nicola nodded. 'I remember Marc taking me there to show me the stone the first time he brought me here. I know he adored his mum, so to be close to her will be perfect.' She kept the thought that it was far too soon for mother and son to be reunited in this way to herself.

* * *

The next morning, Nicola woke up to find the sunshine pouring into her room through the window she'd deliberately left unshuttered overnight. She lay there for several moments absently watching a series of white puffballs of cloud scurrying across the blue sky and disappearing out of sight as she thought about the coming morning. Hopefully the ritual of scattering Marc's ashes wouldn't be too upsetting for Oliver.

Once she was up and showered, Nicola made her way downstairs. Oliver was already in the kitchen chatting away to Odette and Josephine, a plate of croissants and a bowl of milky coffee in front of him.

'These are great, Mum,' he said. 'Can we get croissants at home?'

Nicola laughed. 'I'm sure we can, but I doubt they will taste the same as French ones – they never do. And these are particularly delicious,' she said, helping herself to one.

After breakfast, Odette took Oliver off to help her feed the chickens and to do a few other small chores around the farm, whilst Henri saw to the sheep. Nicola stayed in the kitchen to help Josephine prepare a light lunch for when they all came back from the olive grove: French onion soup with the traditional croûtons sprinkled on top, crusty bread with chunky home-made pâté, and slices of tarte tatin to finish off with.

Sylvie and Raoul arrived shortly before noon and the seven of them made their way to the top of the olive grove terrace, with Henri carrying the urn leading the way, Oliver at his side. Nicola at the back was grateful for Raoul's strangely comforting presence alongside her. The chatter between everyone gradually became more subdued, and by the time they arrived at the top of the olive grove, everyone was silent.

There was a new granite memorial stone sunk into the ground a few feet away from Bernadette's. Marc's full name, Marc Henri Jacques, carved into the stone, followed by his dates. Nicola could feel the tears welling up. Such a short life for someone who had tried to do good in the world and had so much more to give.

She looked across to her son. Oliver was standing statue-like, his gaze fixed on the stone, whilst Henri's quiet words floated on the air. 'Proud of my son... too late for regrets... back on the farm... never forget you... will try to live a good life in your memory... rest in peace.'

Watching Oliver, Nicola prayed that she'd done the right thing in bringing him here and letting him be a part of this final farewell to the father he'd adored, even if his father had been selfish in an extreme sense in the way he lived for the last few years. He could have spent more time with his only son, but he'd chosen not to. Chosen instead to help strangers. Listening to Henri's goodbye words to his son, Nicola realised just how angry and resentful she felt about the injustice of the way Marc had died. All he'd ever wanted was to help others less fortunate than himself. Guiltily, she pushed the thoughts away.

Henri was silent for several seconds before bending and picking up the urn. Taking the top off, he shook the container gently and as the ashes fell towards the ground, Nicola found herself mouthing the words 'From ashes to ashes, from dust to dust,' spoken so often at English funerals.

Henri continued to gently shake the urn until it was empty when he replaced the lid and put it on the ground beside the stone. Josephine and Odette wiped their eyes before Josephine moved across to Oliver to give him a tight hug and Odette did the same to Nicola.

'C'est fini,' she said with a sigh. 'Now we must honour his memory and be kind.'

Nicola nodded as she saw Oliver moving towards her. His face was tear-streaked and although he looked sad, he appeared to be calm as he gave Nicola a small smile.

'You all right?' she asked.

Oliver nodded. 'I'm glad we came, even though this has been hard. I didn't let Dad down.'

Wordlessly Nicola opened her arms and gave Oliver the tightest hug.

* * *

Nicola saw little of Oliver for the next few days. Henri, it seemed, couldn't get enough of him, insisting they spent as much time together as possible. He took Oliver to far-flung corners of the farm, talked to him about the olives and the vines grown there, showed him the traditional meadows where, in summer, the grass would be joined by wild flowers, daisies, poppies, buttercups and clover, making the fields a haven for wildlife as well as making tasty hay. On several occasions, Henri took him down to the village, proudly introducing him to everyone he met as 'mon petit garçon.' Josephine and Odette, desperate to spend time with Oliver as well, started to teach him to play boules on a rough patch of ground at the top of the drive.

Oliver himself had blossomed since they'd arrived, throwing himself into farm life with gusto. From bottle-feeding baby lambs, collecting the eggs from the chickens, to using the pres-

sure hose to wash down the yard with typical young boy enthusiasm trying to soak anyone who dared to come close. Nicola
sensed he was a happy boy again, one who at mealtimes
devoured everything he was offered.

As the days went by Nicola slowly relaxed, realising she'd
overreacted to Henri saying he intended teaching Oliver about
his heritage. He simply wanted him to feel a part his French
family, like any normal grandfather would, the differences
between him and his son pushed to one side as he bonded with
his grandson. If only Marc had been here to witness it.

While Henri kept Oliver busy, Nicola spent her time walking
down to the village, exploring the surrounding countryside and
generally immersing herself in a slower, French countryside way
of life. A life that in some respects seemed left over from a bygone
age despite the modern machinery in the fields that had long ago
replaced numerous men with their horse-drawn implements
working the land.

She enjoyed, too, the company of the aunts, helping them
prepare meals and with some of their farm chores, as well as
making sure she and Oliver did the washing up after mealtimes.
Nicola loved joining them as they relaxed over morning coffee
and cake at the kitchen table, or enjoyed a glass or two of rosé in
the evening. As she sat there, happy in the aunts' company at
those times, she found herself wishing visits like this could have
happened while Marc was alive.

Oliver helped Henri to pull a box of old family photographs
out of the loft one afternoon and they all spent hours hunched
around the kitchen table poring over them. There had been a
Jacques family at La Prouveresse for nearly two hundred years
and Nicola could see that Oliver was fascinated by the history of
the farm and proud of his connection to this family. She knew
Marc would have welcomed his son and his father becoming

close, that there was a possibility the next generation could heal the rift. With Nicola's own parents being dead before he was born, Oliver had never known his maternal grandparents. At least he had relatives in his life now, even if he would only see them occasionally. Accepting Henri's invitation to visit had been a good thing, she decided.

8

One evening when Oliver was in his room and Henri had gone over to the farm workshop to repair a broken implement, Nicola glanced at Josephine as they both sat with a glass of wine out on the small terrace. 'Where's Odette tonight?'

'She's recently been elected to the village council. Tonight is her first meeting of the social and agriculture committee. Much to Henri's displeasure. He doesn't hold with women in politics. It is a good job they're not on the same committees.'

'You've never wanted to be on the village council?' Nicola asked.

'Non. I like a quiet life these days. I know from what Henri says some of the meetings can get très argumentative. Odette, on the other hand, will be in her element.'

Nicola smiled. This week, she'd realised the twins, although close as only twins can be, were totally different in character. Extrovert Odette was never happier than when she had people around her, whereas Josephine was content in the sanctuary of the kitchen, baking and with just her family around her.

'Henri is rather old-fashioned in some of his views, isn't he?'

Nicola said. She'd deliberately stayed in the background for the last few days, happy to give grandfather and grandson the space to get to know each other.

'It takes a lot to make him change his mind, for sure. You have to remember though that France has always been a rather patriarchal society. Women here didn't get to vote until 1944 and Henri is of the generation that still thinks men should rule the world – despite Odette and me trying to convince him otherwise.' Josephine gave a short affectionate laugh. 'Sylvie, she also tries.'

'Gosh, 1944 – that was twenty years after England,' Nicola said, astonished.

Josephine nodded. 'Henri accuses us of being bossy, but really he is a very bossy big brother. He took on the role of head of the family when our father died because it was expected of him and became even bossier.' Josephine sighed and briefly closed her eyes. 'I think the truth is that deep down he cares too much for us but also he worries about what other people think and say. Something I know to my cost,' she added quietly.

Nicola looked at her and waited, but Josephine shrugged.

'It was a long time ago, best forgotten,' and picking up the wine bottle, she poured them both a top-up. 'Peut-être one day I will tell you about the biggest mistake of my life.' Josephine swallowed a large mouthful of her wine before giving Nicola a sad smile. 'C'est la vie,' and deftly Josephine turned the conversation away from herself by saying how much she and Odette had enjoyed playing boules with Oliver.

Even though it was early in the year, every day they ate lunch outside, sitting in the enclosed small garden area at the back of the farmhouse. Weathered painted furniture, pots of lavender

and rosemary, sweet-smelling old-fashioned roses, trailing geraniums tumbling down the stone wall, bougainvillea climbing
the pillars that the rusty hinges of the ancient wrought-iron
gates were embedded in, it had a gentle faded Provençal
atmosphere. This, together with the spectacular view out over
the countryside to the Maritime Alps on the horizon, made it
one of Nicola's favourite places on the farm. She could imagine
how wonderful it would look in the height of summer when
everything would be flowering, and she itched to get her hands
busy pulling weeds out, pruning and snipping cuttings. When
Josephine and Odette confessed they struggled to find the time
to tame the wilderness of the petit jardin every spring ready for
the summer's growth, Nicola resolved she'd make it nicer for
them before she left.

It wasn't until the afternoon of the penultimate day of the
holiday that she had the chance to put her plan into action.
Josephine and Odette were each busy doing their own thing and
Henri had taken Oliver down to the village, so Nicola knew she
had a couple of free hours to garden in peace. Armed with a pair
of secateurs, a truc, a spade and a small hand fork, all of which
she'd found in one of the farm's outhouses, she made her way to
the small garden.

Humming happily to herself as she worked, she thought
about the holiday. There had been a definite good vibe about the
whole week. Now he'd been here once, Oliver was sure to want to
come again which would please everyone. Nicola had to admit
too, that she'd had a good holiday and Oliver had certainly
enjoyed getting to know everything and everybody.

Henri, less antagonistic than she'd been expecting, had
seemed happy in his own grumpy way to be back in touch with
them. There had been no talk of the 'urgent business' he'd
mentioned in his letter. As the week progressed Nicola had

decided it must have been the scattering of the ashes that he'd been referring to and wanted settled.

She took a step back to gauge whether she'd trimmed the bougainvillea enough or whether she should do more.

'Tu like to work in the garden, Nicola?'

Startled, Nicola turned. Henri was sitting at the wooden table, a carafe of rosé wine and two glasses in front of him. She wondered how long he'd been sitting there, silently watching her.

'Yes, I love it. I'm lucky it's my job.' Gaining her college diploma in horticulture from the RHS all those years ago had been a proud moment but something she hadn't put to much use before she married Marc. After Marc had joined Médecins Sans Frontières, she'd unearthed the certificate and offered her services to a local garden centre. Throwing herself into work was a way of distracting herself from worrying about Marc and it wasn't long before she was leading a team of gardeners.

'Ah, I forget. Marc, he told me once you have a certificate in horticulture, yes?'

In spite of herself, Nicola smiled at his pronunciation.

'You will join me in a glass of wine,' Henri said. 'We celebrate a good vacances and then we discuss.'

Without waiting for her reply, he poured two glasses.

Nicola sipped her cold wine and waited. So there were matters d'urgence to discuss after all.

'I decide to make Oliver my heir,' Henri said.

Nicola looked at him, surprised at his words. 'That is very generous of you. Have you told Oliver?'

'Non. We make arrangements first. You and I do that, then peut-être we tell him later if necessary.'

'I'm sorry, Henri, but I don't see what arrangements have to be made? Or where I come into them. Surely you simply have to make a will leaving La Prouveresse to Oliver, sign it, pass it to your notaire for safekeeping, and when the time comes, he informs Oliver.'

Henri looked at her. 'I have conditions before I do that.'

Nicola gave a rueful smile. Of course, with Henri there would always be conditions. He hadn't mellowed that much.

'And do these "conditions" affect me as Oliver's mother?'

'Oliver has to come and live here if he is to inherit the farm.'

'What? He's a child and he lives with me in England.'

'If he is to inherit, he has to live here. He is half French. He needs to speak the language. Get to know the farm in all its seasons.' He stared at her. 'That, as you English would say, is non-negotiable.'

Nicola took a deep breath and looked at Henri. 'So, have I got this correct? You're asking us to give up our life and home in England, where Oliver was born, where he has friends and feels secure, and move out here to live?' She paused and gave Henri a puzzled look. 'Why now, Henri, after all this time, why now do you choose to connect with your grandson?'

Henri gave her a defiant look. 'Oliver, he is a Jacques. He belongs here. He's old enough to come without you if you no wish to come. Josephine and Odette they would happily look after him, so you have no worries. Bien sûr, you can visit whenever you like,' Henri added.

'How generous of you,' Nicola said, knowing that Henri was unlikely to catch the sarcasm in her voice. 'What if Oliver doesn't want to come and live here?' she demanded.

'He will,' a confident Henri replied. 'The holiday has been good. He has a special feel for the farm – unlike his father.' A frown crossed Henri's face.

'But a holiday is different from living here permanently. No, I'm sorry, Henri, but I can't agree to this. As a parent, all I want is for my son to live a happy and fulfilled life around people who love him. If, in a few years, when Oliver has finished school, you still want him to inherit the farm, he'll be old enough to talk things through with you and decide for himself.' Nicola put her glass on the table and went to move away.

Henri put out a restraining hand on her arm.

'The offer is for now, Nicola. I no make it again. You refuse and leave...' Henri shrugged. 'You throw away your son's inheritance. I will make sure he knows you refused to safeguard his future by your selfishness. I wonder what his reaction will be.'

Nicola stared at Henri in disbelief as he gathered up the bottle and the glasses and walked away. No wonder Marc couldn't wait to leave.

After Henri had left, Nicola tried to carry on with her gardening, but her mind was in turmoil. Piercing a finger on a sharp bougainvillea thorn, she groaned in frustration and threw the secateurs into the basket and leaned against the wall, biting hard on the finger, not only to stop the blood but also to keep her tears at bay, while she gazed unseeingly at the view.

What an impossible situation. Was she right to refuse Henri's offer so swiftly? Should she at least have discussed it with Oliver?

She shook her head. No, she couldn't place such a momentous, life-changing burden on a thirteen-year-old boy. It was a decision she had to make on her own.

But what would Oliver's reaction be when Henri told him she'd turned down La Prouveresse on his behalf? Would he listen when she pleaded she'd done it for the best? Or would he accuse her of being selfish and not wanting to give up her own life in England?

Was that why her immediate reaction to Henri's offer had been no? She'd dismissed it as moral blackmail and refused to even consider the possibility of allowing Oliver to come to France to live without her. But the logistics of changing her life, living in

a foreign country, were frightening. The house would have to be
sold, her job at the garden centre given up. Besides, wherever he
lived, Oliver still had at least another five years' schooling ahead
of him, probably followed by three years at university. He was a
bright boy and would surely want to try for a degree.

Fleetingly, Nicola wondered how Marc would want her to
react to his father's demand. She knew that despite refusing to
take over the farm from Henri, part of Marc's heart had always
belonged here in his family home. She knew too of the huge
amount of courage it had taken for him to defy his father and be
the one who broke the accepted father to son hereditary rules by
walking away. His biggest fear, which was hers too, would be
Henri forcing Oliver into living a life he didn't want, like he'd
tried to do with Marc. But what if Oliver was a throwback to
generations of Jacques and had the farming gene deep in his
DNA? And actually wanted this life.

Dimly in the distance, Nicola heard the village church clock
striking the hour. She had to go and get ready for tonight's family
dinner. Josephine, Odette and Sylvie had insisted that Henri book
a table tonight and treat everyone to a farewell dinner at
L'Olivieraie to celebrate the holiday. Something Nicola had been
looking forward to but now she wished it was just a quiet family
supper in the farmhouse kitchen, the atmosphere between her
and Henri was sure to be tense.

She was unlikely to get a chance to talk to Henri privately at
the dinner, but if she did, she promised herself she'd try to
persuade him to change his mind, to make his offer again, when
Oliver was older.

Nicola forced herself to smile normally at Oliver as he came
running into the garden.

'Mum? Papa Henri told me to come and find you. He said you
might have some news for me. Have you?'

9

L'Olivieraie restaurant was busy when Henri ushered his party inside, after much laughter, hand shaking and air kissing with everyone they knew as they made their way through the restaurant to the large round table that had been reserved for them. Nicola finally found herself sitting between Josephine and Claudine, Sylvie's daughter, with Raoul, her brother, on Claudine's other side. Henri, to her relief, was on the opposite side of the table. Sylvie on his left and Oliver on his right.

'Nicola, I'm so pleased you brought Oliver for this holiday,' Josephine said quietly. 'We will keep in touch more now, n'est pas?'

'If Henri has his way, we'll be doing more than that, won't we?' Nicola answered, fiddling with her wine glass. Earlier she'd guiltily managed to dodge Oliver's 'have you got news for me' question by smiling and saying, 'you'll have to wait and see.' Inwardly she was still cursing Henri for putting her in an impossible situation.

Josephine looked at her, puzzled.

'What do you mean?'

'This inheritance business,' Nicola said. 'Surely Henri has told you his plan?'

Josephine shook her head. 'Non. Henri can be very secretive at times. You will have to tell me.'

Nicola bit her lip. Why hadn't Henri told his sisters of his plans? The farm was their home after all.

It wasn't her place to tell them.

But looking at Josephine's concerned face, she felt the need to confide in her. Ask her what she should do.

Taking a deep breath, she said quietly, 'Henri wants Oliver to inherit La Prouveresse, but he's insisting that, to do so, he has to come and live in France now. If he doesn't, he'll disown him like he did Marc. He's even suggested that he comes here without me.'

Josephine stayed silent as Nicola continued.

'I can't decide what to do. If we stay in England, he loses his inheritance and so much more. His family, a place where he can be close to his father. And I get the blame.' Nicola shook her head. 'Why can't Henri just make Oliver his heir without this ridiculous residency clause?'

'Would living in France be that bad?' Josephine asked quietly.

Nicola shook her head and smiled. 'It would be wonderful – even better in lots of ways. But I can't let Henri run Oliver's life the way he did Marc's before he rebelled. It wouldn't be fair.'

Josephine patted her arm in a comforting gesture as she looked across the table at Oliver and Henri talking animatedly together. 'Only you can decide what is best for both of you. All I can say is, it would be lovely to have you both here and,' she leant forward to whisper conspiratorially in Nicola's ear, 'I promise Odette and I help you keep Henri in his place. We no let history repeat.'

'Thank you, Josephine,' Nicola said.

As Josephine turned to talk to Odette on her other side, Claudine spoke to Nicola.

'It's nice to see you again. Do I gather you're thinking of coming to live in France?'

'You overheard?' Nicola put her finger against her lips. 'I've not decided – I haven't even mentioned it to Oliver yet. There are a few obstacles in the way.' She took a sip of her wine. 'How are you, Claudine?'

On the two occasions they'd met years ago, a tentative friendship had been formed, but distance, as well as the estrangement between Marc and his father, had stood in the way.

'I'm fine. I'm back here house-hunting. Philippe, my husband, starts a new job in Nice soon, but we both prefer to live here rather than there, so he's going to commute. If you do come to live at La Prouveresse we must get together.'

'That would be good,' Nicola said. Having a friend of her own age from the beginning would help ease her into French life, she was sure.

'Is one of the obstacles a boyfriend by any chance?' Claudine whispered.

'No boyfriend,' Nicola said, shaking her head, realising she hadn't missed Andrew this week at all. The holiday had gone by in a flash, with no thoughts of home – until Henri's bombshell. Before she could say any more to Claudine, she saw Henri getting to his feet to propose a toast.

'Please raise your glasses to my petit garçon, Oliver. Wherever he lives, whatever he does, whatever life throws at him, may his future be filled with the happiness and prosperity he deserves.'

He looked at Oliver as he spoke, but as everyone raised their glasses, his gaze turned directly to Nicola, as though daring her to challenge his words.

She smiled brightly at him, took a sip of wine and promised

herself that somehow in the hours before they left, she would try to talk him into changing his mind. Otherwise...

10

The idea came to Nicola in the middle of the sleepless night that followed the farewell dinner. As dawn broke, she slipped out of bed, dressing quickly in jeans and a comfy hoody before tiptoeing downstairs. Only one way to discover if it was a feasible idea or a non-starter was to go and take a look. Investigate the possibilities before dismissing it as one of those middle-of-the-night thoughts that seem like a wonderful idea only to fade away as the sun rises.

Quietly, she crept through the house and silently closed the door behind her. Outside, the sky was tinged with a rosé hue as dawn began to filter over the mountains. Despite the early hour, the air was warm and Nicola felt a surge of well-being as she made her way down the farm drive before taking the short cut across the sheep field in the direction of 'Le Jardin de Dominic'.

Three minutes later, she was pushing open the old wooden back gate of the pépinière that Raoul had inherited. She'd walked past it several times during the past week and had been tempted to take a look out of interest, but the timing had never been right;

she was either hurrying back to help the aunts or rushing to watch Oliver and Henri as they played boules in the village.

The weather-worn wooden nameplate, minus a securing screw, was hanging vertically and banged against the gate as Nicola pushed it open. An overgrown path wound its way past some outbuildings and round the side of the cottage before linking up with the main path that finished between two overgrown oleander bushes on either side of the front door.

Nicola wandered slowly around, deep in thought. Last night, when she'd finally managed to corner Henri on his own, he'd flatly refused to even consider settling for seeing Oliver during the school holidays.

'Non, Nicola. He comes to live in France or he loses his inheritance. There's plenty of room at La Prouveresse for both of you if you decide to accompany him.'

'Oliver is definitely not moving over here on his own, Henri. He's far too young. If he comes, I come too.'

Henri had shrugged. 'I'm sure we can all live together in harmony. You will let me have your decision before you leave, oui?' And Henri had returned to Sylvie, leaving Nicola seething at his arrogance.

Shortly afterwards, the party at the restaurant had broken up and they'd returned to the farm. Nicola and Oliver said goodnight to everyone and went to their rooms. As Oliver was getting ready for bed, Nicola had popped her head round the door.

'So, you've enjoyed this week?'

'It's been brill, Mum. I'm really glad we came. Papa Henri can be a bit grumpy, but I think he likes me.'

'Oh, I'm sure he does,' Nicola replied.

'We talked about Dad a bit,' Oliver said, glancing at her. 'Papa Henri says he wishes they'd been able to talk to each other more

– got to know one another better. He said he doesn't want to make the same mistakes with me as he did with Dad.'

Nicola processed this information silently.

Oliver continued, 'He says that he'll always be willing to listen and try to help if I've got a problem. Although, with us in England and him here in France, I can't see how he could ever be much help, can you?'

Nicola watched her son's face grow thoughtful.

'We are coming back though, aren't we, Mum?' he asked, looking anxiously at Nicola. 'It's been fun. I really like France.'

Nicola had stopped short at asking him how he'd feel about the two of them moving to live in France. Only when she'd decided what her answer to Henri's demand was would she sit down with Oliver and talk things through. It wasn't fair to burden a thirteen-year-old with such life-changing decisions.

Now, as she walked around the neglected smallholding in the early-morning light, she considered the future, consoling herself with the thought that at least Oliver had said he liked France. If her idea did prove to be feasible, hopefully he would be pleased.

Nicola kicked some soil loose before bending down and running it through her fingers. Good rich loam, should be fertile stuff, she thought. The overgrown blackberry bushes and other fruit bushes certainly looked healthy enough, just in need of a good prune. The remains of the old garden layout were still visible in places through the overgrowth. Close to the back of the cottage, Nicola traced the outline of the old flower-beds, still defined by their original terracotta edging stones. There were a number of old earthenware pots standing on the paved terrace near the kitchen door, their plants long gone. Nicola visualised how they must have looked in the past, filled with lavender and rosemary, the flowers filling summer days and nights with perfume.

Two small interlocking ponds where water had once tumbled soothingly over a rocky waterfall were visible from the terrace. Tall lily plants seemed to be thriving in the marshy, silted-up ground.

Nicola imagined eating breakfast out here on summer mornings, sitting in the cool of an evening, listening to the inevitable frogs and watching the dragonflies flitting over the surface of the pond. It could be a little paradise.

The rest of the land, about seven hectares that had grown vegetables for the local market in the past, was seriously overgrown. The framework of a large polytunnel was silhouetted at the far end, a lone piece of torn plastic flapping in the wind. Against a boundary wall, a dilapidated greenhouse gave cover to an ancient vine, its trunk twisted and thick with age, shrivelled grapes hung in bunches from its leafless stems. Nicola's fingers itched to pull them off, to tidy up the vine, ready for a new growing season.

She stopped for a moment in the topmost corner of the garden, looking at the smallholding's position in relation to the village. From where she stood, she had a good view of the main road leading to the beginning of the village itself. Visible through the trees on the opposite side of the road were the buildings of a run-down campsite by the small river that wound its way down through the gorge towards the Mediterranean.

Nicola stood still, listening to the faint, early-morning sounds of the village drifting towards her on the light breeze. The noisy shutters of both the boulangerie and café were being pushed up, letting the smell of baking baguettes out and teasing her nostrils with the tantalising promise of fresh coffee and croissants for breakfast.

A few cars passed the front of the cottage, commuters en route to work in Nice. But one or two were going in the opposite direction towards the village – including Raoul's. Idly, Nicola wondered where he'd been so early – or had he been out all night?

She made her way back towards the cottage and the outbuildings, cautiously pushing open the door of the first shed she came to. Inside were the remnants of an old life: rusty garden implements, a bicycle, a wrought-iron garden table and chairs, a large leather trunk, damp cardboard boxes beginning to spill their contents.

One corner of this building had obviously served as a workshop. A bench with a vice and some old tools still stood in one corner. One of the other outbuildings had clearly been used for animals. The feeding trough was still attached to the wall and there was a small chicken coop in there. Broken bales of straw and hay littered the floor.

Deep in thought, Nicola pulled the door closed. Everything was so run-down, it would take weeks, possibly even months, to clear the land and produce anything. All the outbuildings were in need of urgent maintenance – drainpipes were falling off walls and tiles were missing from their roofs in places.

Nicola bit her lip in frustration. It would be a real challenge to clear the land, sort out the buildings and make it all useable again. And she hadn't seen inside the cottage itself yet.

The idea that, in the middle of the night, had seemed so feasible and exciting began to seem silly and unattainable as the early-morning sun rose. A pinky orange glow was spreading across the sky as Nicola studied the stone-built cottage. Structurally, she thought, the cottage looked sound, certainly in better repair than the outbuildings. The pale green paint was peeling off the shutters and the front door, but to her untrained eye at least the roof looked okay.

Nicola was trying to rub some of the grime off one of the

downstairs windows in an attempt to see in when Raoul suddenly appeared.

'Want to look inside?' he asked, holding out a large iron key.

'How did you know I was here?'

'Saw you in the garden when I was driving home.' He inserted the key into the lock. 'Are you going to tell me why you are wandering around here?'

Nicola didn't immediately answer his question.

'You're out and about early,' she said instead, as Raoul opened the door.

Inside, the cottage was dark and smelled musty, but, as Raoul pulled one of the downstairs shutters open, the sunlight streamed in. Now Nicola could see through to the kitchen that ran the width of the cottage and the two rooms on either side of the small hallway. The rooms were empty and there was nothing but a large porcelain sink in the kitchen.

As she explored the ground floor, Nicola began to feel excited again. Despite its unkempt appearance, the cottage had a good feel about it. Nicola sensed, with some tender loving care, it would make a sweet, if quirky, home.

'You and Henri seemed a bit distant last night,' Raoul said unexpectedly.

Nicola turned away and started to climb the steep wooden stairs to look at the bedrooms without answering.

'Your mother was upset when you left the party early last night,' she commented, attempting to avoid Raoul's observation.

Raoul gave a shrug. 'She knew where I was going.'

Nicola, sensing that Raoul didn't want to answer personal questions any more than she did at the moment, let it go and the two of them continued to look around in silence.

Upstairs, the rooms were as dirty and dusty as those on the ground floor, and the small old-fashioned bathroom with its stained bath and sink was uninviting. But there was a wonderful view of the mountains at the back of the village from the main bedroom.

As they stood side by side looking out at the snow-capped mountains, Raoul sighed.

'Nicola, it's six o'clock in the morning. Why are we standing in an empty cottage looking at the view?'

Nicola, deep in thought, turned slightly and looked at him. 'Would you sell this place to me? Or possibly rent it initially?'

'Of course,' Raoul replied instantly. 'But why would you want it?'

Nicola shrugged non-committedly. 'I've been thinking it might be better for Oliver to grow up in France – to have his family around.'

'Has Henri been putting the pressure on?' Raoul asked shrewdly.

Nicola nodded. 'Just a bit.' She looked at him and then decided she had nothing to lose by being honest with him. 'Between you and me, Henri wants to make Oliver his heir on the condition that he comes to live in France – with or without me.'

'Don't let him take over, Nicola,' Raoul said quietly. 'Oliver's your son. Henri smothered Marc when he was young. He may have learned from that mistake, but, knowing Henri, that won't stop him from trying to interfere in Oliver's life in much the same way.'

'I know,' Nicola sighed. 'And that's the main reason I'd want a place of our own – if we come.' She glanced around. 'At least this place would give me something to do – getting the house fixed up and sorting the garden and the land. Eventually it could even give me an income if I grow produce to sell.'

She began to make her way back downstairs. Le Jardin de Dominic had so much potential, a home for them both and, in time, an income from the land, but selling everything and moving to France was a big step. If she was really honest with herself, there was nothing to keep her in the UK and moving here would give both her and Oliver a fresh start with people around them who cared about them. Even if Henri himself had a particular way of showing it. Besides, family was family and didn't Oliver deserve the chance to get to know his only relatives?

'Anyway, I don't know if I can afford it yet. How much are you asking? It may be out of my price range – I gather you've got some secret investment in mind for the money?'

There was a short silence before Raoul spoke.

'As you've been so honest with me, I'll tell you something in confidence too,' he said. 'D'you remember your last visit with Marc when I'd just been involved in a terrible tragedy skiing off piste?'

Nicola nodded. She remembered it well. The whole village had been shocked by the accident that killed a young married man from a nearby village. At the time, Raoul had been working at the ski resort, and subsequent investigations had placed some of the blame on him for failing to take the necessary safety measures. Nicola remembered being struck by Raoul's almost casual acceptance of the situation. Whilst he acknowledged he had been at fault, he had seemed somewhat detached. It was the main reason she'd never really taken to him in the past. She couldn't understand how he could continue skiing off piste as if nothing had happened; as if he didn't care that a man had died.

'Didn't he leave a widow and a young child?' Nicola asked, wondering why Raoul had decided to mention the tragedy now.

'Marie and Luc. He's fourteen now,' Raoul explained.

He looked at Nicola seriously.

'I've decided to sell this place and use the money to set up a trust fund for Luc. I don't need the money – and it would give him a better start in life.'

Nicola was stunned. So there was a softer side to Raoul Traille after all.

'That's incredibly generous of you, Raoul. How much were you hoping to raise selling this place?'

When Raoul told her the figure he had in mind, Nicola realised selling her house in England would give her more than enough to buy it and have some left over to live on while she did the place up. She could even do it without touching Marc's insurance money which she'd put into a trust account earmarked for Oliver at a later date.

'Is that the correct market price?' she asked Raoul in disbelief. 'Not a special price for me?'

'It's the price in the immobilier's window,' Raoul replied. 'You can check. I'm even open to offers on it.'

Nicola shook her head. 'No. The price seems more than fair, particularly in view of what you hope to do with the money.'

Raoul nodded and held out his hand. 'Would you like to shake on it now? I can withdraw it from the immobilier today then.'

Nicola took a deep breath and looked around at the unkempt cottage. She had hoped to return to La Prouveresse with time to think about it. But, somehow, she had a gut feeling this place was right for her and Oliver. She could picture them living here – making a new life for themselves – while securing Oliver's inheritance.

'There is one thing – it may take some time for my house in England to sell. I don't know how quickly I shall have the money.'

'Not a problem,' Raoul said, still extending his hand. 'I know the money will arrive.'

'Can you do me a favour and keep this to yourself for a couple of hours?' she said, slowly holding out her own hand. 'I need to talk to Henri and Oliver before the news becomes general knowledge.'

As Raoul's hand enveloped hers, he smiled. 'D'accord! It's a deal. Let's go and seal it with a coffee and a croissant in the village. I'm starving.'

Nicola stood on the path outside waiting for Raoul to lock the cottage door, feeling shell-shocked. What on earth had made her take such an impetuous decision, so unlike her? She could only pray it wasn't a decision she would come to regret.

11

Josephine looked up from the stove where she was preparing breakfast as Nicola pushed open the door and walked into the kitchen.

'Salut, Nicola! You're out and about early. You couldn't sleep?'

'A bit too much wine last night, I think,' Nicola replied. 'Thought a walk in the fresh air might clear my head.' She helped herself to coffee from the pot on the range.

She needed to talk to Henri and Oliver before she told anybody else about the deal she'd just made with Raoul.

'Is Henri around?' she asked nonchalantly. 'I'd like to talk to him.'

'Over in the barn as usual,' Josephine replied, without looking up.

'Shall I take him a mug of coffee?'

Josephine glanced at her but said nothing, simply filling the mug Henri used for his morning coffee and handing it to her.

In the barn, Henri had one of the ewes out of the pen and, holding her between his legs, was checking her over.

'Bonjour,' he grunted.

Nicola placed his mug on top of a bale of straw and stood drinking her own coffee, waiting for him to finish.

Finally, Henri let the animal go and straightened up to look at Nicola.

'So, you've decided?' he asked, picking up his coffee.

Nicola nodded. 'I can't throw Oliver's inheritance away before he's old enough to decide what he wants to do – so I will bring him to live in France. But,' she held her hand up as Henri went to speak, 'I have a condition or two of my own.'

Henri looked at her, his eyes hard and expressionless.

Nicola tried to ignore the way her heart was thumping. She had to stand up to him from the beginning if things were to have any chance of working out. 'I agree there is no point yet in telling Oliver he is to inherit the farm, but I want it in writing that he is to be your heir. No changing your mind on a whim and disowning him, Henri, if Oliver does something to upset you once we are here.'

She paused for a second or two, expecting Henri to protest. When he didn't, she continued.

'I also want you to understand there is to be no interfering in his day-to-day life like you did with Marc. You are Oliver's grand-father – not his father. I make the decisions about what he does or does not do.'

'Anything else?'

'One more thing. Raoul has agreed to sell me Le Jardin de Dominic. Oliver and I will live there and not here, at La Prou-veresse.'

'Oh, there's no need for that,' Henri said irritably. 'There's plenty of room here.'

'There's every need, Henri,' Nicola insisted. 'I know Oliver will spend a lot of time up here with you and his aunts, but we need our own space too.' Nicola paused and generously tried to soften the blow a little. 'There's also the small point that the farm may be Oliver's future – but it isn't mine. If I'm to give up everything in England, I need a home and a life of my own over here. Those are my conditions,' and Nicola waited for Henri's reaction.

There was silence whilst they both eyed each other warily. Finally, Henri spoke.

'I'm not saying you're right about not moving into La Prouveresse, but I can see your point,' he said grudgingly. 'In the meantime, I'll get my notaire to draw up the necessary papers confirming Oliver as my heir.' He hesitated before wiping his hand on his trouser leg and holding it out towards Nicola. 'Merci, Nicola. I know we both want what is best for Oliver. I hope you will be happy living here in France.'

Nicola gave an uncertain smile as she shook his hand. She just hoped she wasn't making the biggest mistake of her and Oliver's lives.

* * *

Nicola told Oliver she needed to talk to him and wanted to show him something. Oliver kicked at the gravel on the path as the two of them made their way down towards Le Jardin de Dominic after breakfast.

'It was the last chance to go to the village with Papa Henri and do things with him,' Oliver moaned. 'You could have talked to me on the plane this afternoon.'

'I could, but I prefer to do it here, privately,' Nicola answered. 'You've really enjoyed being here this week, haven't you?' She pushed open the broken gate of 'Le Jardin de Dominic' as she spoke and gestured to Oliver to go in.

'Been cool. Why are we going into this dump?'

'It's not a dump... well, it is, but it won't always be one.' Nicola crossed her fingers, took a deep breath and prayed that Oliver would like the news she was about to give him. 'Papa Henri has suggested we come and live in France permanently,' Nicola said quietly, watching for his reaction. She'd decided to give Oliver an edited version of the truth, say that Henri had suggested, not coerced, her into agreeing.

Oliver's eyes widened and he looked at her, shocked. 'Leave England and come here to live forever?'

Nicola nodded.

'Can we? Living on the farm would be brilliant.' Oliver's face lit up with delight as he looked at Nicola.

'Ah, but we won't be living on the farm. We'll be living here, so not too far away. I'm buying Le Jardin de Dominic from Raoul.' Oliver's smile vanished.

'Mum, have you seen the state of this place? It's like a tumble-down cottage abandoned in the woods from one of those Grimms' Fairy Tales you used to read to me.'

'It's not that bad. Come on, have a look inside.' Nicola pushed the big key, that Raoul had insisted she kept, into the lock and led the way indoors. 'There's nothing that a good clean and some paint can't fix. Raoul assured me the roof is in a good state and that's one of the most important things.'

The look that Oliver gave her at that moment reminded her of Marc. It was a look that said 'spontaneity is good but please don't be stupid.'

'Have a look upstairs,' she said. 'The middle bedroom will be yours.'

While Oliver was upstairs, Nicola wandered around down-stairs, mentally working out possible plans for renovating the cottage and trying not to worry about Oliver's comments about the place. She could knock down the hallway walls and make the living area open plan. The kitchen at the back would need updating, as would the bathroom. It would all take time, of course, but there was so much potential to the place. The thought of creating a real home for the two of them in this quirky French cottage was exciting.

'That bathroom is gross,' Oliver said, coming back downstairs. 'But the bedrooms are okay, I suppose.'

'Come and have a look at the terrace and the ponds,' Nicola said, opening the kitchen door. 'I'm looking forward to tackling the garden – and the rest of the land, of course.'

Standing there watching Oliver inspect the ponds, Nicola thought about the last twenty-four hours and the major, life-changing decision she'd taken on behalf of them both.

'It will be a new beginning for the two of us,' she said quietly. 'I know it will be hard at first for both of us, learning a new language, you going to school in a foreign country, leaving your friends behind, me getting to grips with sorting this place out but I think your dad would like to think of us, you, being here.'

'D'you think there are frogs in the ponds?' Oliver said.

'I wouldn't be surprised.'

'Be cool if there are.' Oliver straightened up, pulled his hoody over his head and ambled back to Nicola with his hands in his pockets.

'So are you happy with the idea of coming here to live?' she asked.

'Suppose. Can I walk into the village and find Papa Henri now?'

Nicola sighed. 'Don't show too much enthusiasm, will you?'

'Living in France will be good, but I'd rather live at the farm than in this dump. Can I go now?'

'This place won't always be a dump,' Nicola protested. 'Make sure you're back by midday. Josephine and Odette are doing us an early lunch before Raoul drives us down to Nice airport.'

Wearily, Nicola rubbed her hand across her face and watched Oliver as he ran down to the road and turned left for the village. Life here in France would be so different compared to their lives in England. Country life was quieter, safer in many ways, and would throw up new opportunities for Oliver if he really was a country boy at heart.

Closing the wooden garden gate, Nicola took a last look at the cottage. Deep down she felt a small shiver of excitement. Moving here was going to be good for them both.

* * *

Josephine and Odette were both equally delighted when she told them the news when she got back to the farmhouse.

'It will be so nice to have a boy around the farm again,' Odette said, gently patting Nicola on the arm. 'Beyond our wildest dream. It will be good for all of us, non? Mon Dieu,' she shook her head. 'A chance for old wounds to be buried.'

'Oh la la la,' Josephine said, clapping her hands excitedly before exuberantly giving Nicola a hug. 'I'm so glad you've decided to come. And there was me thinking I'd turn Marc's old room into a sewing room. Now, instead, I'll decorate it for Oliver. Are you happy with the bedroom you've been in this week?'

Nicola bit her bottom lip. 'I'm sure Oliver will love that. I expect he'll be spending a lot of time up here when he's not at school, but we're not going to be living on the farm. I'm buying Le Jardin de Dominic from Raoul.'

Once the sisters had recovered from their initial surprise, they both agreed that Nicola was doing the right thing in keeping her independence.

'Anyway,' Odette said, 'Le Jardin is so close – it's almost a part of the farm.'

'But, Nicola, la petite maison of Le Jardin is in a terrible state. It will be impossible for you to live there immediately. We will clean it before you come back and then help you decorate it, oui?' Josephine said worriedly.

'Oh, I can't ask you to do that,' Nicola said.

'You're not asking – we're offering,' Josephine stated firmly. 'We are so pleased you are coming to live in France.' She wiped the tears from her eyes before enveloping Nicola in another tight hug.

Nicola smiled. She didn't have the slightest doubt that between them, the sisters would have her new home scrubbed clean before she and Oliver returned.

They were a funny pair, over sixty and still sharing the same large attic bedroom at the top of the farmhouse that they'd had as children. These days, between them they did most of the routine work on the farm, as well as looking after Henri. Odette had never married or left La Prouveresse, but Marc had told her that Josephine had married a Parisian, leaving home when she was twenty. She returned a few years later for reasons Nicola had never discovered. From what she had gathered from Marc years before, there had been some kind of scandal that was never discussed. Funny, really; Odette was the noisy, extrovert twin and yet it was Josephine – the quiet, reserved one – who was at the centre of a family secret. This past week Nicola had got to know and to love the twins and she sensed their family love for Oliver included her. Whatever happened between her and Henri, Nicola knew instinctively the aunts would be there for her.

12

Raoul arrived, as promised, after lunch to drive them down to the airport for their late-afternoon flight home to Bristol. Saying goodbye was emotional, but everyone was buoyed up by the fact that they would be returning soon. Even Henri, as he shook Nicola's hand, managed a gruff, 'Au revoir. It will be good to have you here.' Josephine and Odette hugged them both and smiled as they waved them off.

'How long before we come back then, Mum?' Oliver asked, as he wriggled himself into the window seat of the plane and fastened his seat belt.

Nicola shrugged. 'Not sure. A couple of months at the earliest, I should think. There's so much to arrange. And selling the house could take time.'

'I hope we're back in time to help Papa Henri with the hay. He promised I could drive the tractor!' Oliver enthused.

Nicola stared at him, relieved that he was enthusiastic about moving to France but inwardly furious with Henri. How dare he. Tractors were far too dangerous to let inexperienced thirteen-year-old boys loose in the driving seat. Was life going to be a constant battle of wills between her and Henri when they moved over? Well, if it was, Henri would discover early on that she wouldn't be browbeaten into submission. Oliver was her son and there was no way that she'd allow Henri to take him over, or rule his life like he had Marc's.

'He did? We'll have to see about that,' Nicola said non-committally.

Oliver shrugged, clamped his headphones over his ears and disappeared into his own noisy world for the flight.

When the stewardess trundled the buffet trolley up the aisle, Nicola bought sandwiches, crisps, a carton of juice for Oliver and a glass of wine for herself. Afterwards, she settled down with a notebook to make a list of the things she would need to organise in the coming weeks and months. By the time the plane landed, she'd filled six pages.

Wheeling their luggage out to the arrivals hall, Nicola was grateful to see Andrew waiting. As he spotted them, his face lit up with a huge smile. Nicola returned the smile but inwardly quaked at the thought of telling him her plans. She could only hope that he'd thought about things while she was away and accepted the fact that the two of them didn't have a future together as a couple.

But it was Oliver, not Nicola, who broke the news to Andrew as they pushed their luggage trolley through the car park.

'Is Frisby okay? Papa Henri has two barn cats, but they're not friendly like Frisby. They're just mousers really. And, guess what? We're going to live in France. Mum's going to sell the house and buy this dump of a smallholding. But I'm going to spend more time on the farm with Papa Henri.'

Nicola closed her eyes in dismay. She'd wanted to break the news to Andrew herself, gently.

'Frisby is fine,' Andrew said, before turning to look at Nicola with an expression of bewilderment on his face. 'Tell me Oliver's joking?' he pleaded quietly. The look on Nicola's face told him it was no joke.

'Andrew, I can explain. But not now. Not here,' Nicola said, attempting to calm him down.

He turned away without a word and began to stack the luggage into the boot of the car. Meanwhile, Nicola climbed inside, praying that Andrew wouldn't try to discuss things on the way home. She simply couldn't talk about it in front of Oliver. If moving to France meant that their friendship with Andrew was going to be sacrificed, she, at least, owed him the truth, but he had to understand that her options had been limited.

The journey home was quiet, the atmosphere strained. Oliver, realising that his news had upset Andrew, retreated behind his earphones, and Nicola sat silently, looking out of the window.

Once home, Oliver disappeared up to his room and Nicola pulled the 'thank you' bottle of wine she'd bought for Andrew out of her case. But he refused to take it.

'No, thank you, not until you tell me what's going on,' he said sadly. 'Why are you moving to France? What happened while you've been away?'

* * *

The rain on Tuesday evening did nothing to lift Nicola's spirits as she prepared supper for herself and Andrew. She knew the evening was going to be difficult. Andrew had only spoken to her once after he'd rejected the wine she'd brought him from France, demanding to know exactly what was going on, as if he had the right to be consulted. When she'd shaken her head, refusing to discuss things with Oliver within earshot, he'd turned and left.

'I'll ring you,' he'd said. It was two days before he rang, suggesting dinner to 'talk this French business through', and

Nicola had quickly opted for home territory, not wanting to have a public scene in a restaurant. Tonight he was sure to want answers, and Nicola doubted he would be happy with the ones she was going to supply. Oliver was spending the evening with a friend and so she and Andrew had a couple of hours to themselves.

Nicola bit her lip. Was it her fault, this change in his feelings towards her? Had she turned to him for help too many times? Had she given Andrew the impression that she could care for him as more than a friend since Marc died? Whatever had caused the change, she'd be glad when the evening was over and Andrew had accepted that a platonic friendship was all he could expect from her.

Unusually, Andrew rang the doorbell when he arrived and waited for her to open the door. Normally, he opened the door and shouted out his arrival.

'Hello, Nicola. How are you?' he asked as he shook the rain from his coat.

'I'm fine,' she said. She attempted to give him her usual welcome cheek kiss, but Andrew had already moved away from her into the hallway.

She sighed.

'Supper will be about ten minutes. Would you like a glass of wine?'

'What I'd really like, Nicola, is to know what is going on,' he said bluntly.

Nicola poured two glasses of wine and silently handed one to Andrew.

'I'm sorry Oliver blurted out the news before I had a chance to explain what had happened in France. Oliver doesn't know the real reason behind our move either, so what I'm about to tell you is in confidence.'

Andrew raised an eyebrow in surprise. 'So how do you justify uprooting him from everything, everyone, he knows?' he challenged.

Nicola shrugged. 'I edited the truth and told him that Henri wanted us closer. The fact that he'd loved living on the farm and doing things with Henri made it a welcome suggestion. I also promised him we'd have a better life over there.' Nicola replied. 'And I do think we'll both benefit from a new beginning now that Marc has gone forever.'

'Just how did you edit the truth?'

'I didn't tell him about Henri wanting him to inherit the farm on the condition that he moves to France and spends the rest of his childhood there, with or without me.'

Andrew took a sip of his wine as she continued.

'Initially, I told Henri there was no way I'd even consider his demand. Then he threatened to tell Oliver I had thrown his inheritance away – that I, alone, was responsible for depriving him of the farm.'

There was a silence and Nicola sighed.

'I couldn't discuss it with Oliver – he's too young to make such a decision.'

Andrew continued to look at her, his face expressionless. 'And this smallholding you're buying?'

'Le Jardin de Dominic, it's on the edge of La Prouveresse land,' Nicola explained. 'And it's my independence from Henri. I refused to live on the farm, which is what Henri wanted origi-nally. I'm going to need a life of my own over there.' She glanced at Andrew, a small smile on her lips.

'You know I've always wanted a smallholding. This move will, at least, give me the chance to use my qualifications.'

'Tell me something. If you'd been in a new relationship with someone before you went to France, would you still be talking of a new life in another country for you and Oliver?'

Nicola stared at him for several seconds. 'Yes, I would still have to go. Oliver's needs come first, and always will,' she said quietly. 'In all honesty, I don't understand why our moving away is upsetting you so much. You've seen how my life has changed over the years, especially since Marc died. Moving to France is just another unexpected throw of the dice. You and I are good friends and I'll always be grateful for all the help you've given me, especially with Oliver, and there is no reason we can't keep in touch; we'll only be a short plane ride away.'

'I was hoping that in time you and I would become a couple, face the future together,' Andrew admitted quietly. 'The more I've got to know both you and Oliver, the more I've...' he paused. 'The more I've come to care deeply about you both.'

'Oh Andrew, I'm sorry, but I've never felt that way about you. I'm very fond of you, but like I said before, I think of you more as my big brother.'

'So basically you're telling me that you will only ever think of me as that?'

'We can only ever be friends,' Nicola said, as gently as she could. 'I'm trying to do my best for Oliver here and I feel Marc would approve of my decision to take his son to France. Besides, I'm not looking for a new relationship with anyone.' She took a deep breath. 'Right. Supper will be ready. Let me dish up and we'll eat.'

A moment or two later, they were sitting in silence at the kitchen table, both lost in their own thoughts as they ate. It was Nicola who broke the silence.

'Oliver has really missed not seeing you since we've been back. Please don't punish him because you're angry with me. You've been such a stable influence on his life, particularly since

Marc,' she shrugged. 'It will be weeks before we leave, it would be good if you were still around as his friend.'

Andrew sighed. 'I need to say sorry to him and, yes, I will be around.'

Inwardly Nicola gave a sigh of relief. 'Think of my moving away as your opportunity to meet someone who will love you the way you deserve.' She gave him a hopeful smile. 'And you have a standing invitation to come and visit whenever you like.'

Andrew was silent for several seconds. 'I don't think I can bear to do that, not for some time anyway,' he admitted. 'I'm happy to stay in touch with Oliver over the internet but when you leave for France a clean break from you would work better for me.'

Nicola nodded and accepted what he'd said with a smile. She'd be sad to lose his friendship but he was right. A clean break once they were in France would be easier to handle all round.

13

The sun was shining as Josephine drove the ancient farm van down the track, tooting the horn cheerfully as she passed Henri and Odette busy tending the vines in the small vignoble, before turning left and making her way down to the village. It was a route she could almost drive blindfolded, she knew its twists and hairpin bends so well. Sometimes, like today, she stopped the van by the small religious shrine hidden in the undergrowth at the side of a large oak tree.

Local legend decreed that the half a metre high shrine, constructed like a drystone wall with a niche shelf in the middle, had been built in 1916 by the mother of a local lad off to the trenches of World War I in the hope that the Virgin and Child statue she placed on the shelf would keep him safe. No one knew for sure whether he survived or not, but over the years the shrine had become an important place for villagers to come and whisper their worries. Flowers and other tokens were left regularly, alongside the statue on the shelf, and locals who had grown up in the village before moving away always paid it a visit on their annual visits home.

When Josephine returned from Paris that last time, the shrine had become her solace. In those early days, she'd been a daily visitor, whispering her regrets, and later her hopes, to the statue. Of course, nothing had changed, but she drew comfort from murmuring things out loud she couldn't even share with her twin. Her visits were less frequent these days, but she never came empty-handed and this morning was no different. Today's offering was a small bunch of wild flowers she'd picked from one of the farm meadows.

Placing the flowers alongside the statue, she closed her eyes and stood back in secret thought. If only it wasn't too late for her dream to come true.

Opening her eyes, she took a deep breath. Time to get on with life again as it was, not how she wished, longed, for it to be.

* * *

The village square was busy with the small midweek market. Josephine hummed absently to herself as she parked and locked the van and began to make her way towards the stalls. She'd been coming to this market for more years than she cared to count, but it was always a delight – except for that year when it wasn't. The time when she'd known her old friends and neighbours were judging her when they only knew half the truth. Today the sun was shining and in a couple of weeks Nicola and Oliver would be here; life was good.

Josephine wandered around happily for some time looking at the various stalls before buying the things she needed, including the cheese, pork fillet and some cream for supper. Passing a stand where a young potter had made a display of terracotta dishes, she bought an oval one. Nicola had asked her for the recipe for the rich potato gratin that usually accompanied their Sunday lunch and this dish was exactly the right size. It would make a perfect 'Welcome to your new home' present.

Finally, she stopped to chat with her friend who ran the artisan soap stall and treated herself to some bars of her favourite, lavender.

'Trois, s'il vous plait,' she said. She knew Odette liked it too, and she'd put the other one in the bathroom at Le Jardin after they'd cleaned it.

Placing the soaps in her bag, she said her goodbyes, turning away just in time to catch a glimpse of Raoul hurrying past on the other side of the square.

Josephine got the distinct feeling Raoul had seen her and was avoiding her. She watched thoughtfully as he disappeared into the café. Why had he ignored her? She was very fond of Raoul and he was invariably pleased to see her whenever they bumped into each other. He'd spent a lot of time up at La Prouveresse as a boy with Marc and she and Odette had always treated him as a second nephew. Whenever they met, he never hesitated to give them both a cheek kiss and a hug.

For a second or two, Josephine was tempted to wander over to the café and say hello but decided she didn't have the time – she had to get to the supermarché before it closed for lunch. Besides, she was probably imagining things. It was just that Raoul was too busy to stop, unusual but nothing sinister in it. Josephine pushed the thought out of her mind and tried to concentrate on the rest of her shopping.

At the supermarché, her basket was soon full of all the things she'd been unable to find at the market and she joined the queue at the checkout, glad to put it down on the floor while she waited to be served.

'You're having a grand cleaning session up there at La Prouveresse by the looks of it, Josephine.'

Turning, Josephine smiled at Sylvie.

'Non. It is for Le Jardin de Dominic. Tomorrow Odette and I will begin to clean the place, ready for Nicola and Oliver.'

Sylvie frowned. 'But Raoul says they are going to live at the farm after all. At least until Henri has had all the building work done.'

'Pardon?' Josephine said. 'What are you talking about, Sylvie? I didn't know Nicola had asked Henri to organise any building work at Le Jardin.'

There was a short pause before Sylvie answered, clearly embarrassed.

'Raoul's selling Le Jardin to Henri now, not Nicola. Apparently, Henri made him an offer he couldn't refuse.'

'I bet he did,' Josephine said under her breath. 'Sylvie, please excuse me. I have to go home.'

Furiously, Josephine pushed her way out through the queue, not caring she was leaving her shopping behind on the supermarché floor.

* * *

Odette was in the kitchen looking at some farm paperwork and looked up in surprise when Josephine burst in ten minutes later.

'What's wrong?'

'You won't believe what Henri's done now,' and Josephine quickly told her twin what Sylvie had told her. By the time she finished, Odette was on her feet and closing the farm account books.

'Right. I'll sort this out.' And Odette was gone, slamming the kitchen door behind her. Ten seconds later, she was in the barn confronting Henri.

'I am so cross with you, Henri Jacques – why the hell can't you stop meddling?'

Henri glanced up briefly from the piece of machinery he was working on before he shrugged and gave a nod. 'You've heard then? It's a business deal. Le Jardin borders La Prouveresse – it seems stupid not to join the two together. The extra eight hectares will be useful. And with the field next to it being developed, it's a good investment.'

'And Nicola and Oliver? What were you planning for them?'

'I thought they could live up here while the cottage is renovated, then they can move into it – if they still want to, that is. They might want to stay up here with us by then.'

Odette regarded her brother thoughtfully. 'Now, you listen to me, Henri Jacques. In the first place, Josephine and I know why Nicola has agreed to bring Oliver to live here.' She paused. 'We've both been feeling guilty ever since Nicola told Josephine about the pressure you put on her to give up her life in England and move here. But the thought of having her and Oliver living here is so exciting and wonderful that we decided to say nothing. Perhaps we need to have that conversation with her.'

Henri remained unresponsive as Odette went on.

'I take it you didn't intend to tell Nicola about you buying Le Jardin de Dominic before she got here? You simply meant to present her with a fait accompli when she arrived and had nowhere else to go? Well, Henri, it won't work. You can't control their lives when they get here. Have you learned nothing from the past?'

Odette sighed. She'd been hoping that Henri would respond to her last remark, but he was silent. She moved closer to her brother.

'Josephine and I are looking forward to them coming as much as you. But if you don't stop this ridiculous business deal with

Raoul and let him sell Le Jardin de Dominic to Nicola as agreed, one of us will telephone Nicola and tell her the truth you conveniently omitted to mention. Then the whole thing will be off, anyway. We'll continue to live our separate lives and you'll never get to see your grandson growing up.'

There was a long silence as Odette and Henri stared at each other. Henri was the first to turn away, his shoulders dropping.

'Do we understand each other, Henri?'

Henri nodded. 'Oui.'

'Good. One more thing. Josephine and I plan to start cleaning Le Jardin tomorrow, ready for Nicola and Oliver. There's no reason now why we shouldn't do that, is there?' she asked quietly.

'I'm sure Nicola will be very grateful to you both,' Henri said, avoiding his sister's gaze.

'I'm sure she will too,' Odette replied. 'Now, you have a phone call to make, and then I think Josephine will have lunch ready.'

Henri covered the machine he'd been working on and they both returned to the farmhouse.

Walking back across the yard, a thought troubled Odette. Nicola might be grateful for the cleaning of the cottage, but Henri's decision to deceive her and Oliver was another matter. She could only hope that Nicola would forgive her and Josephine for playing a part in it when she learned what Henri had done and the lies he'd told. The truth would inevitably be revealed – it always was.

14

Nicola watched thoughtfully as the 'For Sale' sign was replaced by one with SOLD emblazoned across it in large letters. The six weeks since they'd returned from France had been frantic. Nicola had given in her notice at work, told the school that Oliver would be leaving, made sure their passports were up to date, taken Frisby to the vet's for her inoculations and pet passport, and started the mammoth task of packing.

The house had sold far quicker than she'd ever expected, which she'd taken as a good sign that she was doing the right thing. The new owners were first-time buyers with no chain to worry about and had wanted to take possession at the end of the month – giving her just three weeks to get everything packed and organised before she and Oliver said goodbye to their old lives and moved to France at the beginning of May.

Hopefully everything was going to plan over there too. The last time she'd spoken to Raoul, he had been quite distant and wasn't able to confirm many details. He couldn't even give her a date for signing the contract, so it looked as if they would have to live up at La Prouveresse for a day or two when they arrived. That would please Josephine and Odette – and Henri, of course, but the quicker they could move into Le Jardin the better.

Nicola was packing up the latest box of books ready to go to the charity shop when the telephone rang.

'Allo, Nicola? It's Josephine. How are you?'

'Fine thanks. Nothing wrong is there?' Nicola asked, somewhat surprised. Josephine had never phoned her before.

'Non. I just wondered if you have a date for your arrival yet?'

'I think it will be about April 30th or maybe the first of May. The only problem is, I haven't heard anything official about Le Jardin. The last time I spoke to Raoul he simply said it was all in hand and that, in France, these things take time.'

'Oui, they do,' Josephine agreed. 'There was a small local problem concerning Le Jardin too, but that has now been dealt with.'

'He did tell me though, that I can move in whenever I want to, not to bother waiting for the notaire and the money.'

'I think Raoul expects the papers to be ready at the end of the month, or maybe the first week of May, so the date is perfect. Odette and I have cleaned the cottage, but you will stay up here with us for a day or two, yes? Peut-être even a week or so?'

'Please, Josephine, if it's not a problem. The furniture won't be arriving until a couple of days after us. Do you think Henri could find some yellow or white paint for me? I'd like to paint a few walls before the furniture is in place.'

'No problem. I will tell Henri to get some and put it in the cottage ready for when you arrive.'

Nicola smiled at the authoritative tone in Josephine's voice. 'Thank you. I'll pay you when I get there. Do you know anything about the local problem with Le Jardin?' Nicola continued curiously.

'Some red tape,' Josephine said. 'You know how we French

love our paperwork. I'm sure Raoul will explain the delay when he sees you.'

Nicola was about to ask how Henri and Odette were when Oliver rushed in, slamming the door behind him and running upstairs to his room.

'Josephine, I'm sorry, I've got to go. I'll talk to you again very soon.'

Oliver's bedroom door was firmly closed when Nicola went upstairs. She hesitated before knocking gently.

'Can I come in?' she asked quietly.

Oliver was lying on his bed, hands clasped behind his head, trying not to cry.

'What's the matter?' Nicola asked, sitting on the bed.

'Everything! I don't want to go to France any more,' Oliver said, jumping up off the bed and going to look out of the window. 'And you can't make me,' he went on, turning to face her defiantly.

'I'm afraid I can,' Nicola said. 'But what's suddenly happened to bring this on? Only a few weeks ago you were really excited at the thought of living in France.'

Oliver shrugged. 'I thought it would be exciting living where Dad grew up, but all my friends are here. And they've thrown me out of the school band. Mr Wilkinson said there was no point in me even going to rehearsals now that I'm leaving. He gave my place to Josh and he can't play the drums for toffee. Chloe won't come roller-skating with me tonight because, oh… just because.'

Listening to the tirade, Nicola sighed. She'd been waiting for Oliver to realise what moving to France would really mean – changing schools, giving up his after-school activities, leaving his friends behind – all this as well as having to adapt to a new country and a strange language when they got there.

'Well, Mr Wilkinson has a point. We leave in a couple of

weeks and Josh will need to practise with the band. I'm sure there will be a school band for you to join in France – perhaps even better than the one here. As for Chloe, if you tell her she can come for a holiday once we're settled in, I'm sure she'll start counting the days.'

Nicola paused.

'We'll work out an itinerary – show her all the sights.'

'I still don't want to go,' Oliver muttered.

Nicola bit her lip. 'I'm afraid not going is no longer an option. The house is sold and I'm committed to buying Le Jardin de Dominic from Raoul. I know it will be a big change for both of us – a real challenge – but it should be good too.'

'Why do we have to go over there to live? Even Dad didn't want to live there and it was his home.'

Nicola smothered a sigh. 'I've told you. Papa Henri suggested it, and having considered everything, I think it's the right thing to do. We'll have a better life in France. You'll get to know your relatives and learn another language and I'll be able to run a small-holding – something I've always wanted to do.'

'But why can't you do that here? Andrew could help you if we stay here.'

'Cottages with land here are too expensive, even small ones,' Nicola said. 'Besides, Andrew's got his own life to lead. Talking about Andrew, why don't you message him and ask him to supper tonight?'

Andrew hadn't been to the house for a meal since the night of the dinner and she couldn't help but feel guilty about that. He'd seen Oliver several times, taken him to a couple of football matches he had tickets for, but his frequent daily visits and eating with them had stopped. An invite for supper coming from Oliver rather than herself wouldn't send out the wrong message and she realised Oliver was clearly missing their old friendship.

'If you want,' Oliver said sullenly. 'I'm not very hungry.'

'Not even for a pizza?' Nicola coaxed. 'Message Andrew and find out if he'd like to come for supper.'

Back downstairs, she made herself a cup of coffee and sat sipping it thoughtfully. Oliver's worries had reopened all her own doubts over the move. He was right; Marc had never wanted to return to France to live.

'The family would suffocate me, particularly my father,' he'd always said. 'You wouldn't believe how patriarchal these old French families can be. No, I'm definitely better off away from there.'

There was no way she was going to let Henri Jacques suffocate Oliver. He was her son and she was determined to make a success of this new life for them both whilst safeguarding Oliver's inheritance – without any interference from Henri. He was the grandfather, not the father, in this instance and he'd have a fight on his hands if he tried to take control of things.

Pensively, she looked out of the window. Since the evening when Andrew had advocated a clean break because of the move, they'd only spoken on the phone once or twice. She realised he was trying to distance himself from her in an effort to make the break easier, but she did miss his friendly presence.

The phone rang half an hour later.

'Nicola, it's Andrew. Listen, Oliver has invited me to supper and I wanted to check—'

'Please come, Andrew,' Nicola interrupted. 'Oliver needs to see you. He's not very happy at the moment and he's missing you not being around as much as usual,' she said.

There was a short silence at the other end of the line before Andrew asked.

'Is seven-thirty all right?'

'Thanks. And, Andrew?' Nicola paused. 'You still have the

spare key – use it.'

* * *

Oliver was still upstairs when Andrew arrived clutching a bunch of flowers and a box of chocolates.

'Peace offering,' he said, handing them to Nicola. 'I'm sorry I haven't been in touch with you. I've been trying to sort things out in my mind.' He looked at her and sighed. 'Nicola, I hate the thought of you going to France. I also hate the fact that you will no longer be a part of my everyday life – but I can't bear the thought of losing contact with you altogether. I don't think a clean break when you leave is an option. Please may I at least have visiting rights in your new life?'

'I'd like that,' Nicola said with a smile. 'And I know Oliver will too.'

A wry smile flitted across Andrew's face. 'A couple of weeks for you to settle in and then I'll be the first guest at Le Jardin de Dominic. Okay?'

The doorbell rang at that moment and Nicola jumped up.

'The pizzas are here.'

A few minutes later, as the three of them enjoyed slices of pizza, Andrew glanced at Oliver.

'Bet you're getting excited for France.'

'Don't want to go,' Oliver mumbled through a mouthful of pizza, looking down.

Andrew glanced at Nicola, his eyebrows raised. When she shrugged in response he took a deep breath.

'Why not? You liked France and the farm when you went.'

'All my friends are here. You're here. I'll have to learn French, which is hard.'

'You'll make new friends. Learning a new language when you

live in the country is different, still hard but using it every day you'll learn quickly. I bet when I come for a visit in a few months you'll have so much to tell and show me.'

'You're coming to stay with us?'

Andrew nodded. 'Of course.'

Nicola, listening to the two of them, was grateful to Andrew for being so upbeat about their move to France, seamlessly taking Marc's place in comforting and encouraging Oliver like he'd done so often in the past.

Nicola and Oliver stood and watched as the furniture van disappeared down the road and out of sight. Nicola put her arm around her son's shoulders.

'Just think, the next time we see that we'll be in France,' she said.

'They will look after Frisby properly, won't they?' Oliver asked anxiously.

'Of course. Bill, the foreman, told me he loves cats. He's got one even older than Frisby. I've given them lots of her favourite food. I suspect she'll eat and sleep all the way down – that's much nicer than being put in the noisy hold of a plane. Come on, let's get our things. Andrew will be here any moment.'

'It's strange to think we'll never come back here, isn't it?'

Nicola looked at him quickly but didn't say anything. As they dragged their suitcases to the front door, Oliver looked thoughtful.

'Are you sad at leaving this house, Mum?'

Nicola nodded. 'A bit. Your dad and I were very happy here in the beginning. You were born here.' She glanced at Oliver and realised he was close to tears. 'You know, Oliver, the bricks and mortar aren't important. It's the memories we take with us. And we've both got some happy memories of this house, haven't we?'

Oliver nodded. 'Yes. And once we've left, I won't keep expecting Dad to walk through the door – even though I know he's never coming back.'

'Oh Oliver, come here,' Nicola said, putting her arms around him and hugging him tight. 'I miss him too and I do understand. This new life in France will be good, you'll see. We'll make some more happy memories together.'

A toot from a car horn made them both jump and the next moment Andrew was striding up the garden path.

'Hi. Give me hand with the luggage, Oliver, while your mum locks up – then we'll be off.'

Once at the airport, Andrew waited with them until they'd checked in and Nicola had their boarding passes.

'Before you go, please listen to me, both of you,' Andrew began. 'Nicola, if things don't work out for any reason, you know my home is there for both of you – no strings. And Oliver, any time you want to see United play, I'd be more than happy to have you stay and take you.' He gave Oliver a hug and turned to give Nicola a tighter one. 'I'm going to miss you both so much.'

Nicola swallowed hard. She was useless at goodbyes.

'Things will be fine, Andrew. We'll miss you too, but you're coming over for a visit in a few weeks as soon as the cottage is straight,' she said.

She turned to Oliver and caught hold of his hand.

'Right, our adventure starts here. Let's go.'

Nicola smiled a final goodbye at Andrew before turning away. She held Oliver's hand tightly as they both walked through the security gate and on into the departure lounge. The clock was ticking down on their new French life; there was no going back now.

15

It was early evening when they landed at Nice airport and both Nicola and Oliver were pleased to see Raoul waiting for them in the arrivals hall.

'Welcome back to France,' Raoul said, kissing Nicola on the cheek and shaking Oliver's hand.

Taking the luggage trolley from Nicola, he waited for the automatic doors to open and then led them towards his car.

'Claudine sends her best wishes by the way. She was planning on coming down with me to meet you – to give you a proper welcome to France – but she's not feeling too good this evening.'

'Oh, nothing serious, I hope,' Nicola said.

Raoul shook his head. 'No, I don't think so. Anyway, she said she'd be up to see you at either Le Jardin or the farm tomorrow.'

Outside, the air was warm and scented with the smell of eucalyptus trees that lined the car park. Nicola took a deep breath. It was so different from the wet weather they'd left behind.

'Is everything progressing okay with Le Jardin?' she asked as they began the drive out to La Prouveresse.

'C'est bon,' Raoul answered. 'The notaire says the papers will be ready for signing this weekend and the Le Jardin will be yours.'

'Good,' Nicola said. 'By the way, what was the little local problem that held everything up?' Oliver, sitting in the back seat, had clamped his headphones back on his head, so she knew he wouldn't overhear their conversation.

Raoul hesitated for several seconds.

'Henri,' he muttered finally.

'Henri? But it's nothing to do with him...' Nicola paused as realisation dawned. She should have known Henri would interfere. He hadn't liked it when she'd refused to live up at the farm with him and the tantes. 'He tried to stop you selling to me?'

'Oui. He really put the pressure on me to sell to him for a while and then I got a phone call saying it was all off and I had to sell to you after all.'

'But, Raoul, we'd shaken on the deal. Why didn't you at least ring me and tell me what was going on?'

There was a long silence and Nicola wondered if he was going to answer her question. Eventually he shrugged.

'To be honest, Nicola, I didn't know what to do. Henri kept insisting that you and Oliver belonged on the farm – that he would see you all right. He was talking about renovating the cottage for you before you moved in. Besides, I kept hoping he would change his mind and eventually he did. I think the twins had a hand in that, mind you,' he added thoughtfully. 'Both of them have been a bit distant with me recently.'

Nicola sat watching passing cars flash by. She might have guessed Henri would try to interfere at this early stage, but at least Josephine and Odette had somehow managed to put a stop to his scheming.

'Raoul, are you absolutely certain that the papers will be

ready for me to sign soon? I won't be able to rest until I know for sure that Le Jardin is mine.'

'You have my word – it's yours,' Raoul said. 'There is just one more thing though.'

'What now?' Nicola's heart plummeted at the thought of more problems before she'd even moved in.

'Last week the local council gave themselves permission to develop the field next to Le Jardin. If you don't want to go ahead with the purchase because of it, I'd understand.'

Nicola sighed. She suddenly felt very tired. The last few weeks had been physically and emotionally draining and now the last thing she needed was to find there were problems surrounding Le Jardin.

'What sort of development. A block of apartments? Houses?'

Raoul shook his head. 'Nothing like that. They plan a tourist information centre with "A Taste of the Countryside" shop: "Le Goût de La Campagne". It won't be that big – a single-storey pre-fabricated wooden building with a small car park.'

Nicola was silent. She'd liked the fact that Le Jardin didn't have any close neighbours but, being set back off a main road, wasn't isolated either. Having a tourist information office next door would inevitably mean people coming and going and more noise from cars.

'What exactly is this shop going to sell?'

'It will promote and sell produce from the local area,' Raoul said. 'Honey, olive oil, wine, apple juice, soap, pottery – anything that is from around here.'

'So, if I can get Le Jardin functioning as a pépinière again, I might have a market right on my doorstep?' Nicola said thoughtfully.

'Oui,' Raoul said, glancing at her. 'It could be good for you.'

'Can I look at the plans anywhere?'

'If you like, I'll take you down to the Hôtel de Ville some time and explain them to you,' Raoul offered. 'Henri will be able to tell you more – he might even know when they plan to start building. He's on the town council, and hoping to become mayor one day.'

Nicola was silent. Right now she was so cross with the way Henri had tried to buy Le Jardin from under her that she was determined not to ask him for anything. It would be difficult enough accepting his hospitality for the next few days until the furniture arrived. She was going to have to carefully watch every move Henri made and make sure she was one step ahead of him. The sooner she could sign the completion papers for Le Jardin de Dominic and start an independent French life, the better.

16

The next morning, Nicola inserted the large key into the front door lock of 'Le Jardin de Dominic' and took a deep breath before turning it. Her next step would carry her across the threshold into her new home and life.

Once inside, she quickly opened the shutters, allowing the sun to come streaming in through the clean windows and casting its light across the newly scrubbed and polished terracotta tiled floors. Josephine and Odette had done an amazing job of cleaning the place and the musty smell of a neglected cottage that Nicola remembered had been replaced by the sweet scent of cleaning materials and bunches of dried lavender and rosemary hanging from the beams. Sniffing appreciatively, Nicola resolved to find thank you presents for them both when she went to the village. Yesterday, when she and Oliver had climbed out of Raoul's car, the twins had welcomed them with hugs and exclamations of how good it was to have them back. Henri had fleetingly said 'Bonjour' before disappearing to do some urgent work on the farm.

Nicola wandered around for some time visualising where the

furniture would go when it arrived. The cottage was smaller than their old home, so she'd decided to bring only the things she couldn't live without and get rid of everything else. In the end, it was the comfy settee, beds, kitchen table and chairs, rugs, books, bookcases and all the white goods from the kitchen that had been loaded into the furniture van with their personal stuff. Enough she hoped to begin turning the cottage into a home.

Standing in the empty kitchen, she mentally planned the best places to put things like the washing machine, the cooker, the fridge and the dishwasher. Not a fan of fitted kitchen cupboards, one of the things she had on her 'want' list was a large dresser with shelves and cupboards that she could 'distress' in a shabby-chic way and give it a perfect home on the back wall.

Seeing two or three tins of paint and several brushes on the floor by the kitchen door reminded Nicola of her plan for the morning – painting the kitchen walls. Ten minutes later, humming happily to herself, she began to paint the long wall a shade the tin described as 'sunshine yellow'. The noise of the tractor at La Prouveresse two fields away drifted down towards her and she glanced out of the kitchen window.

Oliver had begged to be excused from decorating duties, saying he wanted to work with Henri in the olive grove. Much to Oliver's disappointment, Nicola had made Henri promise he wouldn't let him anywhere near the tractor driving seat. The promise had been made begrudgingly and Nicola knew she would need to make sure Henri didn't break it. She was still debating whether to let him know she knew about his deceitful attempt to buy Le Jardin but Henri was doing a good job of avoiding her.

Moving into Le Jardin would inevitably put some distance between themselves and Henri as they made friends and settled into their new lives. Hopefully, there would soon be other influences outside the farm – and Henri – competing for Oliver's attention.

As she neared the end of the back kitchen wall, Nicola heard a car door slam and, seconds later, the noise of the old-fashioned iron knocker on the front door was echoing around the empty house.

Cautiously, she opened the door to find Claudine standing there clutching a plant pot.

'Hi! Raoul said I'd find you here this morning. I wanted to be your first visitor. Can't stay long, as I promised maman I'd pick her up to show her the house Philippe and I have found, but I just thought I'd welcome you to your new home. This needs to go outside.'

Nicola thanked her and, as instructed, placed the potted grapefruit plant on the yet-to-be cleaned patio beneath the kitchen window.

'The blossoms will smell wonderful,' Claudine said. 'I love the wall colour,' she added as they walked back into the kitchen.

'You don't think it's too bright?' Nicola asked anxiously. As the paint dried, it looked far more garish than she'd envisaged.

Claudine shook her head. 'Non. C'est bon. It's cheerful. Besides, it will soon fade. Where's Oliver?'

'Helping Henri,' Nicola said. 'Talking of Oliver, I have to sort something out about schools for him. Any idea where I start?'

Claudine frowned. 'Difficile. He's thirteen, isn't he? There is a senior school in the next village, but all the lessons would be in French. How about the international school down in Nice? Although you'd have to drive him there every day and collect him. And it is fee-paying.'

Nicola pulled a face. 'Not sure about a private school. Marc was always dead against the idea.'

'Why not reserve Oliver a place at the local school then and let him have an extra-long summer holiday this year? All the senior schools will be busy with the baccalaureate in the next few weeks,' Claudine said thoughtfully. 'He can start a new school year in September. He'll probably have made a few friends in the village by then too. And you can ask Henri and the aunts to talk to him in French to help him with his language skills.'

'That's a good idea,' Nicola said thoughtfully. 'It's been a hard year for him. A summer off will give him a chance to come to terms with things – settle in here and then get on with his education. Thanks, Claudine.'

'Bon! I must dash,' Claudine said, looking at her watch. 'Oh, I have a message from Raoul before I forget. He's arranged for two men to come and help move your furniture in tomorrow morning. They'll be here about ten o'clock.'

'I'd better get painting then. Do thank Raoul for me.'

Claudine leaned forward to give Nicola the customary cheek kisses. 'Bonne chance in your new home, Nicola.'

* * *

Forty-eight hours later, Nicola, standing in the chaos that was the sitting-room of Le Jardin, was glaring at Henri and his companion.

'Henri, whatever possessed you to do this without checking with me first?'

'I didn't know I needed permission to give my grandson a present.'

'It all depends on the present,' Nicola snapped. 'Have you told him about it?'

'Non. It's a surprise.'

'Well, that's something, I suppose. You can take it back and he doesn't need to know anything about it.' Nicola took a deep breath and tried to control her anger. After the stress of the last few days, she didn't need this added hassle with Henri.

The furniture van had been delayed on the autoroute and it was half a day late arriving at Le Jardin, throwing everything and everybody behind schedule. The two men Raoul had arranged to help with the furniture couldn't come at the new time and, despite both Josephine and Odette spending the day at the cottage to help with the unpacking, there were still boxes everywhere waiting to be unpacked. Because of the muddle, Nicola and Oliver had been forced to spend an extra night up at the farm instead of moving into Le Jardin as planned. Tonight though, they were finally going to sleep in their new home and Nicola had been desperately searching for the box of bed linen when Henri arrived with his inopportune present.

If only he'd waited until they were a bit more settled before springing this on her. The thing was, she quite liked the look of Henri's companion, but she needed to make him understand that he'd overstepped the mark by not asking her first.

'So, is there a story behind this present?' Nicola asked wearily.

Before Henri could answer, Oliver came running downstairs.

'Bonjour Papa Henri. Oh, you've got a new dog. What's its name?' Oliver ran over and threw his arms around the dog, who licked his face and wagged her tail.

'Mischief,' Henri said with a defiant look at Nicola. 'And she's not my dog. I got her for you. But your maman says you can't have her.'

'No, I didn't,' Nicola protested. 'I just said I wished you'd asked me first.'

'No time. Vètinairé was about to take her to the refuge. The couple who owned her have left France and abandoned her.'

'Can I keep her, Mum?' Oliver gave her a pleading look. 'Pleease?'

Feeling she was being forced into making the decision, Nicola sighed. 'It's a big responsibility, Oliver. She'll need walking, grooming and training, she looks quite young. And what about Frisby? She's barely had time to settle in.'

'They'll get used to each other,' Oliver replied confidently. 'She's never been afraid of dogs. Please. I promise to look after Mischief. She can sleep with me too.'

'If it's a problem having her here, I can keep her up at the farm, be company for Meg, and Oliver can come up there to—' Henri began.

'No,' Nicola interrupted Henri firmly. 'If Mischief is going to be Oliver's dog then she will live down here with us. And he will look after her.' She knew Henri was trying to make her look like the disapproving mother.

'I can keep her then?' Oliver asked.

Nicola nodded.

'Thanks, Mum. I'll take her to meet Frisby right now.' Taking hold of Mischief's lead, he ran from the room with the dog.

'We now have a cat and a dog, Henri. Oliver doesn't need any more pets, or surprise presents, okay? Now, if you'll excuse me, I still have this place to try to finish sorting out.'

* * *

The rest of the day passed in a blur of unpacking, putting things away and arranging things, although Nicola had discovered there was a distinct lack of cupboard space in the cottage.

It was past eight o'clock in the evening before she decided she'd had enough. The rest of the unpacking could wait until tomorrow. Earlier, Oliver had pulled an ancient table out of the outbuilding, scrubbed it clean and placed it on the patio outside the kitchen. Impulsively, Nicola decided it was warm enough to eat their first meal at Le Jardin outside and she threw a bright cloth over the table.

Josephine had made them up a supper picnic basket with one of her special chicken flans and a tarte au citron. There was some crisps and lemonade for Oliver and a small bottle of La Prouveresse wine for Nicola.

'You won't have time to cook,' Josephine had said as she insisted on leaving the hamper in the kitchen. 'And you must eat.'

Now, as she and Oliver sat and ate their supper under a darkening sky, Nicola was grateful for Josephine's thoughtfulness. She hadn't realised how hungry she was, and judging by the way Oliver was tucking in, he was enjoying supper too.

Taking a sip of wine, Nicola felt herself relax finally after the rigours of the past few weeks. It was good of Raoul to let them move in before the meeting at the notaire's and paying the money over. They were finally in their new home. She closed her eyes in an attempt to set the moment in her memory.

Oliver sat with Mischief at his feet while the occasional bat began to flit around the eaves of the cottage. Whatever happened in the future, she must remember this quiet moment as the real beginning of their new lives in France.

'Mum,' Oliver's whisper sounded urgent and Nicola came back to reality with a jolt. 'Mum, I think there's someone at the top of the garden. I can see a light.'

Intruders on their first night in Le Jardin? Surely Mischief should, at least, be growling? But Mischief was oblivious to any unwanted guests. She was still sitting happily at Oliver's feet, ready to pounce on any stray crumbs.

Apprehensively, Nicola looked around the garden. Oliver was right. There was a flashing light over near the boundary wall. And one by the back gate. And yet another one by the olive tree.

'Oh, Oliver. It's not an intruder. We've got fireflies. How wonderful is that?'

Together they watched as more and more lights began to weave and dance around the garden. They were everywhere.

'It's like having fairies at the bottom of the garden dancing to an invisible orchestra,' Nicola whispered. Even Oliver was enthralled by the show they were being treated to.

The light display went on for nearly fifteen minutes before slowly fading, leaving half a dozen flickering lights in solitary splendour before they, too, disappeared and the moon alone lit the garden.

'Wow,' Oliver said. 'That was amazing.'

It was indeed, Nicola thought as she began to clear away the supper things. A wonderful, unexpected welcome to their new home and surely a good omen for the future? She could only hope so.

17

'Merci beaucoup, Madam Jacques, la pépinière Le Jardin de Dominic is now yours. I hope you and your son will be very happy there,' and the notaire stood up and shook Nicola's hand. 'I understand you have the cottage key already? These are the other keys belonging to the smallholding.' The notaire handed her a small bunch of rusty keys.

'Thank you.' As she placed them carefully in her bag, Nicola felt an overwhelming sense of relief. Nearly a week after arriving in France, Le Jardin de Dominic was finally hers. She and Oliver could safely begin their lives in their new home.

She glanced at Henri, who'd insisted on accompanying her to the lawyer's office.

'Just to help. Your French is not up to the legal phrases, is it?' was all he'd said when she'd questioned the necessity of him coming.

Nicola had to admit that her limited French was not good enough for all the official forms she'd had to fill in since arriving in France. But she couldn't help feeling that Henri was looking after his own interests too. As she and Raoul had signed the papers in the lawyer's offices it had felt very much like the point in the church marriage service where the vicar asks if there are any objections. Until she'd actually signed, Nicola kept expecting Henri to intervene in some way.

Now, he moved to her side as they left the notaire's office to walk back to the car.

'Voila! You have your smallholding. I, too, hope you and Oliver will be happy there.'

'Thank you, Henri,' Nicola said quietly, hoping that he meant what he said.

'Good doing business with you, Nicola,' Raoul said, shaking her hand. 'If you have any problems or I can help in any way, just give me a ring,' he added.

Before Nicola could say anything in reply, Henri cut in.

'Now she's here, she's got me and the family for that.'

Nicola tried to conceal her resentment. Henri hadn't shown much family loyalty to them in the past, but now she and Oliver were living in France it was obvious that the renowned Henri Jacques possessive streak was going to resurface.

Raoul glanced at Henri sharply before turning to Nicola.

'Well, you know where I am anyway,' he said.

Nicola looked at them both in turn. 'I appreciate the help I've had from both of you, but I've got to stand on my own two feet. I did in England, so there is no reason why I shouldn't do it out here. Just got to get to grips with things and improve my French quickly.'

Henri ignored her remarks.

'Well, I've got work to do back at the farm,' he said, before striding off in the direction of his car.

Raoul smiled. 'You'll soon pick the language up. And you could always find yourself a French sleeping dictionary.' Nicola looked at him blankly and Raoul glanced at Henri, making sure he was out of earshot, before leaning towards her and saying quietly, 'Take a French lover.'

He smiled as Nicola took a step back from him, her eyes wide open in surprise.

'Raoul, really. You forget I was married to Marc for several years and that didn't do much for my French.'

'Ah, but that was in Angleterre,' Raoul said. 'You were Marc's English sleeping dictionary.'

Nicola glanced at him as a thought occurred.

'You're not suggesting you and I...?' She needed Raoul as a friend, nothing else.

Raoul shook his head.

'Unless?' He glanced at her mischievously and laughed at the expression on her face. 'I'm teasing, Nicola. Now, can I give you a lift back to Le Jardin?'

'Thanks, but I left Oliver up at La Prouveresse with the aunts. Henri is taking me back there to collect him, so I'd better catch up with him. After lunch I hope Oliver's going to help me do some more sorting out at Le Jardin. I can't believe how quickly the time has gone since I arrived. There's been so much to organise.'

As they hurried towards Henri in the car park, a large Range Rover swished past them before parking a few metres away from Henri's car.

'Ah, Nicola. Somebody you need to meet.' Holding her arm, Raoul led her purposefully over towards the man who was getting out of his car.

Nicola glanced at him suspiciously.

'Raoul, what are you up to?' She hesitated, remembering how flustered she'd felt at his 'take a French lover' joke earlier. 'You're not trying to...'

Raoul laughed. 'Non, Nicola, I'm not trying anything.' And he walked over to the man.

Standing to one side, Nicola watched as Raoul and the man greeted each other enthusiastically with much hugging and handshaking.

The man's sultry Mediterranean looks and dark, bohemian hairstyle seemed at odds with his businesslike suit and shiny leather shoes.

As she watched and waited for Raoul to introduce her, something tugged at Nicola's memory. Was it possible she already knew this man?

Amid the torrent of quickly spoken French, Nicola caught the occasional word.

'Anglaise... Marc... Henri... Le Jardin de Dominic.'

Raoul was clearly explaining who she was before he turned to her. 'Nicola, meet Gilles Bongars. He's the surveyor in charge of the new "Le Goût de la Campagne" and Tourist Centre.'

'Enchanté, madame.' The hand that shook Nicola's was strong and held her fingers in a tight grip before releasing them. 'You like me to discuss the proposals with you?'

Nicola nodded. 'Please,' she replied.

Both Raoul and Henri had gone over the building plans with her in the mayor's office the other day, but she was still unsure about certain things. Perhaps Gilles would be able to answer some of her questions.

'I'll be on site this afternoon at four o'clock. We meet then?'

'Thank you,' Nicola said. 'I'll look forward it.'

'So shall I, madame,' Gilles answered seriously, before saying goodbye to them both.

Henri tooted his car horn impatiently and Nicola turned quickly to Raoul. 'Goodbye and thank you.'

'Good to do business with you, Nicola. I'll bring Luc up to meet Oliver soon. They're about the same age – hopefully they will be friends.'

'Oliver would like that, I'm sure,' Nicola said. She hesitated before adding. 'I hope Luc appreciates what you're doing for him.'

Raoul shrugged. 'I hope so too. It's the least I can do.'

* * *

It was nearly lunchtime when Henri and Nicola arrived back at La Prouveresse. Henri went straight to the barn to get the tractor and tools ready for an afternoon working in the olive grove after lunch and Nicola made her way to the kitchen.

Both the aunts were there – Josephine busy preparing lunch and Odette sitting at the large wooden table with Oliver, going through the contents of a shoebox, Mischief under the table at his feet. Everyone glanced up with welcoming smiles as Nicola walked in.

'Hi, Mum. Is Le Jardin de Dominic ours now?' Oliver asked.

Nicola waved the keys in the air triumphantly. 'Yes, it's official! What have you got there?' she asked curiously, looking at the motley collection of items lying on the table.

'Some of Dad's things. Josephine and Odette have given them to me. Look, Dad had a catapult – and there's an old diary he kept when he was growing up. I'm not sure whether I ought to read that or not,' Oliver said worriedly. 'I expect he thought it was going to be private for ever and ever. I've got another photo of him now, too – skiing. Odette has said she'll take me skiing at Isola 2000 next winter if I want.'

Nicola glanced across at Odette, surprised. 'You still ski?'

'Oui, of course,' Odette said. 'These days I have the padding not to hurt too much if I fall!' She laughed, glancing down at her ample figure.

The twins insisted that Nicola and Oliver stayed for lunch and when Henri joined them Josephine produced a bottle of sparkling crémant from the fridge.

'We celebrate your new lives here in France,' she said as she gently eased the cork out with a satisfying pop before filling four glasses and a small one for Oliver. 'To the future.'

Sitting there as everyone around the kitchen table, including Henri, raised their glasses to toast the future, Nicola felt a surge of confidence flood her body. Moving to France had been the right decision for both her and Oliver and now that she owned Le Jardin she could begin to put down new roots and give Oliver the secure life he deserved.

18

Later that afternoon, driving back from the village in the farm van having done a big supermarché shop, stocking the kitchen for the first time, and passing the Le Goût de la Campagne site, Nicola saw Gilles Bongars getting out of his 4x4. Guiltily, she remembered his offer to show her the plans at four o'clock. Quickly stopping and winding down the window, she called out, 'Hi. I'm sorry, I'm running late. I need to unload my shopping. I'll be as quick as I can.'

Gilles raised his hand in acknowledgement. 'No rush.'

Nicola carried the shopping into the kitchen and quickly put the fresh food in the refrigerator and the frozen food in the freezer. The rest could wait.

Carefully pulling the front door closed behind her, Nicola made her way across to the site, where Gilles was waiting for her. For the next twenty minutes, he walked her around, explaining what was going where and patiently answering all of her questions.

Building work would begin in the next few days, but because it was a pre-fabricated wooden chalet-type building, it would be erected very quickly. Gilles expected the tourist information office desk to be open in time for the main tourist season.

'It will take time to organise and set up the farmer's co-operative as well as getting the handicraft producers together. And finding the right person to manage the place won't be easy. Because it's going to be a tourist information centre as well, staff will have to speak at least two languages.'

One of Nicola's biggest worries had been the amount of extra traffic the place would generate, but Gilles couldn't see that being a problem.

'The entrance and exit driveway are being situated at the furthest point from Le Jardin de Dominic,' he said.

Finally, it seemed all her questions had been answered.

'Thank you so much for taking the time to explain things to me,' and Nicola gave a relieved sigh.

'My pleasure,' Gilles said and he glanced over at the cottage. 'You've got a lot of work on your hands with that place.'

'I'm beginning to realise that,' Nicola laughed. 'Perhaps you can recommend a good builder when I'm ready?'

'Possibly, if not probably. With my surveyor's hat, on I'm happy to help, especially if you're planning on anything major.'

'Basically, I'm hoping to knock down the dividing walls inside to make one open space downstairs and modernise the bathroom. I'd also like to do something with the attic eventually.'

'Why don't I come across and take a look now?' Gilles said with a smile.

'Are you sure you don't mind? I feel I've imposed enough on your time already.'

'It's not a problem,' Gilles answered, cutting through Nicola's protests. 'I've got a quick call to make and then I'm finished for the day. So why don't you head over to the cottage and I'll join you in a few minutes?'

'Okay. I'll get some coffee going.'

When she opened the door to his knock five minutes later, Gilles was standing there with a basket arrangement of flowers.

'I hope you like these,' he said, smiling as he handed it to her. 'A small housewarming present – to wish you bonne chance with your new life.'

'Thank you,' Nicola said. 'That's so kind of you.'

Gilles hesitated. 'I was so sorry to hear about Marc's death. I knew him years ago – he, Raoul and I were all in the same year at college. I'm sure you and your son must miss him.'

Nicola gave him a rueful smile. 'Yes. We do both miss him. Although in recent years he was away for months on end working with the relief agency, Oliver always knew he would be home at some point. Accepting that he'd never come home again was hard, especially for Oliver.'

'It's hard when someone you've been close to is no longer around,' Gilles said. 'For whatever reason.'

He didn't expand on his words, but Nicola sensed a personal sadness there.

'This is the first time I've been in the cottage,' Gilles said, breaking the silence that had fallen between them. 'I can't believe you only arrived last week – it feels like a well-loved home already. It's certainly got lots of atmosphere and I love those beams with the bunches of lavender and rosemary hanging from them. Right, is this one of the walls you want to demolish?' he asked, taking a small hammer out of his pocket and tapping it.

'Yes, one of them, although I suspect it will be a couple of months before I can make a start on knocking things down. I need Oliver to feel settled and at home here before I start making changes.'

Gilles wandered around downstairs for some time, measuring, tapping and making notes. 'I don't see a problem,' he said finally. 'The two walls you plan to demolish are not supporting walls. I just want to take a quick look at the attached outbuilding because I think you could also put a doorway in the side wall and incorporate that as an extra room if you wanted to.'

'I hadn't even considered the possibility but that is a good idea,' she said, smiling.

When he came back in, he was shaking his head. 'Yes, it is possible, but the outbuilding itself is in a terrible state and I doubt it's worth saving. But if you ever want to put a veranda – sorry, in English, a conservatory – on that side of the cottage, it would be the perfect place.'

'Maybe in the future when I've got to grips with both the cottage and the land,' Nicola said.

'D'accord. Now, I will look at the attic?'

'I warn you, upstairs is untidy – we're still living out of suitcases because I didn't bring any wardrobes from England. The hatch to the attic is in the small bedroom, but I haven't taken a look yet,' Nicola explained as she led the way upstairs and opened the door of the small bedroom. 'Oh, are we going to need a ladder? Because I haven't got one. Not even a stepladder.'

'Let's see if we can open the hatch first,' Gilles said, picking up a rod of stainless steel with a hook in it that was propped in a corner of the bedroom, inserting it into a loop in the hatch and slowly pulling it open to reveal a folding ladder. 'Voila,' and he carefully clicked the ladder into position. 'Would you like the first look?'

Nicola shook her head. 'Not very good with ladders – you go, please.'

Gilles pulled a small pocket torch out before climbing up the ladder and disappearing into the attic. 'Hey, it's good up here. It has a floor – and there's plenty of headroom.'

'Is it empty?'

'Yes.'

Moments later, a dusty but smiling Gilles climbed back down and rejoined her on the landing.

'You'll need to do something about proper stairs, but two windows back and front in the roof and voila! You will have a large space under the stars. It would make two more good-sized rooms with room for a small bathroom also.' He unlocked the ladder and began to push it back in place.

'As easy as that?' Nicola said, smiling back at him – his enthusiasm was so infectious. Suddenly she realised why Gilles had seemed so familiar that morning when Raoul had introduced them. He reminded her of Marc, with the same dark Latin looks, the same charm and the same enthusiasm for life.

'Downstairs inside you have no need of permission, but for the windows in the attic you do. I will draw up the plans and submit them for you, yes?' Gilles asked as he followed Nicola downstairs.

'I'm honestly not in any hurry. Besides, I can't ask you to do that.'

'I offer, you're not asking. I love drawing plans, it's the best part of my job.'

'Are you sure it's no trouble?'

'For me, it's a little job. I bring the plans next week for you to see before I submit them. D'accord?'

'D'accord, and thank you very much, Gilles.' Looking at him, standing there covered in dust, Nicola laughed. 'You have a cobweb in your hair,' she said.

'Cobweb?' Gilles looked at her, puzzled, as he put his hand up to his head.

'A spider's web from the attic – here, let me get rid of it for you,' Nicola said, reaching up and carefully brushing it away. It was, she realised, an oddly intimate gesture to do for someone she barely knew and she dropped her hand quickly. 'How about that coffee I offered you,' she said and turned to lead the way back downstairs.

* * *

'Mum, did you know there's an orange tree in the garden?' Oliver asked as he helped Nicola make a start on clearing the garden of old junk later that evening.

Already there was a large pile by the front gate – the remains of an iron bedstead, rotten window-frames, a pushchair and an ancient lawnmower, amongst other rubbish all waiting for the council to come and collect.

'Really?' Nicola said absently, as she tried to move a particularly stubborn piece of rotten wood. 'Where?'

'Up by the back boundary wall. I think there's a lemon tree up there too.'

'And we've got the grapefruit tree Claudine gave us as well. Looks like we're going to have a real orchard. Let's hope they all produce lots of fruit.'

Nicola glanced at Oliver. He'd been rather quiet all evening and she was about to ask him if there was something on his mind when she heard the shrill ring of her mobile in the kitchen.

'I'll get it,' Oliver said, running towards the cottage. 'It's Andrew,' he called out from the kitchen door a few seconds later.

Making her way towards him, Nicola could hear Oliver telling Andrew about the things he'd been doing on the farm and the fact he wasn't going to school until September.

'Well, he seems happy. How about you?' Andrew said when Oliver finally handed over the phone.

'Yes, I'm happy, if tired,' Nicola said.

'How are things going out there? Henri not ruling your lives? Are you settling in all right?'

'Things are just fine. We're in the cottage now,' Nicola replied and told him a bit about the last few days and the fact that 'A Taste of the Countryside' centre was being built next door.

'Sounds as if you'll have an outlet for all your stuff straight away,' Andrew said.

'How are you?' Nicola asked. 'Still planning on coming out here to see us soon?'

'I can't wait,' Andrew said. 'Might have some exciting news when I do come. Look, I'd better go. I'll ring again next week. Don't forget if there is anything you want me to bring over when I do come, let me know. Take care. Speak again soon.'

Ending the call, Nicola realised that while she'd talked about the new centre and the plans the surveyor was drawing up for Le Jardin, she hadn't mentioned Gilles Bongars by name to Andrew. But then, why should she?

'Mum?'

'Yes, what is it?'

'It's Dad's birthday next week, isn't it?'

Nicola nodded, looking across at Oliver.

'Have you planned anything?' he asked.

'Things are very different now, Oliver,' Nicola said gently. 'I don't think celebrating Dad's birthday this year...' Her voice trailed away. She didn't know what to say. With all the business of moving to France, she'd completely forgotten about Marc's upcoming birthday. She'd always made a special occasion of the day, whether he was home or not. She'd known he'd be celebrating wherever he was in the world and had wanted Oliver to be able to join in, even at a distance. But surely Oliver wouldn't be expecting to celebrate Marc's birthday the first year after his death?

Oliver looked at her seriously. 'I know nothing will bring Dad back. But d'you think, just this year, we could have a special birthday tea up at La Prouveresse with Papa Henri and Josephine and Odette? And maybe Raoul could come too, because he was his best friend.' There was a pause before Oliver continued quietly. 'I like being in the place where he used to be and talking to people who knew him and can tell me about him. I miss him.'

'Oh, Oliver,' Nicola said, her voice tinged with sadness. 'I'll ask Josephine and Odette. If it's not possible up at the farm, we'll certainly do something here. Now come here and give me a hug.'

Holding Oliver tightly, Nicola fought to keep the tears at bay.

'Your dad would be so proud of you.'

19

Not yet midday but the heat from the sun shining in a cloudless blue sky was already intense as Nicola made her way slowly up the farm drive to La Prouveresse.

Stopping to look back at the view, she could just make out the roof of Le Jardin now partially obscured by the leaves on the trees of the small copse at the back of the house. Standing there, deep in thought, Nicola breathed in the beauty of her surroundings, realising that the stillness, which engulfed the Provençal country-side in summer, was beginning. Soon it would be too hot to work outside in the midday sun.

Oliver had already been busy giving Henri a hand harvesting the silage and storing it in the clamp. Now the shorn fields were turning brown under the heat of the sun and Nicola watched as swallows wheeled and darted for the tiny insects hovering above the small stream that ran alongside the hay field.

Taking one last look, Nicola turned and walked the last fifty metres to the farmhouse.

Henri was in the kitchen with the sisters as she pushed open the kitchen door.

'Bonjour, Nicola,' Josephine said. 'You are good today?'

'Yes, thank you,' Nicola said. 'Although I'm in desperate need of a second-hand dresser for the kitchen and a couple of wardrobes. I'll never be straight otherwise. Do you know anywhere local that sells things like that?'

Both Odette and Josephine turned to give Henri a questioning look for several seconds before Odette turned back to Nicola and broke the silence.

'There's a brocante in one of the village back lanes, but it is more bric-a-brac than furniture. You need the dépôt-vente about ten kilometres away or even Emmaus in Nice. I take you to the dépôt-vent if you like?'

'Thank you. I was wondering, has Oliver mentioned this weekend to you? Marc's birthday?'

Everyone shook their heads and Henri glanced at her sharply. 'Non.'

'The thing is, I've always made the day special for Oliver whether Marc was at home or not. More often than not, he was away,' Nicola paused. 'Oliver obviously realises that this year is different, but he still wants to do something on the day...' She took a deep breath before continuing, 'He'd like to have a special meal up here and talk about your memories of Marc. I know it's painful for everyone, but I think Oliver really needs to remember his Dad's birthday this year with people who knew him.'

It was Henri who broke the silence that followed her words.

'Marc's dead and gone,' he said. 'Nothing is going to alter that. Oliver needs to get on with his life.'

'I think that's what he is trying to do,' Nicola said slowly. 'Coming to live here, where Marc was born and grew up, has simply made him want to know more about his father. To learn about things that he would have learnt from him in the course of a proper lifetime relationship. Things that will help to keep his memory alive for him.'

Nicola looked at Josephine and Odette.

'You've already helped so much by talking about his father to him. Giving him that box of Marc's things.'

She turned to look at Henri. 'You know, it might help you to talk about Marc too. Remember him in a positive way.'

Henri regarded her stonily. 'I remember Marc in my own way. I don't find it necessary to be forever talking about him.'

It was Josephine who said, 'Henri, you – we – have so many more memories of Marc than Oliver. It can't be wrong to share them with him. I think a special dinner on Sunday celebrating Marc's life is a good idea.'

'I agree,' Odette said. 'He is only a boy, Henri, whose whole world has been turned upside down since he lost his father and Nicola brought him here to be closer to us, his family and his memory. The least you can do is have a little understanding.'

Ignoring Henri's mutinous face, she turned and spoke directly to Nicola.

'It's so good having you both living here and anything we can do to help make you and Oliver happy in your new life, I and Josephine will do. We all know it wasn't an easy decision for you to come and live in France, don't we, Henri?' she said, turning directly back to her brother.

There was complete silence, broken only by the buzz of the kitchen boiler for several seconds.

It was Henri who broke the silence when, to Nicola's surprise, he looked at Odette, nodded and muttered, 'Oui. Arrange what you like,' before opening the kitchen door and slamming it behind him as he left.

'Voila. It is arranged,' Josephine said. 'Dinner on Sunday will be dedicated to the memory of Marc.'

'You can all come down to Le Jardin if it would make it easier,' Nicola said hesitantly. 'I know Oliver wanted it to be up here in Marc's old home, but if it's going to cause resentment...' Her voice trailed away anxiously.

'Non. It is better here,' Odette said. 'I promise you Henri will come round to the idea.'

'If you're sure, thank you.'

Leaving the twins to their work, Nicola was surprised when Henri, standing by the open door of one of the small outbuildings, called out to her as she walked across the farmyard.

'Nicola, you come see.'

Smothering a 'what now?' retort, Nicola obeyed and followed Henri into a stone building she'd never been in before. An Aladdin's cave that was stuffed with a mixture of house furniture and ancient farm implements. Things that had been discarded by generations of Jacques were now piled up in a haphazard jumble.

'You've got your own dépôt-vente in here, Henri,' Nicola said in amazement, trying to take it all in.

Henri shrugged. 'Nothing worth anything; antiques were sold a long time ago. But there is this old commode de cuisine,' he said, stopping in front of a kitchen dresser. 'You want this?'

'It would be perfect for the cottage kitchen,' Nicola said, taking a closer look. Three open shelves and a deep cupboard on the bottom, with two drawers and a shelf. 'Would you mind though, if I painted it?'

'Do as you wish. Tomorrow I bring it in the trailer. Oliver and Raoul will help. There is a small wardrobe behind it. I bring that too. Okay,' Before Nicola could thank him, Henri had turned and was already striding out of the building.

Walking down to Le Jardin deep in thought, Nicola wondered about Henri's sudden decision to offer her the old furniture. Remembering the looks both Josephine and Odette had given him earlier, she wondered if Henri could possibly be suffering with a guilty conscience over something. The sisters had definitely applied the pressure, agreeing about having a party at the weekend, and almost daring Henri not to fulfil Oliver's request. Their words had seemed to hold an unspoken threat.

Fleetingly, Nicola speculated about what sort of hold the two women could possibly have over their brother before deciding it was no concern of hers. The main thing was Oliver would be able to talk about Marc on his birthday, with people who had known and loved him when he was young. Get to learn a little more about the man who had been his father. Perhaps she too would learn something new about the man she'd loved and married.

As Nicola opened the back gate to Le Jardin, Gilles Bongars drove in off the main road and parked by the front door.

'Bonjour, Nicola. I meet with the mayor next door in an hour, but I have brought some preliminary sketches to show you. You have the time to look?'

'Come on in,' Nicola said, opening the door. 'Raoul has taken Oliver to meet Luc, so I am on my own for lunch. Would you like to join me? Nothing fancy, just salad and tuna.'

'Thank you,' Gilles said. 'I did sketches for the roof windows, the new staircase you will need and also for a conservatory, so when you are ready you have the plans for everything.'

The sketches, when Gilles unrolled them for her to see were amazing, the cottage would be transformed once she had the work done.

'I can't thank you enough for these, or for doing them so quickly,' Nicola said.

After the sketches were rolled up again Gilles gave her a hand organising lunch and they sat down companionably to eat on the terrace under the shade of the large parasol Odette had loaned her from La Prouveresse.

'You are enjoying your new life here in France? You think it will, how you say, work out for you?' Gilles asked as he poured them both glasses of water, having declined to drink rosé with the meal because he had to drive back down to Nice.

'Early days yet, but I think it's going to be okay. My biggest worry is Oliver. Him coming to terms with Marc's death and being happy here is the most important thing.'

'You are lucky to have Josephine and Odette nearby, and Henri too, of course. You're not completely alone in a strange land.'

Nicola didn't like to tell Gilles that whilst Josephine and Odette were always there for her, she never quite knew how Henri was going to react to anything she said or did.

'Although even having family around can be difficult in times of bereavement,' Gilles added thoughtfully. 'They don't always understand that sometimes it is necessary to let the grief out. Be angry at what has happened. Relatives can smother your natural emotions with good intentions, simply to encourage you to get on with your life.'

Nicola glanced at him. Clearly Gilles had seen some tragedy in his life too.

He looked at her sadly. 'One day I will tell you how I know this, but not today. Now,' he said, standing up, 'I must go. Thank you for lunch. Will you allow me to return the favour soon? There's a little restaurant in the next village where I often have lunch when I'm out this way.'

'I'd love that, thank you,' Nicola said.

'Bien. I will ring you soon.'

Watching Gilles drive away, she thought about the sadness she'd glimpsed in his eyes when he'd spoken about the need to let grief out. Whatever tragedy had happened in his life, it had clearly made him receptive to others' emotions.

20

Henri was as good as his word and appeared early the next morning with the two parts of the dresser in the farm trailer, a small wardrobe and Raoul standing hanging on to the back of the tractor. As she was going to paint the dresser, Nicola suggested the best plan was to simply place the two pieces separately in the outhouse where she could work on them and then she and Oliver would assemble the dresser in the kitchen when it was ready.

Between them, Henri and Raoul managed to get the wardrobe up the stairs and into Nicola's bedroom.

'Give me a shout when you want to move the base of the dresser,' Raoul said as he and Henri left. 'That part is heavy.'

'Thanks.'

Over the next few days, Nicola concentrated on trying to get the garden and land near the house in to some sort of order, as well as sanding down the dresser and giving it an undercoat. Oliver gave her a hand in the garden and together they pulled weeds, pruned bushes and cleaned out the silted-up pond. Mischief was happy to join them and contribute by digging holes in the freshly weeded soil. Frisby, curled up in a patch of sunshine nearby, watched with his eyes half closed. Afterwards, Oliver pulled the old bicycle out of the shed and offered to clean it up.

'Be useful for shopping in the village,' he said. 'The basket will hold quite a lot. Save you carrying it until we get a car. I can use it too, until you get me a bike again,' he added with a cheeky grin as he started scraping the rust off the wheels.

After all their hard work, the garden was already starting to look better and Nicola was pleased with their efforts. Next week she intended to bribe Oliver into giving her a hand digging over a patch of the land at the top of the holding.

* * *

On Saturday afternoon, they were just setting out to walk into the village to cheer on Henri, who was playing with the local boules team in an inter-village competition, when Nicola's mobile rang – with a distraught Andrew on the other end.

'Calm down. Whatever has happened?' she asked.

'You know I said I might have some news to tell you? Well, I have, but it's not what I expected.' There was a pause. 'Instead of the promotion I was expecting, I've been made redundant.'

Even though he was a thousand miles away, Nicola could sense Andrew's bitterness.

'I've got a golden handshake, but the fact remains I'm unemployed as of the end of the month.'

'I'm so sorry, but I'm sure you'll soon find another job. Try thinking of the redundancy as an opportunity for you to do something new.' She took a deep breath. 'Why don't you come over here earlier and stay for longer than the week you planned? That way you'll have time to relax and think about your future properly.'

Even as she made the offer, Nicola felt her heart sink. Did she really want Andrew coming to stay for an indefinite time? Living in close proximity could throw up all sorts of problems. The cottage was too small for guests, particularly one who had said he wanted more from her than she was prepared to give. But Andrew had been her friend for a long time and had been at her side through the toughest of tough times, having him to stay was the least she could do in return.

'Not sure that I'm even going to come now,' Andrew said.

'Think about it, anyway. I'm sorry, but I'm walking to the village with Oliver. We're already late. Call me later and we'll talk,' she said. 'Now, cheer up and try to think positive.'

Nicola frowned as she ended the call. Andrew was clearly in a state. She could only hope that if he did decide to come, he'd manage to come to terms with his redundancy before he arrived. The short visit she had been anticipating him to make had taken on a longer, almost, ominous quality.

Oliver had run on ahead while she was on the phone and by the time she caught up with him, he had joined Josephine and Odette, who were watching Henri and his team from the edge of the ground. Nicola found a seat on one of the wrought-iron benches under the shade of the leafy plane trees, and sitting there with Mischief at her feet, she let her thoughts drift as she half-heartedly watched the game.

It was so pleasant, people watching and listening to the cries of joy and despair as players threw a solid steel ball in the direction of the small red jack in an attempt to have their boule land the closest.

Listening to Oliver's happy laughter, Nicola began to relax. It might be early days yet, but she was beginning to believe that she had done the right thing in moving to France. It had given her the smallholding she'd always dreamed of and Oliver the chance of growing up in beautiful countryside, surrounded by family. Their lives were settling down into a gentle rhythm and Oliver was definitely happier. Deciding to give him the summer off had been a good idea. The headmaster at the school, when Nicola had rung to see about reserving a place for Oliver, had been sympathetic when she'd explained the circumstances, agreeing that a stress-free month or two was probably a good idea for his mental health.

Nicola glanced across to see Oliver standing next to Henri who was clearly explaining some rule about the game. She knew it was far too early to tell, but Oliver's relationship with his grandfather seemed to be developing along the right lines. So far, Henri hadn't overstepped any of the boundaries she had in place to stop him interfering in Oliver's life. She sensed that for a proud man of the old school who rarely let his emotions show, Henri was finding Oliver's presence in his life a pleasure, even if it was a challenge to him not to interfere on a daily basis.

Mischief stirred at her feet and barked a greeting as Oliver came running over to them.

'Mum, Grandpa Henri says I can have Dad's boule set if I'm serious about learning to play. He says he'll look it out and give them to me tomorrow evening.'

Ah, tomorrow evening. The dinner party at La Prouveresse to remember and celebrate Marc's birthday. Oliver was looking forward to it so much, but Nicola still had reservations about it after Henri's initial reaction to the idea.

'About tomorrow evening – you won't expect too much will you, Oliver?' Nicola said. 'People, particularly Papa Henri, may be unable to communicate their true feelings and emotions about your dad. I'm sure too, they will all remember him differently. A different side of him.'

'I know that, Mum. I just want to hear about some of the

things he did when he was growing up. There are all sorts of things in his diary that he never mentioned to me.'

'So, you've been reading his diary then?' Nicola asked with a smile.

Oliver nodded. 'I decided Dad wouldn't mind me reading it – even though it's a private thing. It's not as if I'm going to show it to everyone. Although you can read it if you want?' He looked at Nicola.

'Maybe when you've finished it.' Deep down though, Nicola knew she was unlikely to read it. Oliver was clearly getting some solace from reading about his dad's boyhood here on the farm but too much time had passed for her to benefit from reading a young Marc's thoughts.

'Was that Andrew on the phone earlier? He is still coming to see us?'

'Yes. Might even stay longer than we expected him to.' And she explained about Andrew losing his job.

'How long will he stay then, d'you think?'

'I've no idea,' Nicola said. 'It depends on lots of things. He might have to return home quickly for job interviews.' She shrugged.

'If you two get married, he won't want us to go back to England, will he?' Oliver asked, looking at her anxiously.

'Whatever makes you think we might get married?' Nicola said, stunned by the unexpected question.

'Andrew asked me once if I'd mind if you married him.'

'He had no business asking you that,' Nicola said, inwardly furious with Andrew. There was a slight pause before she added, 'There are no plans for Andrew and I to marry and there never will be.' Even after the divorce from Marc, when he'd hoped she'd meet someone else, have more children, Nicola hadn't been interested in a new relationship with anyone. Perhaps at some time in the future she'd fall in love again but Oliver would need to be a lot older before that happened. He was and would continue to be her priority, his feelings paramount. But now Oliver had brought up the subject she couldn't help wondering.

'How would you feel if I did get married again? Would you mind?'

Oliver shook his head. 'No. I like Andrew. He doesn't try to boss me around – he's a friend. But I like it here too. I definitely wouldn't want to go back. So, if you do get married, Andrew will have to come here to live.'

Nicola smothered a sigh. 'I've just told you. Andrew and I will never be getting married so stop worrying about having to go back to England.'

No doubt about it, when Andrew arrived, she would have to reiterate that she didn't think about him in that way and make sure he truly understood the way things were. Platonic friendship was all that she was able to give him.

21

Nicola spent most of Sunday giving the dresser its top coat of the palest olive green paint she'd ever seen. Standing back to look at her handiwork, she gave a happy smile. She'd done a good job; the dresser was going to look amazing in the kitchen. Tonight at the party she'd ask Raoul if he could give her a hand tomorrow to carry it in and help her assemble it.

As Nicola and Oliver walked up to La Prouveresse early in the evening, they could hear voices and soft music drifting in the air from the petit jardin. Josephine and Odette had spent the day turning the small area into a perfect dinner party setting.

The weathered wooden table had been covered with a gaily patterned Provençal cloth and laid with the best china and glasses. Josephine and Odette had persuaded Henri to weave some fairy lights in among the bougainvillea and yellow citronella candles were already flickering away in terracotta pots. To Oliver's obvious delight, a small case containing six steel boule balls had been placed on his chair.

'Thank you, Papa Henri. I'll take great care of them. Was Dad a good player?'

'Yes. Played for the junior village team. Star player, so you've got quite a reputation to live up to,' Henri said sternly.

'I'll do my best,' Oliver said seriously.

Nicola glanced at Henri, trying to gauge the mood he was in, but his face was impassive as he silently handed her a glass of wine before turning away to greet Sylvie, who had arrived with Raoul and Claudine.

Nicola sighed. Henri clearly still wasn't happy about this birthday celebration. Hopefully the others would be forthcoming with their memories and Henri would relax as the evening wore on. Even if he didn't contribute any of his own memories of Marc, surely listening to others talking about his son would help him, whether he realised it or not. She did understand that this evening was going to be difficult for him, for all of them, herself included, but being surrounded by friends and family had to help them all get through it for Oliver's sake.

It was Raoul who started things off as they all enjoyed the first course of smoked salmon and salad, by asking Odette. 'D'you remember cooking a salmon the first time we got back from a weekend's camping and fishing up in the mountains?'

Odette nodded. 'Oui. It was delicious. Marc said it had taken a long time to catch it.'

Raoul nodded. 'Mmm. We'd spent most of the day with the others and caught nothing, so we went out at midnight and poached it from another river.'

'Imbeciles!' Henri said. 'If you'd been caught, it would have been me paying the fine.'

Raoul shrugged. 'We were ten. It was an adventure. We didn't stop to think about the consequences. And it wasn't as if we did it again. It was the only time I ever knew Marc to intentionally break the law.'

Raoul looked at Henri.

'Besides, in those days all Marc wanted to do was to please you. We only went poaching because he'd promised to bring you a salmon. He didn't want to come back without one.'

Henri absorbed this information silently.

It was Josephine who said, 'Marc was never one to make idle promises. You always knew if Marc said he'd do something, he would. And usually with lots of enthusiasm. He was such a kind boy.'

'He was so good with the animals too,' Odette said. 'Except for that rogue ram we had one year.'

As Nicola sat listening to Odette and the others reminiscing and laughing about the ram that had butted everything and everybody, her own memories of Marc began to filter back. How happy they'd been in the beginning. The hopes they'd had for the future. Their shared joy at the birth of Oliver.

Then other memories began to drift into her mind.

Her unhappiness as Marc started to distance himself from her, getting more and more involved in his humanitarian work. Her inability to understand why he had to sacrifice his – her – personal happiness. The divorce she'd never wanted.

It was only now she was here, living with Marc's family around her, that she realised how much of her life had been dictated by Marc's wants and needs. Those feelings of anger and of resentment that had begun to surface during the scattering of Marc's ashes nudged their way back to the forefront of her mind. Marc's chosen lifestyle shouldn't have ruled her life to the extent it did, but she was equally guilty of not standing up to Marc more, not arguing for what she wanted. She'd been so determined to protect Oliver at all costs from the fallout of his parents' marriage, she'd allowed her own dreams and desires to be pushed aside.

Now though, she had a chance, a new opportunity, to make her own dreams come true, something she was going to make the most of for her sake and Oliver's. There was no way she was going to allow regrets for things done, or not done, in the past to influence their future.

She glanced across at Oliver as he laughed at something Raoul said, before saying quietly to Odette so he couldn't hear, 'The Marc I knew and loved could also be incredibly selfish. He always wanted things done his way.'

'Took after his father there then,' Josephine said, sotto voce, overhearing, as she placed the roasted leg of lamb on the table.

Nicola stared at her in surprise and then smiled her agreement.

'The Jacques men have always been stubborn,' Odette said in a loud voice, looking at Henri, who ignored her remark as he began to carve the meat.

'I've been reading Dad's diary,' Oliver said to Raoul. 'He mentions you a lot. You were best friends for a long time, weren't you?'

Raoul nodded. 'From the day we first met at the Ecole Maternelle until...' he paused, clearly choosing his words carefully, 'until the day he left. Didn't even tell me he was going. He did write to me though, when he met your Maman. Asked me to be best man at the wedding.' He glanced across at Nicola. 'You looked beautiful. It was a great wedding. I thought you two would be together for ever.' He shook his head sadly.

So did I, thought Nicola, taking a sip of her wine, *so did I*.

Henri, at the far end of the table, muttered something that finished with the words 'Didn't invite me' drifting down towards Nicola as he stared at her.

Nicola bit her lip, not wanting to say out loud. 'You wouldn't have come anyway.'

There was no point in antagonising Henri tonight over something that had happened a long time ago.

'Will I get to meet Pascal one day?' Oliver asked conversationally as he helped himself to some of his favourite sauté potatoes. 'Dad says in his diary he took him sailing a couple of times.'

Complete silence greeted Oliver's remark, but he'd certainly caught everybody's attention with his question.

A question it seemed that nobody was going to answer as the silence lengthened.

Oliver looked at Nicola in the silence and mouthed, 'What have I said?'

Nicola shrugged, bewildered. Pascal wasn't a name she could ever remember Marc mentioning, so she didn't have any idea as to why hearing this name had caused such obvious unease among certain Jacques family members.

Josephine was looking visibly shaken and Nicola intercepted a concerned look Odette gave her sister before finally breaking the silence and saying slowly, 'No, Oliver, you won't meet Pascal. He was a friend who lives in Paris and we lost touch with him a long time ago.'

At the mention of Paris, Nicola suddenly wondered if Oliver had unwittingly stumbled across somebody involved with Josephine's hidden past that Marc had hinted at once.

'Tante Josephine was quite a girl in her youth. Don't know the full story, but apparently years ago she had to leave Paris in a hurry,' he'd once told her.

Now, watching the colour slowly return to the cheeks of the slim, middle-aged woman sitting opposite her and trying to imagine her as a young girl, Nicola could only speculate about the secrets that this reserved French woman could be harbouring. Whatever they were, she hoped that the unexpected mention of this Pascal, whoever he was, hadn't brought too many unhappy memories to the surface. Both the aunts had been so kind to Oliver and herself, she'd hate to hurt either of them.

It was Claudine who brought everybody's thoughts firmly back to Marc.

'Does anyone remember the punk band Marc played in and I sang with?' She glanced at her brother. 'I know you do because you were upset they wouldn't let you join. Made my life a misery for months.'

'Marc practising the drums in the barn made our life a misery too,' Henri said dryly. 'The noise was deafening at times. But when he improved, we used to play the occasional piece of jazz together. I remember enjoying that,' he added quietly.

'I played the drums in the school band back home... back in England,' Oliver said. 'I really enjoyed it. Hope I can join one here. If not, Luc plays the guitar as well, so we might start a group.' He looked at his grandfather. 'I've never heard you play the sax. Dad told me you were really good. Do you still play?'

Henri shook his head. 'Non.'

Oliver hesitated before asking quietly, 'You won't teach me to play the saxophone then?'

Henri looked at him unhappily before sighing. 'Peut-être. If I ever find the instrument.'

Oliver, taking his grandfather's words as a definite yes, said, 'Great. I'll help you look for it.'

Nicola smiled and shook her head in amusement. Oliver was getting more and more like Marc every day. Not just in looks but also in the way he reacted to people. Getting his own way was a skill that Marc had possessed in abundance.

'I remember going to jazz evenings down in Nice,' Claudine said. 'Great fun. Marc always reckoned none of the saxophone players were anywhere near as good as you, Henri.'

Raoul laughed. 'You two really did go and listen to the jazz then? I always thought it was just a ruse for you to spend time together away from family.'

Claudine nodded. 'It was, but the jazz was too good to miss. Oh, and those romantic late-night strolls along the Promenade des Anglais. I wouldn't have missed them for anything, but even then Marc was planning to leave.' She fiddled with her wine glass and took a long drink before glancing at Nicola and continuing, 'I lived in hope that he would either change his mind or at least ask me to go with him. Mais non,' she shrugged. 'I was to wait here for his return. That was one promise he didn't keep,' she added quietly, almost to herself as she lifted the glass to her lips again. 'And then, when he did return, he was a married man. Did you know I was his first ever girl friend?' she asked suddenly, looking across at Nicola.

Nicola nodded. 'Yes, and I know he was very fond of you. He wanted us to meet and hoped we'd be friends.'

'First love is always bittersweet, isn't it?' Claudine said before she swallowed another mouthful of wine.

'Ça suffit,' Sylvie said, crossly taking Claudine's glass away and saying something to her in rapid French as she placed a plate of food in front of her. 'Eat not drink,' she ordered her daughter.

Nicola didn't understand all the words that Sylvie used to scold Claudine, but the action spoke for itself. Enough is enough.

Nicola didn't reply to Claudine. Marc had been her own first bittersweet love and she was becoming increasingly afraid that he would turn out to be her only true love.

When she'd said to Josephine and Odette that remembering Marc's birthday would be hard for everyone, she hadn't bargained on just how painful the experience of hearing other people's memories of her husband would be for her personally. Or how the love she'd once felt for him would once again rise to the surface and threaten to destabilise her attempts to create a new life without him.

She'd thought she'd mastered her feelings about Marc, but here she was feeling insanely jealous over what had clearly been a teenage romance long before the two of them had even met.

Absently, Nicola took a piece of bread from the basket and broke a piece off as she tried to rationalise her thoughts and stifle the jealous feelings that were surging through her body.

'Ah, Nicola, it was a long time ago,' Josephine said quietly, taking Nicola's hand in hers.

Nicola looked at her in surprise.

'If Marc had really loved Claudine, he would have come back for her, but it was you he loved and married. Enjoy the memories of the good times you had together.' Josephine paused. 'Sometimes it is hard to look at things dispassionately and get on with life, particularly when you've been hurt by a lost love, but, believe me, Marc's love for you, and Oliver, was one of the mainstays of his life – despite how he failed you.'

Nicola smiled weakly, but before she could say anything, Oliver, who had overheard the quiet conversation, broke in resentfully.

'If he loved us so much, why did he leave us alone so much? If he hadn't, he wouldn't have been killed. We didn't drive him away like...' his voice broke and he hesitated. 'Like Papa Henri did,' and he glared at his grandfather angrily. 'It doesn't matter what any of you say,' he said, his voice tremulous. 'Why couldn't he let us be a normal, proper family? Why did he need to help strangers and not be with his own family?'

Brushing tears away from his eyes, Oliver turned and ran out of the petit jardin.

Instinctively, Nicola rose to follow him, but Henri said, 'No,

Nicola. It is time I had a few words with my grandson. I alone will go.'

Nicola sank back down onto her chair, hoping that whatever 'few words' Henri was about to have with Oliver wouldn't make the situation worse. She watched in silence as Henri left the petit jardin to find Oliver. There was little point in asking him to take it easy with Oliver. She knew Henri would deal with the situation in his own way whatever she said. Nicola could only hope and pray he would, at the very least, be kind.

Odette, ever practical, stood up and began to clear the table.

'Josephine has made Marc's favourite chocolate cake for dessert. I will fetch it,' and Odette disappeared into the lengthening shadows towards the farmhouse.

'Nicola, please don't worry. Henri will be gentle with Oliver, I promise you,' Sylvie's quiet voice broke into Nicola's thoughts.

Nicola looked at Sylvie uncertainly. Gentle wasn't a word she'd normally associate with Henri.

'I'm beginning to think this dinner party for Oliver to talk to everyone and share their memories of his father was a bad idea,' Nicola said wearily. 'I know I've learnt more about Marc's life than I really expected,' and she glanced across the table, where Raoul was talking quietly to Claudine. Turning back to Sylvie, Nicola said, 'As for Oliver, rather than helping, it's simply stirred up all his negative feelings again. Just when I was beginning to think he'd started to come to terms with everything. I dread to think what he's accusing Henri of now,' and Nicola shook her head worriedly as she looked at Sylvie.

'Deep down Henri is very big-hearted. He will be hurting for Oliver, as well as himself. If they can just talk about their feelings to each other, it will help both of them so much,' Sylvie said. 'This whole Marc business has hurt Henri as much as Oliver,' she sighed. 'Maybe more,' she glanced at Nicola. 'He realises he was to blame for a lot of the bad feeling between him and Marc. His biggest regret now is that he will never be able to say sorry to Marc.'

Sylvie watched as Odette placed the chocolate birthday cake and a large cheeseboard on the table.

'Since you bring Oliver here, Henri begins to live again. Oliver is his new purpose in life,' Sylvie said.

'But that isn't necessarily healthy or good,' Nicola protested. 'He'll try and control him like he did with Marc.'

'Non,' Sylvie shook her head. 'This time he knows he must tread gently. He already listens more and tries not to insist his is the only way to do things.' She smiled at Nicola. 'Believe me, Henri is not the same as he was. Oh, he's still stubborn and chauvinistic, but he's changed, hasn't he, Odette? He knows he mustn't repeat the mistakes of the past.'

Odette nodded as she began to cut the cake into portions. 'Oui. He still likes to have the last word if he can, but he's getting used to not having it,' she laughed.

'Having you both here has really made a difference, you know, Nicola. To all our lives,' Josephine added quietly. 'I maybe shouldn't say this, but I think Marc treated you very shabbily over the last few years by allowing the relief agency to take over his life so much and I'm glad you didn't reject us all and refuse to bring Oliver to live in France.'

'You know I couldn't do that, Josephine,' Nicola said, looking at her. 'Staying in England wasn't an option that Henri gave me.'

'Nicola, there's something that maybe we ought to tell you,' Josephine said quietly. 'The thing is—'

'Listen,' Sylvie interrupted urgently. 'Is that what I think it is?'

Everybody stopped talking to listen as the mournful notes of a saxophone drifted towards them on the warm night air. As they listened, the tentative notes became stronger and within minutes Gershwin's 'Summertime' was filling the air.

'Henri's found his saxophone after all these years,' Odette said, with tears in her eyes. 'I'm so happy. Now things should get better all the time. Henri was always more content when he could lose himself in his music.'

As the notes of 'Summertime' died away on the night air, other haunting tunes followed and everyone remained silent, listening to the impromptu concert. Finally, as the bats started to flit around the roofs of the outbuildings illuminated by the moon, the music stopped. The party atmosphere, spoilt when Oliver had shouted his broken-hearted questions at everyone, had been replaced with a sense of calm, of acceptance, as the music wafted towards them.

A few minutes later, Henri and Oliver arrived back in the petit jardin side by side, Henri with his arm around Oliver's shoulder and Oliver carrying his grandfather's saxophone.

All signs of tears had disappeared from Oliver's face, but Nicola could see he was still rather subdued. Resisting the urge to put her arms around him, which she knew would embarrass him in front of everyone, she simply asked, 'You okay?'

Oliver nodded. 'Papa Henri and I had a long chat about Dad and other stuff.' There was a short pause before he said, 'Mum, can I change my name? Papa Henri says as I'm growing up in France, I should use the French version of my name. It just means putting an extra "i" in it and pronouncing it differently and I'd really like to do it.'

Nicola looked at him, remembering the light-hearted argument she and Marc had had over their new son's name. Marc had wanted the French version of his name on his birth certificate and she'd protested, saying Oliver would be growing up in England and the additional 'i' would only confuse people. In the end,

Marc had reluctantly agreed to the English version. But now Oliver was living in France and would be going to a French school perhaps it would be better.

Thoughtfully, Nicola picked up her glass. 'Shall we raise a glass to the extra "i" then? To the French version of Olivier. Hip hip hurray.'

Everyone laughed and raised their glasses. 'To Olivier.'

22

In an effort to keep her mind off the painful memories that the dinner party had opened up, Nicola again threw herself into work at Le Jardin for the next day or two. She was determined to try and get a vegetable plot dug over and the small greenhouse attached to the granite boundary wall cleaned out and fresh compost dug into its beds before Andrew arrived. Not that he'd given her a definite arrival date yet.

There was also the question of getting the small bedroom in the cottage habitable for his visit. The only piece of furniture in there at the moment was the old sofa bed she'd brought from England. At the very least, the room needed some drawers and hanging space for clothes.

'Have another look in the small barn,' Odette said when Nicola mentioned the problem. 'No more wardrobes, but somewhere in the jumble there are a couple of hanging rails and a set of drawers. If they're any use, I'll get Henri to bring them down.'

A day later Josephine, sitting on the back of the tractor clutching a rolled-up rug, came down with Henri. The two hanging rails, a set of drawers and a small cane bedroom chair that Nicola hadn't noticed in the barn were all balanced in the trailer.

'Thought this might be useful too,' Josephine said, lifting the cane chair off the trailer.

Once everything was unloaded, Henri climbed back on the tractor. 'Got to get back. Vétérinaire is due.' He looked at Josephine, muttered. 'Don't forget,' and disappeared back up the lane to La Prouveresse in a cloud of smelly tractor exhaust.

Nicola looked at Josephine and sighed, 'Don't forget what?'

Josephine shrugged helplessly. 'I've told him it's none of our business, but you know Henri.' She paused before continuing, 'He wants to know how close you are to this man, Andrew. Olivier has talked about him a lot. Henri thinks you might be planning to marry him.'

'Why didn't Henri ask me himself? He's not usually so diffident about being nosey.' The thought, 'or annoying me to my face' flashed through Nicola's mind.

'He's trying hard not to upset you by asking questions. Gets me to do his dirty work instead,' Josephine laughed. 'But you don't have to tell me if you don't want to. And I don't have to tell Henri either. I can tell him I forget to ask.'

'Andrew is an old friend of Marc's. Marc asked him to keep a friendly eye on Olivier and me as he was away so much. Andrew was there when Marc died and he was very good with Olivier.' Nicola was quiet for a moment. 'He's been a good male role model for Olivier but...' she sighed. 'But I know he wants to marry me. He's even asked Olivier how he'd feel about it, can you believe.'

'And you? Do you want to marry him?'

'I am very fond of Andrew as a friend, but I don't love him and I'm certainly not in love with him. He knows I think of him as the big brother I never had. So, you can tell Henri I don't have any feelings for him and I'm certainly not going to marry him. I suspect though, he still might try to change my mind when he's here.'

Josephine was silent, concern etched on her face. 'You must do what is best for you, Nicola. No one else, not even Olivier. For you. Follow your instincts and things will work out somehow in the end. Now, I give you a hand getting these things upstairs, n'est pas?'

It was only after Josephine had left that Nicola remembered she hadn't asked her what it was she had been about to tell her at the dinner party when Henri's music had filled the air and interrupted the conversation. Whatever it was couldn't be that important, Nicola reasoned philosophically to herself, otherwise she was certain Josephine would have remembered to mention it.

* * *

Gilles telephoned early the following morning. 'I have to come to Le Goût de la Campagne and I wondered whether you were free today for the lunch I promised you?'

'That would be lovely, thank you,' Nicola said.

'Bien. I pick you up at 12.30.'

Nicola had barely put the phone down when it rang again. Claudine.

'Fancy meeting up for a coffee in the village café?'

Nicola laughed. It was going to be a sociable day. 'I'd love to. Can't be too long though. I have to get back. I'm having lunch with Gilles Bongars and he's picking me up at 12.30,' Nicola said.

'In that case, see you in half an hour. Can't have you being late for a date with the gorgeous Gilles,' Claudine said, laughing.

'It's not a date,' Nicola protested. 'Just a thank you for the lunch I gave him the other week.'

'Ooh, a regular date,' Claudine teased. 'See you soon.'

Nicola smiled to herself as she put her bag in the bicycle basket ready to cycle into the village to meet Claudine. A date indeed. It was just Gilles returning her hospitality, that was all.

Nicola was about to close the garden gate and set off for the village when her phone rang again. This time it was Andrew. Stifling a sigh, she picked it up.

'I'm about to book a flight, but I thought I'd better check first that it's still all right if I come over?'

'Of course. Oliver is looking forward to it. We both are,' Nicola added hastily. 'How long are you planning to stay?'

'Just over a week.'

Inwardly Nicola gave a relieved sigh. She'd been anticipating longer. A week was easily manageable. 'I hope you're not expecting luxury accommodation. The cottage is livable but needs some work and the spare room is small. A box room really, with your old friend the put-you-up.'

'It'll be fine. I need a complete change of scene and I just can't wait to get away from everything and get my head straight.'

'We're about an hour into the back country. Do you want me to see if someone can meet you?' Nicola said.

'No thanks. I'll hire a car. That way I'll be able to get out of your hair and explore on the days you're busy. Directions for the satnav would be good though. See you in a week then.'

'See you in a week,' Nicola echoed his words. Was hiring a car and talking about exploring on his own a good omen? He had sounded quite upbeat on the phone. Maybe Andrew's visit wouldn't be the problem she was anticipating.

* * *

Surprised by the number of people who already recognised her as a local, addressing her by name, 'Bonjour, Madame Jacques', Nicola wandered around the small market before making her way past the fountain in the town square towards the coffee shop.

Claudine was already seated at one of the pavement tables with an empty demitasse cup in front of her. Smiling, she raised a hand in greeting as she saw Nicola.

'Coffee or a glass of rosé?'

'Water, I think,' Nicola said. 'It's too hot for coffee and too early for wine. For an English woman anyway,' she added, glancing around and seeing half carafes of wine on nearly every table.

Claudine ordered water and another coffee before asking, 'How's Olivier after the party?'

'Quiet.'

'Do you know what Henri said to him?'

Nicola shook her head. 'No, not really. Something about we all make mistakes and everyone has regrets in their lives.' She gave a resigned shrug. 'At least he and Henri are still talking. Henri seems to be making a real effort with Olivier. They've gone out together this morning. Another grandfather-grandson sort of bonding trip.' The waiter placed her water on the table at that moment. 'Merci,' she said before taking a sip.

'Raoul told me about a car that might suit me and Henri's taken Olivier with him today to give it the once-over. Not that Olivier knows any more about cars than I do. I'm praying the trip turns out okay, in more ways than one. I really do need a car and I need Olivier and Henri to have a good relationship. Otherwise life will be just too difficult.'

'I'm sure Olivier will come to terms with things soon. He's young and he's got so much to look forward to here. And Henri,

well, he must have learnt something from the mistakes he made
with Marc.'

'I certainly hope so,' Nicola said, then hesitated. 'Claudine,
can I ask you something? Do you know who Pascal is? I don't like
to ask Josephine or Odette, they were clearly upset on Sunday at
the mention of his name, and Henri would just fob me off, I'm
sure.'

'Pascal, the guy who took Marc sailing?' Claudine shrugged.

Nicola nodded. 'I'm just curious. Marc obviously enjoyed the
time he spent with him, but the mere mention of his name on
Sunday seemed to throw everybody into a state. It's not someone
Marc ever mentioned to me when talking about his life here.'

'I vaguely remember his visit, but I don't know much about
him. Some sort of connection by marriage to Josephine. I think
he only came that one summer. You need to talk to Maman. She
knows everybody's darkest secrets. Including mine,' Claudine
added softly and she pushed her empty coffee cup away. 'Nicola, I
want to apologise for my behaviour the other evening.'

Nicola shook her head. 'Claudine, there's no need...'

'There's every need. I want you and I to be friends. I can't
allow the shadow of Marc to come between us.' Claudine fiddled
with her gold chain necklace as she continued, 'I was nineteen
and devastated when Marc left. But the truth is, deep down, I
know that Marc didn't love me. Oh, we had some great times
together, but if I'm truthful, the love was all on my side, not his.
Teenage infatuation, I guess.'

Nicola was quiet, realising how hard it was for Claudine to
talk to her about this.

Claudine hesitated before adding. 'You know Phillipe and I
are having a few problems? One of the reasons we came back
here to live was to try to work things out between us with a less

stressful lifestyle. I'm afraid I drank too much wine on Sunday and all those memories with everybody talking about Marc somehow made my teenage dreams seem more real than the present. Made me wish for that lost world again.'

'Claudine, I don't know what to say, except I hope you and Phillipe work it out,' Nicola said. The small twinges of jealousy she'd felt the other evening listening to Claudine talk about her relationship with Marc had vanished, replaced by genuine, understanding sympathy.

Claudine smiled. 'Things are definitely better. Luckily, he couldn't come on Sunday so he didn't witness my behaviour.' She looked at Nicola apprehensively. 'You won't...?'

'Of course not,' Nicola said quickly. 'The whole thing is forgotten. Look, I have to go, but would you and Phillipe like to come to supper one evening soon? An old friend is coming for a visit from England. I'd like you to meet him.' She didn't add that having friends around would make it easier to entertain Andrew.

'That sounds wonderful. Let me know which evening and I'll make sure Phillipe is home early.'

Cycling home, Nicola tried to put thoughts of Andrew's impending visit out of her mind. A depressed and belligerent Andrew wouldn't make for an easy guest. Hopefully he would have calmed down before he arrived and if not, she suspected she was in for a difficult time.

Sighing, she put the bicycle away in the shed before going indoors. She had time for a quick shower and a change of clothes. What to wear posed a problem though. She wanted to look good but didn't want to be overdressed for a village restaurant. After a lot of debate with herself, she went for white jeans, a pale blue shirt, denim jacket and her wedge sandals. Never one for a lot of make-up, she opted for mascara and her normal lip salve.

Hearing a car arrive, she ran downstairs, determined not to let her worries overshadow the treat of being taken out for lunch, or of getting to know Gilles Bongars better.

23

The restaurant where Gilles had booked a table was a mere half-hour drive up the road from Le Jardin de Dominic but seemed to exist in a time warp.

From the moment she walked across the drawbridge over the River Var and under the arch into the ancient moated village of Entrevaux, Nicola was fascinated by the place. Tall, thin sixteenth-century houses lined narrow lane after narrow lane, occasionally opening out into a small square. Window boxes with their tumbling red, white and pink geraniums clung precariously to sills. Narrow alleys were ablaze with colourful flowers.

'This is the picture-book image of a French village,' Nicola said. 'It's beautiful.'

As they made their way through the village, Gilles pointed out the Vauban Citadel high above it.

'The village was an important place back in medieval times,' he said. 'And even in the seventeenth century, it guarded a highly strategic approach from the south.'

'It looks like quite a climb,' Nicola said, craning her head to see the fortress properly.

'Another day we will be brave and do it, but today, on your first visit, you must see the church,' Gilles said, leading her past some olive trees towards a plain wall with a simple doorway.

Walking through the ordinary nondescript entrance into the ancient Notre-Dame-De-L'Assomption, a cathedral until the end of the eighteenth century, Nicola gasped as she saw the breathtaking beautiful Baroque interior.

'But the outside was so ordinary,' she said and Gilles smiled.

Wandering back down through the village, Nicola kept stopping to look at the houses and to wonder about the people who had lived in them through the centuries.

'I feel as if I should be wearing a long dress and a wimple on my head,' she said.

'You must come and see the medieval parade when everyone dresses up and the place looks as if the clock has been turned back hundreds of years. You could even join in,' Gilles said. 'There is so much going on those days.'

The restaurant Gilles liked was on the main square, where a tall tree gave welcome shade and the water from an old fountain soothed as it tinkled into its granite trough.

'What a magical place,' Nicola said as they took their places at one of the outside tables set up in the square.

'After lunch, we take a stroll in the hidden medieval gardens,' Gilles promised.

'Will we have time? Don't you have to be back at work?' Nicola said.

Gilles shook his head. 'Today I make sure I have the afternoon free,' he said, smiling at her. Nicola returned his smile. He was good company and she was happy at the prospect of spending the afternoon with him.

The popular restaurant was busy, with a mixture of tourists and locals enjoying the good food and chattering away in a mix of languages. Several people stopped by their table to say hello to Gilles and shake Nicola vigorously by the hand when he introduced her.

Gilles smiled apologetically. 'It is because of my job. Everybody wants me to be their friend. To remember them when they apply for planning permission.'

Nicola laughed. 'I'm sure it's more than that.'

Le patron came to the table and took their order personally, promising Nicola she was in for a treat when she chose Daube à la Provençal, the 'plat de jour'.

They shared a small carafe of wine and laughed companionably at the antics of a small child at a nearby table.

'Do you have any children?' Nicola asked.

Gilles shook his head. 'Non. I've never married and I've always thought children needed to be a part of that whole scene. Not an item on their own. And sadly, I've never met the one person I wanted to spend my life with,' he added quietly.

Nicola took a reflective sip of her wine. 'In an ideal world, I agree about children, but it doesn't always work like that,' she said, a sorrowful look clouding her face.

'Oh, Nicola, I'm so sorry. I didn't mean to upset you. I know sometimes things go wrong however hard you try personally,' and Gilles reached out to cover her hand with his. A gesture Nicola found strangely comforting, before Gilles let her hand go.

As they lingered over their coffee, Gilles said, 'I have two tickets for a jazz concert a week this Saturday. Would you like to come with me? I could pick you up about six, drive down to Nice, have dinner and then go to the concert. Couldn't promise to get you home before 10 o'clock though.'

'Thank you. Sounds fun. I'm sure the aunts will enjoy having Olivier for the evening and... OH,' Nicola broke off in midsentence as she remembered Andrew's visit.

'You are already doing something that evening?' Gilles said.

Nicola shook her head. 'No. It's just that I have a friend coming to stay next week.' She smiled at Gilles. 'But I'm sure Josephine and Odette won't mind entertaining an extra person for the evening.'

How Andrew would react to her leaving him at the farm and going to a concert with Gilles was another matter. It could be a good thing, though, it might help Andrew realise that she was making new friends and enjoying life here in France.

* * *

Later that same afternoon, Nicola began to make her way up to the farm. Olivier had messaged to say that Henri said the car was a bargain and was arranging for it to be delivered in a few days and she wanted to give him the money he paid out. The temperature was in the thirties and she was glad of the slight breeze that was gently stirring the leaves of the two tall eucalyptus trees standing sentinel-like at the bottom of the drive by the letterbox. She stopped to check for post and to cool down for a few seconds in the shade of the shadow the trees were casting across the track. One official-looking letter was in the box, addressed to Henri.

Nicola glanced at the letter curiously. It had a Parisian postmark and the address of a firm of lawyers stamped across it. Knowing that Henri used a local firm of notaires, Nicola couldn't help wondering what the letter might be about as she pushed it into her bag.

As she strolled up the drive, she could see Henri and Olivier walking back from the small vineyard on the edge of La Prouveresse land. The vines there were already heavy with the grapes that would provide the prized bottles of house wine at the end of summer and Henri would have been anxiously checking them over.

The farmhouse was deserted when Nicola reached it and she found Josephine and Odette sitting in the shade of the petit jardin sharing a jug of iced home-made lemonade.

'Nicola, you will join us, yes?' and Josephine handed her a glass without waiting for her answer.

'You are ready for your friend to arrive next week?' Odette asked.

'As ready as I'll ever be.'

'Bon. You bring him for supper the day he arrives, yes? Sylvie will be here too.'

'Thanks. I thought on Sunday we'd go to the fete in the village, are you going?'

'Oui, of course.' Josephine and Odette chorused together.

'Even Henri will go. It's a tradition.'

The mention of Henri reminded Nicola why she was there.

'Will you give this to Henri for me please. It's the euros for my car,' she explained as she fished in her bag for the envelope containing the money. 'Oh, and this was in the box as I came up.'

Josephine frowned as she took the letter and saw the post-mark and said quietly, 'It's from Paris,' before glancing at her sister.

At that moment, Henri and Olivier arrived and Josephine silently held it out to Henri.

He brushed aside the offer of a glass of lemonade as he opened the letter and read its contents before handing it back to Josephine.

'Your past is catching up with you. You'd better ring them,' he said curtly. 'Find out what it's all about once and for all. Don't want them turning up here.'

'Can't you ring them for me, Henri?' Josephine asked

anxiously as she read the letter. 'After all, it's you they've written to asking for information about my whereabouts. Can't you find out why they want me to contact them? And then I'll ring them.' Josephine bit her bottom lip before looking at her sister and brother and asking, 'You don't think the gendarmes want to interview me again after all this time, do you?'

Nicola, wishing she was anywhere but here in the small garden, looked between the two sisters and Henri as she listened to the intriguing conversation. Why on earth would law-abiding Josephine be afraid of being interviewed by the gendarmes? In fact, why did the gendarmes want to interview her at all?

24

'Andrew should be here about five o'clock,' Nicola said. 'So I hope you won't be too late back.'

'We won't,' promised Olivier. 'Raoul says we should be back by six o'clock at the latest.'

Nicola had planned that both she and Olivier would be at home to greet Andrew when he arrived. But then Raoul had said he and Marie, Luc's mother, were planning to spend the day in Nice with Luc and would she and Olivier like to join them?

'Bit of skateboarding along the Promenade des Anglais for the boys, you and Marie could do some shopping while I see to some business and then lunch at a special little bistro I know.'

Tempting though the offer was, Nicola felt she had to say no. She couldn't risk not being back in time for Andrew's arrival.

'Just give me the directions in case I can't get to grips with the satnav and I'll see you late afternoon,' he'd said during their last phone call. Nicola knew in Andrew talk that could mean any time between three and six o'clock so she had to stay close to home.

Having waved goodbye to Raoul and the boys after breakfast, Nicola fetched Mischief's lead and set off for the village. She needed a baguette and some basil for the tomato salad she was making and the dog needed a walk before the day got too hot.

The Taste of the Countryside site was teeming with life as she walked past. The main structure was already in place and men were tiling the roof, whilst a bulldozer was busy clearing the ground for the entrance road. Nicola was pleased to see that the building was already blending in with its surroundings. A large placard had been placed near the edge of the main road with the words 'Ouverture Prochaine' emblazed across it.

Once back at Le Jardin, Nicola spent the rest of the morning in the garden, sowing the newly dug vegetable plot with some early winter vegetables and beginning a small herb garden to the side of the kitchen.

At midday, deciding it was too hot to work outside, she retreated indoors out of the heat for lunch and the luxury of a short siesta in the cool of her bedroom.

The slamming of a car door and a shouted 'Mum' woke her with a jolt. A quick glance at the bedside clock told her that she'd slept most of the afternoon away. Before she could get off the bed, Oliver burst in, clearly upset.

'Why are you in bed? You're not ill, are you?'

Nicola shook her head. 'No. It was so hot I thought I'd have a short siesta.'

'Andrew not here yet? Raoul came back early especially,' Olivier said.

'No, not yet. I expect the autoroute was busy. Maybe I've missed a message.' Nicola picked up her phone. 'Yes, he's been unexpectedly delayed. He'll be about another hour. Which means you've got time to take Mischief for a walk.'

'Okay. I need to see Papa Henri too. I'll see you later.'

* * *

Nicola was sitting on the terrace reading a magazine when Andrew finally arrived.

'How are you? Everything okay?' she asked as he stepped out of his car and stretched, and she leant forward to give him a welcome kiss on the cheek.

But Andrew had other ideas and pulled her against him in a tight hug.

'Oh, Nicola, I can't tell you how good it is to be here,' he said.

Nicola smiled at him as she moved out of his arms. The belligerent Andrew bellowing down the telephone at her demanding answers that she couldn't give had apparently been left behind in England, but that hug was a little too friendly, she felt.

'You're later than I expected.'

'Yeah, sorry about that. I saw this woman just outside Nice on the N202 thumbing a lift and you know how I feel about the dangers women hitch-hiking put themselves in. Better for old trustworthy me to offer her a lift than someone...' he shrugged. 'Turns out she lives not many miles from Puget-Théniers, so I made sure she got home.'

'That was kind of you.' And so typical of Andrew, Nicola thought.

'Agnes only spoke a few words of English, my French is a bit basic, so thank god for Google Translate on the phone.'

Nicola laughed.

'Where's Oliver?'

'He's gone up to the farm to help Henri with something. By the way, at his request he's now known as Olivier. Come on in and I'll give you the grand tour before I take you there.'

Andrew looked disappointed at this but didn't say anything.

Showing Andrew upstairs to his room, Nicola apologised for it being so tiny.

'Gilles expects the plans to be passed soon and then I can get the builders in to put a spiral staircase in for the attic and convert the space into two more bedrooms and a small bathroom,' she explained as she opened the bedroom door. 'I hope you'll be comfy in here,' she said, going across to the window. 'You've got a wonderful view of the mountains.'

'I'll be fine,' Andrew assured her. 'That put-you-up and I are old friends, like you said. So tell me, who is Gilles?'

'A friend who offered to help me with the plans for this place. He's the local surveyor in charge of the new Taste of the Country-side building next door, so I'm very lucky to have his help.'

Just as Nicola was debating whether to mention her Saturday night outing next week with Gilles or leave it until later, Olivier banged the back door and bounded up the stairs, throwing himself at Andrew in welcome. As Mischief decided it would be fun to do the same, chaos prevailed for several minutes.

Back downstairs, as she made tea for them all, Andrew and Olivier had a lively discussion about the new striker that Manchester United had signed. Andrew was amazed that Olivier was so up to date with his information before he realised that Olivier had his computer permanently on the internet.

'Bet you message Chloe as well every day too,' Andrew teased. 'Your mum seems to have forgotten how to use email, maybe you can remind her from time to time to drop me a message. Although, if things work out, we could all be together a bit more,' and he glanced across at Nicola. 'But we'll talk about that later. Right now, I want to hear all about your new life.'

Nicola tensed at the words 'all be together a bit more'. What exactly did he mean by that? She couldn't ask him now with Olivier there but at the first opportunity she got she would demand an explanation. But by the time Olivier had told him all about his new friend, Luc, and how Papa Henri had found

Mischief for him and Nicola had given him a quick tour of Le Jardin de Dominic's land, it was time to walk up to La Prouveresse for supper, leaving no time for Nicola to tackle Andrew about his words.

As Olivier ran ahead with Mischief at his heels, Nicola tried to warn Andrew about the kind of welcome he could expect from the Jacques family.

'The aunts are lovely. They'll make you welcome whatever. As for Henri, well... he'll probably be fine too. But, on the other hand, he could be rude. Sylvie is going to be there and she keeps him in check most of the time, so hopefully...'

'Is Henri still trying to run your life?' Andrew asked, a definite edge to his voice.

Nicola shook her head. 'Not really, although he does like to know what's going on down to the last detail and soon lets me know if he doesn't approve. Josephine, Odette and Sylvie all reckon he's changed recently.'

'How does he treat Oliver?' This time his voice was sharper, as if he was ready to challenge Henri over his treatment of Oliver.

'They get on well and spend a lot of time together,' Nicola said, realising that the last thing she needed was Andrew tackling Henri verbally about Oliver. 'Thankfully, he's not trying to tell Olivier what he should do as much as I feared he might, but he does have his moments.'

As they neared the top of the drive, they were surprised to see the sisters with Henri and Sylvie, standing in a huddle gazing down over the valley. Henri had the binoculars to his eyes and was muttering away in rapid French under his breath.

'It's the first of the summer fires,' Josephine explained as she pointed across the valley. 'Fortunately, it doesn't appear to be a big one.'

A thin column of black smoke was rising from the forest that lay five or six kilometres above the village. They watched silently as a Canadair plane dumped its cargo of water before turning away to clear air space for the next one.

It was some time before Henri lowered his binoculars. 'Think they've managed to control it. Mind you, the pompiers will be there all night dampening things down. Trouble is, everything is so dry.'

'Does it happen often?' Andrew asked.

'Too often. People don't think,' and Henri glared at Andrew as though he was personally responsible.

'This is Andrew,' Nicola said quickly and introduced everyone.

'Shall we eat?' Josephine said. 'Supper is all ready. Olivier, can you help me carry things to the table please?'

Conversation around the table was general and, mainly in deference to Andrew, in a mixture of French and English. Nicola was surprised by how good Andrew's French actually was.

'I've been taking lessons since you left,' he explained.

'In England you do what?' Henri asked.

'I've been working in the construction industry,' Andrew said. 'But I've just been made redundant.' He glanced at Nicola before continuing. 'It seems an ideal opportunity to rethink my life. Perhaps retrain and do something completely different. Anyway, I've decided to take a year off. My redundancy money is enough to live on if I'm careful. Thought I'd divide my time between the UK and France, if that's all right with you?' he said quietly, looking at Nicola.

There was no doubting Olivier's delight at this news, but Nicola, although she smiled warmly at Andrew, was inwardly stunned. Was Andrew hoping to move into Le Jardin with them? More importantly, was he expecting her to welcome him with open arms?

25

Sunday morning, and unusually, Nicola was awakened by the noise of traffic going past Le Jardin de Dominic. Sleepily, she glanced at the bedside clock: 6.30 a.m.

Lying there listening, as the sound of the church bell tolling out over the countryside added its sombre bass peal to the early-morning sounds, she remembered it was the day of the fete. And that Andrew was sleeping in the next room.

Nicola sighed. Andrew. His news last night about taking a year off and dividing his time between the two countries had been totally unexpected, leaving her reeling with the hidden implications behind it.

Walking home from La Prouveresse last night under a star-laden sky, she'd tried to tell him as gently as she could that he couldn't stay with her and Olivier indefinitely, if indeed that was what he was hoping.

'It's purely a practical consideration,' she'd said, trying to soften the blow. 'There really isn't enough room. And once the plans are passed, I shall start looking for builders and the cottage will be in chaos for several weeks. Olivier and I will probably decamp up to La Prouveresse, especially when there are walls being knocked down. Josephine suggested it only the other day.'

Andrew was silent for a few moments and Nicola could sense his hurt. As she went to open the back gate leading to Le Jardin, Andrew put his hand out and stopped her.

'Do you like having me here, Nicola?'

'I invited you and this is your first day here and I'm looking forward to enjoying your company for the next week,' Nicola said. 'But the fact remains you can't move in with me, even on a semi-permanent basis. Le Jardin just isn't big enough. If you decide to settle in the area, you have to find your own place.'

Andrew had looked at her silently.

'So I suggest you enjoy your holiday and keep an eye out for places you feel you could live in,' Nicola added determinedly. 'That is, if you are serious about moving out here.'

'Oh, I'm serious,' Andrew said slowly. 'Although I had hoped you'd be a bit more enthusiastic about having me around in your life again.'

Nicola remembered sighing and closing her eyes in frustration at his words. Was that the real reason he wanted to move to France? To be near her. In a strange way, it was beginning to feel like the pendulum had swung the other way – from her needing his help to him being dependent on her being in his life. She wished she could backpedal to the exact moment when things between them had shifted from friendship into this minefield of unexpected, and in her case unreciprocated, feelings, and stop it in its tracks before it had gained momentum.

Nicola had looked at him and tried to banish the guilty feelings about her lack of enthusiasm over Andrew's news, but before she could say anything Andrew spoke again.

'And afterwards? When the alterations to Le Jardin are

finished and there is room, will there still be a problem having me around?'

'Andrew there isn't a problem having you around.' Nicola had paused, trying to choose her next words carefully. 'I enjoy your company, but I did explain before I came to France that even if I stayed in England, we'd only ever be friends. And that hasn't changed. We're friends. Good friends. It will be fun having you here for the next week and I'm looking forward to showing you around,' she hesitated. 'But if you do decide to come and live in the area, it would be too easy to slip into being regarded as the local English couple and neither of us would be free to meet other people and create new independent lives here.'

'Is that what you want, Nicola? An independent life? No ties.'

'No. And yes. The only people I have to worry about at the moment is Olivier and myself. For the first time in almost ever, I can please myself. Do what I want. It's been a long time since I've been able to do that without feeling guilty.'

Now, as the early-morning sunlight streamed into her bedroom, Nicola took a deep breath and, pushing back the bedclothes, got up.

Hopefully, Andrew wouldn't be brooding about last night and they could enjoy their day at the fete without the future of their non-relationship looming over them like a black cloud.

More of an agricultural show than an ordinary fete, the festivities were in full swing by the time Nicola and Andrew arrived to join in the fun. An excited Olivier had gone down with Henri earlier, keen to join in with everything.

Traffic had been banished from the village for the day and the narrow streets were crammed with stalls and stands of every description. Making their way slowly along the crowded streets, soaking up the atmosphere and marvelling at the variety of goods on display, Nicola was amazed at how the village had transformed itself for the fete.

It seemed, too, that all the local farmers and their livestock had come to the village for the day. Flocks of sheep were being auctioned off down in the marketplace and everywhere there was the noise of animals. Cows, pigs, ducks, chickens and goats all adding their own noises to the cacophony of sound that was all around.

Two large Percheron horses were giving rides to excited children and the shooting range set up near the gendarmerie on the edge of the village was a definite hit with the village teenagers.

Already the smell of cooking hung in the air as the socca and the roast chicken vans opened for business. Stalls full of locally produced cheeses added their own unmistakable brand of aromas to the feasts on offer.

At lunchtime, Nicola left Olivier and Andrew watching two men carving intricate designs with powerful chainsaws in tree trunks, which, quite frankly, she found terrifying to watch, while she went and found some ham salad baguettes and cold drinks for lunch. When she returned, Andrew was talking to two women – mother and daughter, Nicola guessed. The younger woman was about her own age.

'This is Agnes, the hitchhiker?' Andrew said. 'And Madame Bernard, her mother.'

'Bonjour,' Nicola said.

Madame Bernard, who spoke a little English, said, 'I not know how to thank your husband enough, he bring Agnes home safe.'

'He's a good friend, not my husband,' Nicola corrected. 'But he is a very kind man.'

Madame Bernard turned to Andrew. 'You come for lunch. I say thank you properly. Jeudi a midi, qui?'

'Merci,' Andrew said and smiled at Agnes as she turned to leave with her mother.

With so much to do and see, the rest of the day passed quickly and it was soon time for the afternoon parade of prize-winning animals. Nicola, Andrew and Josephine fought their way through the crowds to get a good view as a smiling Olivier led Henri's prize-winning ewe around the show ring, the red ribbons of the first-place rosette attached to the animal's halter blowing in the wind.

'He certainly seems to have settled down well,' Andrew said. 'Much more confident in himself. He's grown too. He's taller than you these days.'

Nicola nodded. 'Moving here has definitely helped him put things in perspective, although I think he still misses Marc more than he lets on.'

Josephine agreed. 'But he and Henri are helping each other sort their feelings out.' She glanced at Nicola. 'Are you still thinking of sending him to the English school in September? His French has improved so much, I'm sure he'd cope with a normal French school. I know Henri would like him to go to Marc's old school,' Josephine added quietly.

'Olivier has mentioned it once or twice!' Nicola smiled. 'But it does depend on how good his French is by the end of summer. I've already reserved him a place there, but please don't tell him yet, I want him to keep improving his French.'

26

Up at La Prouveresse on Tuesday morning, Odette pounded the bread dough on the kitchen table, her thoughts anywhere but on her task. These days she rarely made bread, saying the boulangerie needed the business, but there was nothing quite so satisfying as kneading dough, and this morning she needed the physical relief she always got from ten minutes of pummelling the olive bread into shape.

Henri was on the telephone talking in a low voice, the letter from the Parisian notaire in his hand. Josephine had admitted that morning she hadn't done anything about contacting them because she was too scared about the outcome. With a cross 'Tch,' Henri had snatched up the letter from the kitchen table where it lay. Standing at the sink washing up, Josephine was now casting anxious glances at him.

'D'accord. Hold on and I will ask my sister if she will speak to you now.'

Josephine gasped at his words and went white as Henri turned to look at her.

'Relax,' he said gently. 'Nobody wants to arrest you and put you in jail. But you do have a decision to make.'

Both Josephine and Odette looked at him and waited.

'These lawyers in Paris are acting for the Dupont family. They say it would be to your advantage to talk to them. They have some information...' Henri paused briefly before continuing, 'about Pascal that they will only tell you in person.'

'Pascal? Is he... is he dead?' Josephine whispered.

Henri shook his head. 'Non.'

There was a short silence before Henri spoke again.

'Josephine, you don't have to speak to them if you don't want to. I will tell them your decision is no and that you want no further involvement with the Dupont family. They have assured me the matter will finish there.'

'Have you any idea what it is about Pascal they want to tell me?' Josephine asked quietly.

Henri shook his head. 'Non. Now, are you going to talk to them?' and he held the phone out to her.

Slowly, Josephine dried her hands before moving across the kitchen and took the phone from Henri.

'Bonjour. This is Josephine Dupont speaking. I understand you would like to talk to me.'

She listened intently for a moment.

'D'accord. I agree. Merci.'

And she ended the call and turned to face Henri and Odette.

'I have agreed they can write directly to me – that is all,' she said and returned to the sink to finish the washing-up.

Half an hour later, washing-up finished and the kitchen tidy, Henri and Odette out working in the barn, Josephine picked up the letter from the table where Henri had left it, folded it carefully and put it in her skirt pocket. She needed to clear her head and a walk down through the farm to the shrine beckoned.

Josephine swept away with her hands the debris of fallen leaves and twigs that had fallen in the niche before carefully breaking off a long bramble that threatened to grow across the shrine. The next time she came, she'd bring her garden secateurs with her and get rid of the surrounding brambles for good.

She smiled as she placed the offering of the wild flowers she'd picked as she walked down at the foot of the Virgin and child statue. Standing there in silence, letting her thoughts clear, Josephine felt a pang of guilty remorse as she touched the letter in her pocket. She hadn't been totally honest with her brother and sister, saying she'd simply agreed to the notaire writing to her. The notaire had indicated the reason why they were in touch and she couldn't wait for their letter to arrive. Until then, she would hug the secret of the little they had told her to herself.

* * *

Nicola, out in the garden hanging washing on the whirligig, saw Josephine on her way back up to La Prouveresse and waved. To Nicola's relief, Josephine returned the wave but carried on towards the farm. It wasn't that she didn't want to stop and chat with Josephine, it was a matter of having so much to do still in preparation for this evening.

Claudine and Philippe had accepted the supper invitation she'd mentioned to Claudine and in a moment of madness she'd also asked Raoul if he would like to bring Marie and Luc. Luc would be company for Olivier after supper had finished and the adults sat around talking and it would be good to meet Marie properly. She'd thought about inviting Gilles but decided against asking him. As much as she would have liked him to come, Nicola was wary of Andrew's reaction to her inviting an unattached man

– especially one whom she sensed liked her and was already a good friend.

Nicola couldn't remember the last time she'd invited friends for supper in England. With Marc away so much, it had been difficult to organise even an impromptu get-together and they'd slipped out of the habit of entertaining even when he was home. But France was the land of gastronomic temptation and Nicola was determined to enjoy all the culinary delights on offer, as well as to get back into cooking herself.

She'd deliberately invited everyone for supper rather than dinner this evening, in an effort to indicate to her friends that the meal would be a more relaxed affair than dinner, which in France could easily contain five or six courses. Tonight's supper would be delicious but relatively simple: tapenade made with black olives from the farm that Josephine had shown her how to make spread on crisp toast for starters; a main course of pork cutlets roasted in the oven, accompanied by fresh asparagus and dauphinoise potatoes cooked in the terracotta dish Josephine and Odette had given her as a housewarming present; dessert would be a fresh fruit salad with crème fraiche or ice cream. All eaten outside on the terrace under the stars. And wine, of course.

Andrew had taken Olivier off to the Mercantour National Parc for a boys' day out that would involve rock climbing and mountain biking. Stuff that Nicola didn't even like to think about Olivier taking part in, but she knew that it was the kind of trip Marc would have taken him on and that Andrew would take good care of him. They'd set off after an early breakfast and Andrew had promised they'd be back in time to give her a hand with the last-minute preparations. With Olivier out, Mischief had shadowed her all day with a real hangdog expression, clearly missing him.

After a busy morning in the garden and doing the usual chores in the cottage, Nicola made herself some lunch before beginning to prepare the food ready for cooking later and organising the table and chairs on the terrace. Henri had unearthed some extra chairs from the barn and it was a motley collection that she cleaned and placed around the table with its new bright yellow tablecloth patterned with bunches of olives she'd purchased from a stall at the fete on Sunday.

Placing the last of the three candles in the middle of the table, Nicola stood back and regarded it all with a critical eye. It was definitely an informal setting but it looked pretty and inviting, which was the main thing after all. Now to start preparing the food.

An hour after Nicola had placed the dauphinoise potatoes in the oven to allow plenty of time for them to cook, Andrew and Olivier arrived home. She didn't have to ask if they'd had a good day, Olivier was buzzing.

'I went on this aaaamaaazing zip wire, Mum. I didn't think I'd like it, but it was ace,' Olivier told her excitedly. 'Andrew says he'll take me again when he moves over.'

As Olivier bounded upstairs, Andrew quietly admitted to Nicola it had been a good day. 'Although I have to confess I'd forgotten how tiring these activity days can be for anyone no longer young and not in peak condition.'

'Oh, you poor old man, you,' Nicola teased. 'Go and have a reviving shower, you'll feel better. Olivier can have his after you. Everything is under control down here.'

Andrew was back downstairs and opening a bottle of wine half an hour later when Raoul, Marie and Luc arrived, followed two minutes later by Claudine and Philippe. Once everyone was settled with a glass of something to drink, Nicola left them chatting and fetched the warm toast and the tapenade. As everyone helped themselves she wished them, 'Bon appétit' before quickly returning to the kitchen to check on the potatoes and the meat in the oven. Time to steam the asparagus ready for the main course. Once that was on the table, Nicola could relax and enjoy the rest of the evening with her friends.

She enlisted Olivier's help to clear between the two courses and to carry out warm plates for everyone while she placed the food on the table. Sitting there as the evening progressed, glass of wine in her hand, listening to the noise of the cicadas growing quieter as the light faded and the conversation of her friends around the table getting a little louder as the wine disappeared, Nicola realised for the first time in months, years even, she had peace of mind. Moving to France at Henri's insistence was proving to be one of the best things she could have done. Perhaps she should buy him a thank you present. She smothered a smile. A simple thank you one day would suffice.

Olivier and Luc disappeared up to his room as soon as they'd eaten, leaving the grown-ups to talk. As the two newcomers, Nicola and Andrew listened, fascinated, to the other four as they talked about the area, telling them about places off the beaten track that Andrew should visit while he was there.

'One tourist trap you should visit is Entrevaux. It's not far. If you're interested in old buildings, you'll be fascinated,' Raoul said.

'Gilles treated me to lunch there the other day. Wonderful place. I can't wait to go back.' Nicola said. 'So much history in those walls and roads.'

Inevitably the conversation turned to Andrew and his plan to move to France in the near future.

'You should talk to Gilles. He'll know what is available privately, as well as via the immobiliers between Nice and Entre-vaux,' Raoul said.

'He certainly knows a lot of people,' Nicola said. 'So many people greeted him while we were walking around Entrevaux.'

'Sounds like a good contact I need to meet,' Andrew said, turning to Nicola. 'Am I likely to this week?'

Ignoring the look in his eyes and the sharp edge she detected in his voice, Nicola nodded. 'I expect so. He visits The Taste of the Countryside regularly.'

Now was not the time to tell him about her concert date at the end of the week with Gilles.

27

In the days following the supper party, Andrew, to Nicola's relief, took himself off in his hire car exploring the area, and on Thursday he went to lunch with Agnes and her mother. When Nicola asked him how it had been, he smiled.

'It was good. I've promised Agnes lunch at my place, wherever that ends up being once I've moved over.'

'With or without her mother?' Nicola teased.

'Oh, with, without a doubt,' Andrew laughed.

'It's good you're making friends so quickly,' Nicola said with a smile.

Andrew had also collected sets of printed handouts from estate agents near and far and on Friday afternoon he arrived back at Le Jardin earlier than usual, excited and waving a brochure at Nicola.

'You'll never guess what has gone on the market. The perfect place for me.'

'You've found somewhere you really like?' Nicola said, pleased that he sounded so upbeat.

'I've only seen it from the road so far. Look at what it is and where it is.' Andrew thrust the brochure towards her. 'I wanted us to take a proper first look together.'

As Nicola glanced at the estate agent's details, her heart sank. 'That looks like the campsite across the road.'

'It is. How perfect a location for me is that?'

Nicola kept her gaze on the brochure, trying not to show Andrew how far from perfect it was in her mind. Too close, was the phrase screaming through her head.

Andrew though, didn't appear to notice her lack of enthusiasm.

'Come on. Let's go and take a look,' he said.

As they walked down to the campsite together, Nicola tried to rationalise her thoughts. She wished she could feel happier at the prospect of Andrew buying a nearby property but selfishly she knew she didn't want him living in such close proximity.

'It's very run-down,' Nicola said doubtfully. 'I haven't actually seen any campers here at all this year. And what about some-where for you to live?'

'There's a house on the site.'

'But is it habitable? I do know the old lady who owns it moved into the village years ago.'

'Details say the house needs renovating. Could be a good investment, even if it does need a lot of renovation. I can always live in a caravan,' Andrew said.

'Can't see you running a campsite somehow.'

'Oh, I don't know. I like people and it would certainly be a challenge sorting it out.' He glanced at Nicola. 'You could help me,' he said quietly. 'A joint project.'

Nicola shook her head. 'Sorry, but no. Of course I'd help whenever I could but I've got enough on my hands with Le Jardin at present. The campsite challenge would be yours alone. Give you a purpose.'

There was a short silence before Andrew said, 'Well, I'm going to look around the site with an open mind anyway.'

When they reached the padlocked gate at the entrance, Andrew climbed over first, turning to offer Nicola a helping hand although she didn't need it.

A short, overgrown track led them towards some derelict outbuildings, an old-fashioned concrete shower block and a wooden building whose faded sign announced it to be the camp café. To one side and set back was the sad-looking house mentioned in the details, an overgrown wisteria vine crawling along the eaves of the roof, its deep purple flowers hanging below were fading and its roots were littered with dropped petals.

Nicola walked over and peered through one of the windows on either side of the front door and could make out an abandoned old-fashioned sofa and two matching armchairs grouped around a small table in a room with a large granite fireplace. She turned away. In its day it had clearly been a lovely house but Andrew would certainly have a challenge on his hand to renovate and bring it back to being habitable again.

Various narrow footpaths disappeared into the undergrowth where the remains of several caravans could be seen and they walked a little way down a path dwarfed by tall pine trees.

Despite the heat, Nicola shivered. 'This place is so overgrown, it's a bit creepy,' she said. 'I've seen enough. I'm going to leave you to it and go home.'

'I'd like to explore a bit more, see how far the land stretches,' Andrew said. 'I'll see you later, if that's okay,' and he set off down one of the footpaths, leaving Nicola to make her own way down the drive.

As she crossed the road towards Le Jardin, she saw Gilles walking across from Le Goût de la Campagne towards Le Jardin.

'Gilles, how lovely to see you. Have you got time for a coffee?'

'Thank you. Nicola, I have come today to tell you that the plans for Le Jardin have been passed.'

'That's great news. Come on in and I'll make some coffee and you can tell me what I do now.'

They were sitting in the kitchen with the plans spread out on the table before them when Andrew returned. Within minutes of Nicola introducing them, the two men had found a common rapport in their joint interest of the building industry.

When Andrew mentioned he'd been across the road looking at the campsite as a possible project for when he moved to France, Gilles immediately asked if he'd like a second opinion.

'I remember when it was busy all summer, but since then, the outbuildings have been neglected and the house has only had the barest amount of maintenance. I can tell you without seeing the place, any renovation you need to do will have to include rewiring, replacing the plumbing and a new septic tank. The rules have all been updated,' Gilles explained.

'The roof seems okay,' Andrew said. 'Would planning and re-registering the place as a campsite be difficult, d'you think?'

Gilles shrugged non-committedly. 'Shouldn't think so. I'm afraid I haven't got time today, but I'm picking Nicola up tomorrow evening, why don't I come a bit earlier and we can go and have a good look before you make any decisions?'

'Thanks,' Andrew said. 'I'd appreciate that.' He glanced across at Nicola. 'You didn't say you were going out tomorrow. Where are the two of you off to then?'

'A concert in Nice,' Gilles answered easily. 'I'd ask you to join us, but I'm afraid the tickets sold out weeks ago.'

'If it's any consolation, Josephine and Odette are really looking forward to spoiling you and Olivier tomorrow evening,' Nicola said quickly, knowing that Andrew was trying not to show how upset he was at her news. 'Josephine is making one of her famous terrine de lapin aux raisins et pistachios for supper,' she added, inwardly praying that Andrew wouldn't create a scene in front of Gilles.

To her relief, he simply smiled and said, 'Sounds delicious,' before starting to study the plans that were still spread out on the table.

28

When Gilles arrived early the following evening, he came from the Taste of the Countryside and Nicola could see that he was annoyed.

'I cannot believe what has happened there. I have to apologise to you.' And he gestured across towards the Taste of the Countryside site.

Nicola followed his gesture and saw with dismay that most of the fence separating Le Jardin from the building site had been destroyed.

'I am very sorry. The driver of the bulldozer made a mistake. Monday morning I can have men here to repair the fence, but for now and tomorrow I can do nothing. The men have all finished work for the day. I've pulled the fence back as best I can, but it is not good.'

'Please don't worry, Gilles. These things happen. As long as the fence is repaired Monday,' and Nicola smiled philosophically at him. Before Gilles could say any more Andrew joined them.

Nicola watched as Andrew and Gilles set off for the campsite, an uneasy knot in her stomach for some reason. Andrew might be keen to have Gilles' professional advice, but would he say anything to him about his personal reasons for moving to France as they wandered around?

Olivier had already gone up to La Prouveresse when they returned.

'The Tantes are expecting you any time now,' Nicola told Andrew as she picked up her handbag and prepared to leave. 'I hope you enjoy your evening. I'll see you in the morning.'

'I'm sure we will,' Andrew said. 'You look very nice by the way.' And he leant forward to give her a peck on the cheek. 'You enjoy yourself too.'

Sitting at Gilles' side as they drove out of Le Jardin, waving goodbye to Andrew standing on the doorstep seeing them off, Nicola couldn't help but feel slightly guilty at leaving him. Perhaps she should have told Gilles that she wasn't free this evening after all. There would have been other concerts.

'We have a slight change of plan,' Gilles said, interrupting her thoughts. 'The restaurant I wanted to take you to was full, so we dine at my apartment instead. I cook for you.' Gilles glanced at Nicola anxiously. 'Is that okay? I can cook,' he assured her. 'It won't be a takeaway.'

Nicola laughed. 'It sounds fine to me. Besides, I'd love to see your home.'

* * *

Gilles' apartment, at the top of a faded, shuttered building in the heart of Nice's old town, was delightful. Traditionally furnished, and with its four rooms, larger than Nicola had expected, it had the feel of a very comfortable family home.

There were several silver framed photos placed on the shelves in the alcove by the wood-burning stove. One, of a middle-aged couple smiling as they sailed a yacht, Nicola took to be Gilles' parents. Idly, she wondered who the attractive girl laughing into the camera in another photo was.

'My twin sister,' Gilles said, catching her glance.

'I didn't know you...'

'She died the day after that photo was taken,' Gilles said briefly. 'Twenty years ago.'

'Sorry is such an inadequate word, isn't it?' Nicola said quietly.

Gilles nodded. 'It still hurts, but time and life does go on.' He opened a door. 'Now, why don't you wait out here, I'll just be a few moments,' and he gestured her to go through.

Standing on the rooftop terrace as Gilles attended to things in his ultra-modern kitchen, Nicola took in the views. In one direction, she could see the harbour with the Mediterranean beyond and in the other direction, the range of mountains that formed the Alps Maritime.

'What breathtaking views,' she said as Gilles handed her a glass of sparkling wine. 'It must be magic when it's dark and all the lights are switched on.'

Gilles nodded. 'I often come out here at the end of a difficult day and simply stand and stare. Seems to recharge the batteries somehow.'

The dinner he'd prepared was simple and delicious. Salmon and rocket salad for starters, daube au Provençal – 'I knew you liked that,' Gilles said laughing – followed by cup au chocolat and coffee.

By the time they left to walk the short distance to the concert hall, they were totally relaxed with each other. Crossing the busy Rue de Notre Dame, Gilles took Nicola's hand – and continued to hold it until they reached the theatre.

* * *

It was late when the concert finished, but as they emerged into the night, Nicola was amazed by how many people were still out enjoying themselves.

'We have a coffee and then I drive you home,' Gilles said.

Sitting at one of the many pavement cafés, Nicola watched the late-night world of Nice go by. Bars and cafés thronged with people, music from discos and jazz clubs drifted on the still warm night air. The locals mingled happily with the holidaymakers, and there was even a game of boules going on down one of the side streets.

The drive home through deserted countryside passed quickly. Coming to a stop outside Le Jardin, Gilles glanced across at Nicola.

'I have enjoyed this evening. I hope you have too?'

'It's been lovely. Thank you, Gilles. I'm only sorry you have such a long drive home again.'

Gilles shrugged. 'Not a problem.' There was a pause before he said, 'May I ask you something?'

'Of course,' Nicola said, as she got out of the car.

As Gilles came to stand next to her, he said, 'You and Andrew. Are you, how you say, an item?'

Nicola took a quick breath. 'Did Andrew say something to you?'

Gilles shook his head. 'Non, it is something I sense when he looks at you. He is très fond of you.'

Nicola sighed. 'We're old friends. He helped me through a difficult patch in my life, and I am very fond of him too – as a good friend. The big brother I never had. But that is all. I simply do not see him in any other way. I have told him that. Several times in fact.'

'So, if I ask you out again, he will not come and biff me on the nose?'

Despite herself, Nicola laughed at his expression. 'No, he will not come and "biff" you on the nose, I promise.'

'Good.' And Gilles leant forward and gently kissed her. 'Sleep well. I'll see you soon.'

* * *

Slowly getting ready for bed, Nicola thought about the evening and Gilles. She'd really enjoyed herself and hoped that Gilles meant what he'd said about asking her out again.

As for Andrew, she'd thought she'd impressed on him enough the fact that she and he would never be a couple. If Gilles had picked up on the looks Andrew gave her, then who knew who else would assume the wrong thing? The thought of him 'biffing' Gilles on the nose might be amusing in a way, but she'd hate it to happen for real.

* * *

Nicola stirred irritably and tried to shake off the hands that were shaking her violently.

'Go away. It can't possibly be time to get up yet,' and she determinedly clutched her duvet around her.

'Mum. Wake up,' Olivier shouted. 'There are wild boar in the garden. They are ruining everything. Andrew needs your help.'

Nicola sat bolt upright. 'How did they get in?'

'The fence is down, remember?' Olivier said. 'Now come on.'

Once downstairs, Nicola pulled on her wellingtons and struggled to make sense of the scene before her.

'How long do you think they've been in here?' she asked Andrew.

He shrugged. 'Long enough to ruin your vegetable garden and dig up part of your flower beds,' he said, shining the torch through the garden to show her some of the devastation the animals had already caused. 'Right now they are at the top of the garden, rooting around under the trees. As far as I can see, there are two adults and three or four babies,' he said. 'The adults are pretty aggressive. Probably our best plan is to try and herd them back towards the building site, and hope they don't attack us.'

'But there's nothing to stop them coming straight back,' Nicola said, dismayed.

'Papa Henri has an electric fence he doesn't use in the barn – shall I ring him?' Olivier asked.

'Yes please,' Nicola said. 'Although I suspect he's going to be less than pleased to be woken up at,' she glanced at her watch, '3.30 a.m.'

'It's an emergency. He'll understand,' Olivier said confidently.

And he was right. Henri drove down with the electric fence and stayed to help Andrew erect it.

'No point in chasing them off until it's up. They'll only come straight back. Don't know what Gilles Bongars was thinking off not getting that fence put back up yesterday. Should have known the boar would be in here tout suite.'

Once the two strands of wire were in place, the four of them began the nerve-wracking task of chasing the boar out of the garden through the opening they'd left at the top.

'Concentrate on the adults,' Henri said, 'but be careful. They will protect the babies, and we don't want anyone being attacked.'

It took an hour before all the wild boar were out of the garden and they were able to switch on the electric fence to keep them out. Nicola sighed with relief as she watched them disappear into the darkness of the field behind the Taste of the Countryside building site.

'Thanks, Henri. Cup of coffee before you go home?'

'No thanks,' Henri shook his head. 'I'll have something stronger when I get back. Don't forget to ring Bongars first thing – he should at least be told what's happened.'

'Night, Mum. I'm going back to bed,' Olivier said tiredly.

Nicola looked at Andrew. 'I'm going to make myself some hot chocolate. Would you like some?'

'Please,' and Andrew followed her into the kitchen. 'I want to tell you something too.'

Nicola's heart sank. What now?

'How was your evening?' She asked, hoping to delay the conversation, at least for a moment.

'Great. Josephine and Odette were on good form. Really made me feel part of the family. Odette says she'll take me skiing this winter – if I'm not too busy.'

Nicola smiled. 'So, what did you want to tell me?'

'I've decided to buy the campsite,' Andrew said.

Nicola was quiet for a few seconds before she said, 'Are you sure? It's one of the first places you've looked at. There may be something better on the market. Please don't rush into things, Andrew.' She shrugged. 'I doubt that the campsite is going to have a lot of people interested in it. Le Jardin had a habitable house and look how long it was empty before I bought it.'

'But this is a business opportunity, with land,' Andrew insisted. 'Besides, there is nothing else in the neighbourhood on the market. Raoul was at the farmhouse for supper and I talked to him about it. He said it was a good opportunity and I should snap it up. Especially as I need something close to Le Jardin,' he added.

Nicola stared at him and bit back on the words: *But you don't need something close to Le Jardin, do you, Andrew? You can go anywhere. You want to be close for all the wrong reasons.* If he was moving here still hoping they would grow closer, then he was uprooting himself for the wrong reason. What was it going to take to get the message through to Andrew that they would never be more than good friends, however much he wanted more? She took a deep breath.

'Andrew, it's the middle of the night, I'm tired and I really don't want to have this conversation with you now. But please don't expect, or even assume, that things between us will change when you're living here. My feelings for you will not change from friendship to love and the sooner you accept that, the better it will be for both us. Do you understand?'

She stared at him, waiting for his answer. Slowly he gave a resigned nod of his head and a muttered, 'Yes.'

'Good. I'm going back to bed. I'll see you at breakfast – which will be late.'

29

Three days later and Nicola and Olivier were together on the doorstep to say goodbye to Andrew as he slammed the boot of his hire car shut.

Nicola was relieved at how well Andrew's holiday had gone in the end. Once he'd decided he was going to buy the campsite, the last few days of his visit had been taken up in a whirl of meetings and never-ending French bureaucracy. The question of their relationship had been pushed to one side and she'd managed to avoid being alone in his company, but Nicola had known it was only a matter of time before Andrew would raise the subject again. It happened over supper yesterday evening – his last night in France.

'I hope you don't mind, but I've left a few things in the chest of drawers in my room. Seems silly taking all my stuff, especially as I'll be back with all my worldly goods in a month or two.'

Stifling a sigh as she realised it would be churlish of her to object, Nicola had agreed that, no, she didn't mind. Andrew had clearly forgotten that the building work on Le Jardin might start before he returned, and that the room would have to be cleared.

Andrew's voice brought her back to reality as he continued.

'I need to say a couple of things. First, thanks for having me to stay.' He fiddled with his wine glass before looking directly at her. 'Secondly, it's lovely to see you so happy and making a success of your life in France. The move has been good for Olivier too, he loves spending time on the farm. I can only hope my move will be prove to be equally successful for me.' He paused and shook his head as Nicola went to speak. 'I need to say this. A few months ago, I was in a deep rut, both at work and in my personal life. Redundancy was a big shock. You moving here was another. I know you think I'm making a mistake, buying the campsite so quickly and moving over here, and I confess I'd hoped you'd missed me enough to return my feelings and welcome me joining you, but now I do realise that's never going to happen.'

Nicola watched and waited as he took a sip of his wine.

'I know everything about my new life is going to be a challenge – the campsite, renovating the house, learning French, making new friends. You had family and people here who knew and remembered Marc to help you settle – yes, I know Henri is difficult, but the aunts, Claudine, Raoul welcomed you with open arms.' Andrew took a deep breath. 'And that is what I hope you will be when I return – a good friend to me, a part of my family without any strings.'

Nicola smiled. The message seemed to have finally got through. 'In that case, I look forward to welcoming my big brother to France and back into my life.'

Now standing outside the cottage, Nicola watched as Andrew ruffled Olivier's hair by way of saying goodbye. 'I'll see you soon. Look after your mum.'

Turning, he looked at Nicola and opened his arms.

'Goodbye friends hug?'

Nicola stepped into his embrace and returned the hug.

'There is something I forgot to say last night,' Andrew said, looking at her. 'Gilles is a good bloke who likes you and I can see you like him too. I hope the three of us will be friends when I move over?'

'Of course. You take care and travel safe,' Nicola said as Andrew got in the car and drove away. Relief had flooded her body at his words about Gilles. It really did seem as though he had got the message and was moving on, which meant she didn't have to worry about her growing friendship with Gilles upsetting him.

The weeks until his return were likely to be her busiest yet at Le Jardin. Not only did she have to get the house ready for the builders, there was also now the job of restoring the garden after the onslaught from the wild boar. Thankfully, an apologetic Gilles had organised for a far stronger fence to be re-erected so the garden was secure again.

'Hope Andrew gets back soon. It's been great having him here,' Olivier said. 'Okay if I go up to the farm now?'

'Yes, but take Mischief with you,' Nicola said. 'I'm going to be busy in the garden.' Olivier had already given her a hand replanting the plants that had survived being rooted out and left by the boar, but there was still a lot to be done. Including setting up a vegetable plot again. That would have to be her first priority if she was to have fresh produce to sell when Taste of the Countryside opened its doors.

As Andrew's car disappeared from view, Josephine arrived.

'Oh, I've missed saying goodbye,' she said ruefully. 'I'd so hoped to be in time.' She sighed disappointedly. 'Still, he'll be back soon, n'est pas?'

Nicola nodded. 'A couple of months, when the campsite will be his. Although where he's going to live whilst he renovates that house is anyone's guess.'

'Oh, he's organising for a mobile home to be delivered. Didn't he tell you?' Josephine said. 'After he moves into the house, he plans on the mobile home being his first letting caravan.' She looked at Nicola shrewdly. 'Are you not looking forward to Andrew coming to live here?'

Nicola sighed. 'In a way yes, but...' she shrugged. 'I'm afraid he's moving here for all the wrong reasons. I know he says he's fed up with his old way of life and wants a challenge, and he's told me he also accepts that we'll never be more than friends, but I still can't help worrying he is moving to France too fast.'

'Other people's expectations are not always easy to deal with, are they,' Josephine said quietly. 'Nicola, I need to talk to you.'

Nicola glanced at her in surprise. Josephine, normally one of the most level-headed of all the women she knew, was agitatedly playing with the silver cross that always hung round her neck. Clearly Josephine had something serious on her mind.

'Shall we sit down?' Nicola said, wondering what could be on Josephine's mind.

It wasn't until they were both seated at the patio table with cups of coffee that Josephine, glancing apprehensively at Nicola, asked. 'You are happy here in France, aren't you, Nicola? You don't regret coming here? You don't long to go back to Angleterre? To the life you had there.'

Nicola, surprised at the question, didn't answer immediately. Her main concern had always been for Olivier rather than herself, helping him to recover from the death of his father. Moving to France had certainly helped there, he was a different boy to the one he'd been nine months ago. As for herself, she remembered that feeling of having peace of mind which she'd experienced the night of the recent supper party,

'Yes, I am happy here, probably happier than I've been for years. And no, I don't long to go back to England. In fact, I was even thinking of thanking Henri for "suggesting" we came here to live.'

'Ah, it's that "suggestion" I want to talk to you about,' Josephine said.

Nicola looked at Josephine questioningly and waited. There was definitely more to Josephine wanting to talk to her than just making sure she was happy in her new life.

'Odette and I love having you and Olivier here. It's made such a difference to our lives. I'd have hated it if you weren't happy too. But we have been feeling guilty ever since you bought this place,' Josephine gestured around her. 'There is something I must tell you before you hear it from somebody else. You see, Nicola, there's this little fact that Henri conveniently forgot to tell you when he coerced you into coming to live here in France with Olivier.'

30

'Henri, I want a word with you about Olivier's inheritance. Josephine says you lied to me.'

Nicola's voice, even to her own ears, sounded brusque and rude. But she didn't care – she was furious with Henri and determined to tell him exactly how she felt.

Henri, on his way to the barn, stopped and turned to look at Nicola.

'Josephine's told you, has she?' he said. 'I thought she would eventually. Never was one to keep her mouth shut where the truth was concerned.'

'It was a joint decision by the twins to tell me. Josephine was the messenger. Although I don't blame them, I wish one of them had opened their mouths before,' Nicola snapped. 'It would have saved a lot of misunderstanding. And I'd not be here now to give you a piece of my mind!'

'My guess is you'd not be here at all,' Henri said slowly. 'If you'd known the truth, you'd never have come to France in the first place. Even as you agreed to come, you weren't exactly thrilled at the prospect, I remember.'

Nicola looked at him crossly. 'I wasn't thrilled at being coerced into making the decision. That was bad enough, but now I know that you based it on a downright lie, it's even worse. It makes a complete farce of our being here.'

There was a short silence before Henri said quietly, 'I didn't lie about wanting Olivier to grow up here, getting to know his French family. And the truth is, if you'd known the way French inheritance laws work, that Olivier, as my only direct descendant, would inherit La Prouveresse whatever I did, you would never have even considered coming here to live, would you?'

He didn't give her the chance to answer before continuing.

'I'd have seen Olivier a couple of times a year, if I was lucky.' He shook his head. 'I wanted more than visiting rights. I also wanted a chance to try and heal the rift I'd created between us.'

There was silence as Henri looked at her.

'Well, now you know, Olivier inherits La Prouveresse whatever happens. So you can pack up and return to England. Can't expect you to stay; not now you know the truth. Isn't that what you've come to tell me?'

Before Nicola could answer, he turned and walked into the barn, closing the door firmly behind him.

Nicola gazed after him, exasperated. Trust Henri to make sure he had the last word by walking away from the argument. It would serve him right if she did sell up and go back to England.

She sighed. Her initial anger when Josephine had told her the truth about the blackmail had faded somewhat, but she had been determined to confront Henri over his lie, although the fact that he didn't seem the least bit repentant was disconcerting.

And was he really expecting her to leave everything she'd been working on over the last few months, and return to England?

Hesitantly, Nicola turned and walked across the yard to the

farmhouse. She had this sneaky feeling that Josephine had been avoiding her ever since telling her the truth the other day about the French inheritance laws, and she needed to put things right between them.

Both Josephine and Odette were pleased to see her though, even if Josephine did look a bit wary.

'I've just spoken to Henri,' Nicola said quietly. 'And told him I know the truth about Olivier's inheritance.'

Odette glanced at her quickly. 'Nicola, we both feel so guilty about this whole affair.'

'Please don't, Odette,' Nicola said quietly. 'If anybody should feel guilty, it's Henri, but quite clearly he doesn't have a guilty feeling in his body. He didn't even attempt to apologise. He also seems to expect me to hotfoot it back to England, taking Olivier with me now that I know the truth.'

Josephine gasped. 'You're not going, are you?'

Nicola shook her head. 'No. But knowing that I can leave without Olivier losing his inheritance if things don't work out at Le Jardin de Dominic is a big relief. And at the very least it means that I don't have to...' she hesitated, not sure if the sisters would understand the phrase, 'pussyfoot around Henri any more.'

'Have you told Olivier what Henri did?' Josephine asked.

'No,' Nicola shook her head. 'He didn't know the real reason behind us coming to France, so there's no point. He and Henri are building a good relationship – I wouldn't want to spoil that,' Nicola said, realising the truth of what she'd just said. Despite Henri's mistakes with her, she'd never come between Olivier and his grandfather.

'Henri means well,' Josephine said slowly. 'It's just that sometimes he goes the wrong way about it.'

Nicola smiled sardonically. 'That's so true.'

* * *

For the next few days, Nicola was busy, not only finishing clearing up the mess caused by the wild boar, but also planting some new stock in the salad and vegetable plots she was trying to establish. There was also the small matter of getting some quotes for the building work she wanted done from the builders Gilles had put her in touch with.

Raoul, calling in unexpectedly at Le Jardin one morning, found Nicola busy digging over a plot of land she'd earmarked for some winter vegetables. Despite her protests, he immediately offered to finish the job for her while she and Olivier tied up some tomato plants that had escaped the rampaging boar.

Afterwards, Nicola poured some cold drinks and they all sat out on to the patio.

'Thanks for that. Now, to what do I owe the honour of this visit?' Nicola said gratefully.

'Have you decided yet which school Olivier will be going to?' Raoul asked unexpectedly.

Nicola looked at Olivier crossly. 'Have you been moaning to Raoul?'

Olivier looked sheepish, but it was Raoul who said, 'Not moaning exactly. He just mentions it every time he sees me,' he laughed. 'But seriously, Nicola, you will have to make a decision soon – it's the first week of August and "la rentrée" to school is already on everyone's mind.'

'Mum, I really want to go the French school and not the English one down in Nice,' Olivier said.

Nicola sighed, and decided to tease them both a little bit. 'Oh Olivier, I'm not sure. I know your French has come on by leaps and bounds, but will you understand lessons like, science, say, in

French? Some subjects are hard enough to understand without struggling with the language.'

'Papa Henri and the aunts will help me translate things, if there is something I don't understand,' Olivier said confidently.

'They were at school a long time ago,' Nicola replied. 'They won't be familiar with the sort of work you can expect to be doing.'

'I still think I'll cope,' Olivier said stubbornly. 'Luc will help me too. So please – I really want to go to Dad's old school.'

Raoul looked at Nicola. 'Why not let him go for a term and see how he gets on? If it doesn't work, then in January you can send him down to Nice.'

'That's exactly what I thought I'd do,' Nicola said, trying not to smile as she looked at Olivier. 'So I phoned the school a few weeks ago and reserved you a place. The headmaster was very understanding and assured me they would take care to make sure you could cope. Give you extra French lessons if necessary.'

Olivier punched the air with his fist before jumping up and giving her a hug. 'Yes. Thanks, Mum. I'm going to message Luc,' and the kitchen door banged behind him as he ran indoors.

'Don't worry,' Raoul said. 'Everyone will help and you can always ring me.' He glanced at Nicola before continuing. 'Olivier's school wasn't the only reason I called in,' he said quietly. 'I need some advice,' he paused. 'And I thought as an outsider, with the experience you've had, you would be the best person to ask.'

31

The Taste of the Countryside building next door was progressing rapidly and Gilles was there almost daily as the hot summer days continued to pass, supervising and checking on things.

Invariably, these visits were early-morning ones and Nicola became used to Gilles knocking on the door of Le Jardin, holding fresh croissants, just as she was putting her morning coffee on. Olivier had usually disappeared up to the farm by then, but Gilles always brought extra croissants for him. The mornings he didn't appear she missed him and the days seemed strangely long. She enjoyed his company and he'd become a really good friend. He did warn her though, that his involvement with the building was nearing its end.

One morning, Gilles arrived a little later than usual and invited her to have a coffee in the new building.

'The Tourist Office is finished and is open and they have a serious coffee machine that needs testing,' he explained as they walked over. 'The idea now is to finish the fitting out of shelves in the display area of the rest of the building and order the stock. This way both sections will be open for the remainder of the summer season, but the official opening will be delayed until sometime in early December.'

Gilles pushed open the door and ushered Nicola in.

'Morning, Ann-Marie,' he called. 'I've brought Nicola Jacques from Le Jardin de Dominic to meet you.' He turned to Nicola. 'Ann-Marie is the manageress of Le Goût de la Campagne as well as the Tourist Office.'

Ann-Marie came out from behind the counter and shook Nicola's hand. 'Gilles tells me you hope to sell some of your produce here eventually.'

'What with the boar digging up and trampling over every-thing and now the heat shrivelling everything up, I'm way behind schedule for selling anything. This year a few tomatoes might be the sum total of things,' Nicola said. 'Next year though, I hope to be better organised. I was thinking too, once the building work is done, I will have at least one room available and I was wondering about registering to offer bed and breakfast next summer.'

'Good idea. When you're ready to register, let me know,' Ann-Marie said. 'Gilles, can I have a quick word?'

While Gilles and Ann-Marie were talking, Nicola wandered over to look at a display of framed photographs fixed to the wall by the door. A mixture of black and white and coloured photos showed the history of life in the area from around the begin-ning of the twentieth century, through to the present day. One in particular caught her eye. Four people gathered around a tractor with a trailer full of grapes on a farmyard that looked like La Prouveresse. Nicola squinted at the figures. Surely that was Henri and the twins? The woman alongside Henri had to be Bernadette, Marc's mother. Further along the wall a sepia photograph was surely Le Jardin de Dominic taken between the wars.

Nicola turned as Gilles joined her. 'Look at these two photos.

They're amazing. Can I buy copies anywhere? I'd love to have them hanging in the cottage.'

'It was Ann-Marie's idea to have the photographs on display and the plan is to have copies for sale once the place is fully functioning. I'll put an order in for you, but you'll have to be patient a little longer.'

Gilles opened the door and they both turned to call out 'Au revoir' to Ann-Marie as they left.

Walking back towards Le Jardin de Dominic, Nicola said, 'I need to say thank you for all the builder contacts you gave me. I've gone with Pierre from Entrevaux. His quote seemed to cover everything and I liked him.'

'He's the one I hoped you'd choose. Did you mention my name? When does he hope to start?'

'I did drop your name into the conversation,' Nicola admitted. 'He's promised to start fairly soon. Much to the aunts' delight, Olivier and I are moving up to the farm, I can't face living in a building site, so I'm going to start packing a few things to take with us and clear the space downstairs. There's not a lot of furniture to worry about, just a sofa and a coffee table, which Olivier and I can move to one side.' Nicola pushed open the garden gate.

'How is Olivier?'

'He's happy now I've told him he can go to the senior school in the next village rather than the international school in Nice,' Nicola said. 'Luc has given him a copy of the list of stationery I'll need to buy him. It's a mind-bogglingly long list.'

Gilles laughed. 'Every summer it is the same. Everyone is still on holiday but "la rentrée" dominates the supermarkets and everyone's thoughts. I remember my maman's frantic searches each August for a particular notebook that a certain teacher wanted.'

'Claudine assures me that the place to go to is the big hypermarket outside Nice, so we're going to have a day out there soon. August is turning out to be a surprisingly busy month.' She looked at Gilles hopefully. 'Have you got time to stop for lunch?'

Gilles shook his head. 'Sadly no. I have a midday rendezvous in Nice, so I have to leave soon. Today is my last official day with Le Goût de la Campagne, so sadly I will not be seeing you so often. I will ring you soon and we arrange a date, yes?' He caught hold of her hands. 'I realise we haven't known each other very long and I don't want to presume anything too soon but, already we seem to have something special between us. And Nicola, even if I can't drop in to see you, please remember I'm only a phone call away if you need me. For anything. I will be there.'

'I'll remember, and thank you.'

'Bien,' and Gilles placed a gentle kiss on her cheek. 'Au revoir for now. I will ring you soon.'

Nicola waited as he got in his car and drove away, a happy smile on her face.

32

A day later, Nicola and Claudine prepared to drive to Nice to buy Olivier's school clothes and all the stationery he would need for his new school. Olivier himself had spent the night at Luc's and was catching the small Train des Pignes from the village and would meet them at the hypermarket and then travel back with them.

'Are you sure you want to drive?' Claudine asked as she settled herself into Nicola's car. 'We could always go in my car.'

Nicola shook her head. 'No, it's fine. I need to get used to driving on the wrong side of the road in different places. I'm happy locally, but busy roads are different. I'm relying on you to navigate for me by the way. I don't know my way around Nice.'

Travelling down the N202, they were forced to stop by temporary traffic lights at several sections where the road wound its way alongside the river on their left and sheer rocks on their right. Nicola gazed in disbelief at the small figures of workmen scaling the roadside cliffs as if they were enjoying a quick abseil.

'That looks so dangerous. What are they doing?'

'Preparing for winter. Every year there are landslides and

rockfalls along this route so they fix these huge steel nets to catch them in an effort to make it safer. Look,' Claudine pointed up and towards the cliff face at the side of them. 'There's a high net there.'

'Do these nets work?' Nicola asked.

'Mostly. Depends on how unstable everything is and how big the falling rocks are.'

The traffic light changed to green and Nicola followed a stream of cars as they edged their way past the vans and trucks of the roadworks.

By the time Nicola was turning off the main road and negotiating the large parking area of the hypermarket, Claudine had filled her in on all the gossip from the village and given her some surprising news of her own.

'I'm pregnant,' she told Nicola happily. 'Isn't it wonderful?'

'Congratulations.' Nicola glanced at her friend curiously. 'Is Phillipe pleased?' she asked, remembering the problems in their marriage Claudine and Phillipe had been experiencing earlier in the year.

Claudine nodded happily. 'He's thrilled too. Me not getting pregnant was one of our problems. He'd always said he wanted at least two children. The only person who doesn't seem happy for me is my dear brother, Raoul. He's strangely quiet these days.'

'I think he's got problems of his own,' Nicola said quietly.

Claudine looked at her. 'Has he been talking to you?'

Nicola nodded. 'He asked my advice, as an outsider,' she added quickly, not wanting to hurt her friend by telling her that Raoul had confided in a stranger rather than his own sister. 'He seemed to think I would know how to solve his problem.'

'And did you?'

'Not really,' Nicola said, wondering how much she could say

to Claudine without breaking Raoul's confidence. 'My experiences with Andrew and Olivier are totally different to—'

'Ah,' Claudine interrupted. 'It's Marie, isn't it? She's turned him down again.' She sighed. 'Every year he asks her to marry him – and every year she says no. Did Raoul want you to have a word with her?'

'No,' Nicola said quietly. 'Raoul's problem is Luc. Marie has said she will marry Raoul – once he and Luc have a better relationship. He wanted my advice on how he could establish the sort of relationship he's seen that Olivier and Andrew have. At the moment, despite Raoul doing his best, Luc apparently does nothing but hurl insults at him and refuses to even discuss the situation.' There was a short silence while Nicola concentrated on parking, before she said, 'Olivier says Luc has simply turned his mind against Raoul marrying his mum and is determined to make life as difficult as he can for him.'

'So, what did you say to Raoul?'

'What could I say? Other than, give it time.' Nicola sighed. 'But I do feel sorry for Marie, stuck in the middle.'

'Yes, you're lucky that Olivier has accepted Andrew so well,' Claudine said thoughtfully. 'When you two finally get married—'

'Hey, I'm not marrying Andrew,' Nicola protested.

'But that's why Andrew is moving over here, isn't it? So you two can build a new life together – at least that's the impression he gave us all the night of the supper party.' Claudine looked at Nicola anxiously.

Nicola suppressed a wave of frustration at Claudine's words and shook her head. 'Andrew was Marc's good friend and Olivier has always had a good relationship with him, even when his dad was alive. Before he left the other day, Andrew and I talked seriously about our friendship and I got him to finally accept the fact that that is all we will ever be to each other – good friends. Please tell Raoul that – and anybody else who thinks Andrew and I are a couple – we are most definitely not.'

* * *

The day before the builders started knocking down walls in La Jardin de Dominic, Nicola and Olivier moved up to the farm. Josephine and Odette were delighted to have them both staying there again. Nicola soon slipped back into the habit of helping the sisters like she had on that first visit at the beginning of the year. Even Henri went out of his way to be affable and make Nicola feel welcome – no mention was made again of her returning to England.

First thing every morning, she returned to Le Jardin to feed Frisby, check on the builders' progress and to spend time gardening before it got too hot to work outside. Working on the land she'd cleared for vegetables, she could see the cars driving into the parking for Le Goût de Campagne using the new entrance road, but thankfully, as Gilles had assured her, they were too far away to be a problem.

In the evenings, Henri occasionally went down to Sylvie's for a couple of hours, leaving Josephine, Odette and Nicola to do their own thing until bedtime. Nicola enjoyed those evenings spent listening to the twins reminiscing, either sitting around the old wooden table in the farmhouse kitchen, listening to the muted sounds of Olivier practising the saxophone that Henri had started to teach him to play, upstairs in his bedroom or out in the petit jardin.

One evening when the mosquitoes had driven them inside, she asked them both, 'Do you ever wish you'd moved away from the village, lived different sort of lives?'

Both the sisters looked at her for several seconds without

replying and then, to Nicola's dismay, Josephine got up and left the kitchen.

'I'm sorry,' Nicola said, embarrassed, looking at Odette. 'It's none of my business. I shouldn't have asked. And now I've upset Josephine.'

Odette smiled at her as she said quietly, 'Do you know the saying "Bien dans sa peau"?'

'Happy in my skin?' Nicola said, slowly translating the words.

Odette nodded. 'Yes. I'm content enough with the way things are. A husband and children of my own would have been good, but it was not to be – the children part anyway. You never know, I might still find a husband!' She laughed, before adding soberly, 'But Josephine now, she's not been happy in her skin since she returned from Paris, although she hides it well.' Odette looked at Nicola thoughtfully. 'Did Marc ever tell you about Josephine's past?'

Nicola shook her head. 'Only that she was once married and lived in Paris. I don't think he ever knew the truth behind her return to La Prouveresse; he was quite young at the time.'

'Things went terribly wrong for her in Paris. No phone in the farm in those days, so we knew nothing about the trouble she was in. The letters she wrote to us made no mention of the bad times she was living through. It wasn't until she arrived back here unexpectedly that we learnt the full extent of the trouble she was in.' Odette paused. 'When Henri heard the truth, he told her there was no possibility of her returning to Paris. There was no future with the situation she'd got herself into. As for Pascal...'

'Pascal,' Josephine's voice interrupted as she returned, 'begged me to go away with him.'

Moving across to Nicola, Josephine handed her a black and white photograph.

'This is me, in another life a long time ago. And to answer your question, yes, I do wish I'd lived a different life.'

As Nicola looked at the photograph, she knew she would never have recognised Josephine as being the woman in it.

The young, pretty, dark-haired woman standing in the arms of a handsome man and laughing happily up at him was clearly in love with life and the man holding her. The camera had captured perfectly the look of love that the couple were sharing.

'Your husband was very handsome,' Nicola said gently.

There was a short pause.

'Non, Nicola. That's not my husband. It is Pascal – his brother,' Josephine said, sadly brushing away a tear as she took the photograph back from Nicola. 'The love of my life. And the man I should have had the courage to marry years ago.'

33

Nicola had been hoping that she and Olivier would have moved back into Le Jardin before Olivier's first day at his new school, but in the event, Olivier's school term started before the builders had even finished knocking down walls and getting a new steel girder in place across the width of the cottage downstairs.

'Bonne chance, Olivier!' Henri said gruffly as Olivier gulped down his croissant and picked up his schoolbag before dashing out of the La Prouveresse kitchen and down the farm drive to catch the school bus.

Nicola had offered to drive him to school, but Olivier had given an emphatic 'No thanks' to that idea, saying he'd prefer to go by himself on the bus. Nicola was pleased he was so keen to start a new phase of his life independently but couldn't help feeling sad that another stage of her own life was over.

Walking slowly down to Le Jardin after he'd left, Nicola found herself remembering Olivier's first day at primary school. She'd felt bereft that day too, but Marc had been at her side then as Olivier had vanished excitedly into the reception class. Afterwards he'd helped dry her tears and taken her out for the day. So much had changed since then. Today she was on her own.

Nicola smothered a sigh and tried to stop the tears from coursing down her cheeks. Olivier would be fourteen soon. Today was just another step on his way to being a grown-up. It was only a matter of a few more years before he'd be off to university, finding his own way in life, not needing her on a daily basis any more.

'Bonjour, Nicola. Are you all right?' Gilles' gentle voice broke anxiously into her reverie.

Nicola jumped with surprise. She'd been so deep in her own thoughts that she'd arrived at the back gate of Le Jardin without noticing her surroundings and was unaware that Gilles was waiting for her by the gate.

Now, looking miserably at Gilles, she nodded and struggled to speak normally. 'I'm fine really, thanks. It's just that Olivier going off to his new school brought back memories and also made me think about the future – and how uncertain everything in life is.' Nicola smiled tremulously at Gilles through her tears. 'I'm glad the builders haven't arrived yet to see me like this. What are you doing here? Is there a problem at Le Goût de la Campagne?'

'Oh Nicola, ma cherè, come here,' and Gilles pulled her towards him, wrapping his arms around her tightly. He held her silently for a moment before saying, 'I came to see how you were. Have you had breakfast?'

Nicola shook her head, surprised. 'No. I couldn't eat anything – I was more nervous than Olivier.'

'In that case, let's go to the village for coffee and croissants.'

Five minutes later, they were sitting on the terrace of the village café, coffee and apricot croissants in front of them.

'This is so kind of you,' Nicola said, looking at Gilles. 'I'm really grateful for the company too. I've missed our early-morning breakfasts recently,' she added.

'Me too,' Gilles said. 'That's one of the reasons why I came up today.' There was a short silence before Gilles added, 'The other reason is I knew today would be difficult for you with Olivier starting a new school. I don't like to see you unhappy, Nicola.' He slowly reached across the table and took her hand in his. 'I know there is nothing I can do about today – it's one of life's personal milestones for Olivier and you.' He looked at Nicola, his eyes serious. 'But know that Olivier will be fine – and so will you. As for the future – who knows what it will bring?' He paused before continuing hesitantly, 'Please, if I can help in any way at any time, just ask. Promise?'

Nicola smiled through the tears that were threatening to start again at his kind words. 'I promise. Thank you, Gilles.'

He smiled and squeezed her hand tightly. 'Now, I have to spend a couple of hours in Monaco this morning. Why don't you come with me?'

* * *

Nicola sat at one of the pavement tables of the Café de Paris, watching the world go by while Gilles kept his business appointment in an office somewhere along the Avenue de Grande-Bretagne. Gilles had driven up through Monte Carlo before parking his car in a nearby large underground car park and joining her for a quick coffee before heading off for his meeting.

Remembering the comforting hug Gilles had given her that morning and his earlier words about their special friendship, she felt a small glow of happiness spread through her body. She was so lucky to have met Gilles.

Nicola smiled as a group of teenagers posed nonchalantly

close to three Ferraris seemingly abandoned by their owners at the foot of the Casino steps. Liveried security men were making sure no one got too close to the cars but smiled indulgently as souvenir photographs were taken.

A glamorous woman leaving the Hotel de Paris opposite and stepping into a waiting limousine took her attention. Surely it was...

'Seen anyone famous then?' Gilles teased as he greeted her with the customary kiss on both cheeks that Nicola had come to look forward to and expect from him.

He placed his briefcase on the table and ordered two more coffees.

Nicola shook her head. 'Nobody that I can put a name to,' she said. 'But it's been fun watching.'

'I thought we'd have lunch up in the old town of Monaco,' Gilles said. 'We'll take a taxi up to the Place D'Armes and then walk up the ramp way to the Palace. The views out over the principality are spectacular.' Taking her by the hand he led her across to a waiting taxi.

Walking hand in hand up the gentle incline towards the Palace, Gilles pointed out some of the well-known landmarks and gave Nicola a potted history of the small country that was no bigger than Hyde Park in London.

They were too late to witness the changing of the guard on the courtyard outside the palace and Gilles led Nicola down the narrow street towards the cathedral instead. The cool interior of Cathédrale de Notre-Dame-Immaculée provided a welcome respite from the heat, despite having to shuffle around with the crowds anxious to see the tombstones of Prince Rainier and Princess Grace.

Lunch was eaten in a private, hidden courtyard of a small restaurant whose entrance from one of the narrow, tourist-filled streets gave no inkling of the quiet oasis behind it. The crab salad Nicola chose was delicious, but the dessert, dacquoise with almonds, apricots and cream, that melted in her mouth, was sublime. Gilles watched with amusement as she replaced her spoon on the almost spotless plate. 'That was so good.'

As they lingered over coffee, a small brown-eyed girl went silently from table to table offering single stem red roses. Everyone, with the exception of Gilles, declined to buy a bloom.

Wordlessly he presented his chosen rose to Nicola, leaning across to kiss her gently as he did so. Nicola blushed as a ripple of quiet applause broke out at his romantic gesture.

As they began to make their way back down to the harbour through the terraced gardens beneath the palace, Nicola said, 'Gilles, I can't thank you enough for turning this into such a memorable day.'

His arm around her shoulders squeezed her tightly. 'I hope you and I have many more memorable days together,' he said quietly. 'Now, I want you to meet some special people and then I'll drive you home.'

Five minutes later and Gilles ushered Nicola into one of the large luxurious apartment blocks overlooking the Port of Monaco. The concierge looked up briefly with a welcoming smile and a deferential 'Bonjour Monsieur Bongars' before the lift took them up to the eleventh floor.

Standing in the elevator, Nicola suddenly felt apprehensive at the thought of meeting people who lived in such opulent surroundings, however special they might be to Gilles. And why was it so important to him that she met them? She was about to ask Gilles to explain when the lift stopped.

Gilles pulled the safety door aside and pushed open the outer door that opened directly into a spacious apartment. Turning, he took hold of her hand and said, 'Come on. I want you to meet my parents.'

'Your parents? You could have warned me.'

She sensed that Laurent and Stephanie Bongars were as surprised to see her appearing with Gilles as she was to meet them. But they were charming and made Nicola feel very welcome once she'd got over her initial surprise.

'We're so pleased to meet with you,' Stephanie said with a perfect English accent. 'Gilles has told us so much about you.'

Nicola smiled as she shook hands with them both. 'I'm sorry Gilles hasn't told me anything about you, but I'm delighted to meet you!'

'Come, let's sit out on the balcony,' Laurent said. 'Anneka, the maid, will bring the tea.'

'Sorry, Papa, we can't stay,' Gilles said. 'Nicola has to get back for her son, Olivier. I just didn't want to bring her to Monaco and not introduce you to each other. I promise I'll bring her back – and Olivier – another day.'

Sitting beside Gilles as he drove her home, Nicola remembered his words that she was to ring him any time and he would be there for her. Today had proved that. She hadn't rung him, but he'd known instinctively how down she would be feeling and had wanted to be there for her. At this moment she couldn't find the right words to describe exactly how she felt but she knew she was incredibly happy he'd been there for her today.

34

Olivier was already in the kitchen of La Prouveresse when Nicola got back late that afternoon. Josephine, Odette and Henri were all keen to know the details of his first day at school.

Nicola stifled the pangs of guilt about not being home for his return and asked, 'How did it go then?'

Olivier nodded, his mouth too full of baguette and cheese to speak for a second or two.

'Okay. I'm in Luc's team for football. And there is a school band. The teachers seem all right too,' he added as an afterthought.

'Did you understand the lessons?' Nicola said anxiously.

'Mostly,' Olivier answered. 'Papa Henri's going to help me with my biology homework later. Where have you been?'

'Monaco with Gilles.' Nicola said, ignoring the speculative look Henri threw in her direction.

'Andrew phoned earlier,' Josephine said. 'His house sale has fallen through. He's going to be a couple of months late getting here. End of September, beginning of October probably, but could be even later.'

'Hope he has arrived in time for the olives,' Henri said. 'We need all the help we can get then.'

'I can help,' Olivier said.

'We'll need your help before then with the grapes,' Henri said. 'Another few days and they will be ready. It's an early harvest this year, summer has been so good.'

'Evenings and weekend work only for both harvests,' Nicola said. 'You're not taking time off school.'

Olivier pulled a face at her words but didn't say anything.

* * *

Henri was right about the grapes being ready for picking that week and, to Olivier's delight, Henri decided the coming Saturday would be the day.

Traditionally, lunch was always given to all the neighbours who came to help pick the grapes, although as Josephine said, 'These days, it's mainly Sylvie, Raoul and Claudine providing the extra hands. The vineyard is so small now, it takes hours rather than days to pick the fruit. But it's still an excuse for a social get-together.'

Nicola helped Josephine and Odette all day Friday to prepare the extra food that would be required the day the grapes were harvested.

Saturday mid-morning and Nicola placed a hand in the small of her aching back and slowly stretched. It had been an early seven o'clock start heralding a long morning spent out in the open with the hot sun beating down. Her hair under her straw hat was soaked with sweat and clinging to her head, but at last the row of vines Henri had given her was clipped bare of grapes.

Taking a swig from her almost empty water bottle, she glanced along the vines to see how the others were doing. Odette and one of the neighbours were working companionably along the far vine. They too would soon be finished. Raoul and Sylvie were already walking towards the trailer with their last full baskets. Henri was waiting by the tractor, ready to drive the harvest down to the co-operative.

Nicola emptied the contents of her basket into the trailer and began to make her way back to the farmhouse to give Josephine a helping hand with lunch.

Just as she reached the farmyard, she was surprised to see an unknown man getting out of a car parked in front of the barn.

'Bonjour, monsieur. Can I help you?'

The stranger turned at the sound of her voice.

'Bonjour, madam. I am here to see Josephine Dupont. On personal business,' he added quietly.

'Is she expecting you?'

The man shook his head. 'Non. But I am sure she will see me, once she knows I am here.' And he handed Nicola a card.

Nicola smothered an exclamation as she looked at the name on the card. She glanced up sharply at the man. 'I'm not sure—'

'Please. Just tell her I'm here. Waiting.'

Leaving the man standing by his car, Nicola made her way slowly into the farmhouse. She could hear the others making their way from the vineyard and the tractor and trailer chugging up through the field and on down the drive to the village. Nicola wished Odette would hurry up and arrive. She'd know what to do.

Josephine was standing by the stove carefully stirring the soup that was the first course for lunch.

'Bonjour, Nicola. Is it finished?'

'Yes. Everybody is on their way up. Henri has decided to take the trailer straight down to the co-operative and said don't wait for him to begin lunch. Olivier has gone with him.'

'Tch. Henri, he's always the same. Why can't he come with the others.' Josephine's smile faded as she glanced up at Nicola and saw the serious look on her face. 'There is something wrong?'

Silently Nicola held out the card the man in the farmyard had given her. She watched the colour drain from Josephine's face as she read the name.

'He seems to think you'll want to see him?'

'Pascal's here?' Josephine whispered.

Nicola nodded. 'He's waiting outside. If you want to run and hide, I can go and tell him you're not here.'

Josephine shook her head, a smile slowly creeping over her face. 'No. I'd love to see him. But privately. Not in front of Henri and everyone.' Biting her lip, she looked at Nicola. 'What shall I do?'

Nicola thought quickly and then said, 'You stay here and I'll go and tell Pascal to drive down to Le Jardin and you'll join him there. The builders will have gone to lunch in the village, so it should be quiet. It will definitely be messy, but at least it will be away from everyone up here.'

Nicola pressed her house key into a bemused Josephine's hand and quickly ran outside to give Pascal his instructions before anyone else arrived in the farmyard.

'Josephine will meet you down at Le Jardin de Dominic, which is my home. It will be more private than here.'

Pascal looked at her anxiously as she urged him to leave. 'You are sure Josephine will come to me?'

'I promise she'll be with you soon. Ten minutes at the most,' Nicola said. 'Now go before any of the family or Henri arrive.'

'Merci, madame.'

There was no sign of Josephine when Nicola got back to the kitchen. Just her discarded apron on the table and the soup bubbling noisily away on the range. A minute later, as Nicola sliced up the baguettes to accompany the soup, Josephine reappeared.

'How do I look?'

Nicola smiled. 'Beautiful.'

Josephine had changed from her working farm clothes into a pale blue dress and pinned her hair up into a loose chignon. Her eyes were sparkling and her whole demeanour was transformed. She was clearly looking forward to this unexpected meeting with Pascal.

'Thank you, Nicola.'

'Are you sure you don't want me to come with you?' Nicola asked. 'Or Odette?'

Josephine shook her head. 'No. This is something I have to do – want to do – on my own. I'll see you later.' And the kitchen door closed behind her.

Thoughtfully, Nicola carried on putting the finishing touches to lunch. Pascal had struck her as a sincere, genuine man during those few minutes on the farmyard. She hoped his arrival at La Prouveresse didn't mean there was trouble brewing for Josephine.

Odette was the first to arrive back at the farm and looked surprised to see Nicola on her own. 'Where's Josephine?'

Quickly Nicola explained about Pascal's arrival and Josephine's desire to see him by herself.

'Thank goodness Henri didn't meet him in the yard,' was Odette's immediate response.

'Why is Henri so anti Pascal?' Nicola asked curiously. 'Josephine looked thrilled at the thought of him being here after her initial shock.'

Odette sat down at the table, a heavy sigh escaping her lips. 'Oh Nicola, it's a long story, but basically, as Josephine told you, Pascal was the love of her life.'

'But she was married to his brother?' Nicola said.

Odette nodded. 'That was part of the problem.'

As she took a breath, about to explain things to Nicola, they both heard voices coming across the farmyard.

'We'll talk later. Meantime, not a word to anyone, while we have lunch. Ooh, how I'd love to be a fly on the wall down at Le Jardin right now...'

35

Half running, half walking down the farm drive before cutting across the field that would bring her out at the rear of Le Jardin de Dominic, Josephine tried to compose the thoughts that were racing around her mind.

When she'd agreed the lawyers could write to her with the news they had about Pascal Dupont, just knowing that he was still alive had been enough to make her heart skip a beat or two. Now, the prospect of meeting him again in a few moments was almost unbearable.

It was nearly thirty years since they'd last seen each other. Nearly thirty years of visiting the village shrine, wishing for his return. And nearly thirty years of pointlessly wishing 'if only' on her part. If only, she'd had the courage of her convictions, listened to her heart and not Henri or the conventional wisdom of the time.

The last time she'd seen him had been the visit Marc had written about in his diary when Pascal had taken him sailing. He'd charmed everyone on that visit and she'd begun to hope against hope that the impossible would be possible. So many times he'd begged and begged her to leave and start a new life with him. Instead she let Henri persuade her that it wasn't right and she would regret it if she went with Pascal.

With the exception of Odette, she'd hidden her broken heart from everyone when Pascal had finally accepted her refusal and left.

If only she'd done as he asked and gone with him. How different her life would have been.

Josephine sighed. It was far too late for regrets.

Now, as she opened the back gate of Le Jardin, she could only hope that Pascal had forgiven her for turning him away. Could this unexpected visit of his possibly be heralding in a future where they would be in contact again? Be friends for the rest of their lives?

But as she saw him standing, waiting for her, she knew that friendship with Pascal, even after all these years, was an impossible dream.

He heard the click of the gate and turned, smiling in relief as he saw her.

'Josie. You came,' he said quietly.

'How could I not?' Josephine asked gently, her heart soaring on hearing him call her Josie. He had always been the only one to call her that and she loved the way he said it.

She felt like a young girl again, her heart skipping a beat as she studied his face, still familiar after all the years, fighting the urge to reach out and touch him. Less familiar was the walking stick he was leaning heavily on.

'Logging accident in Canada years ago,' Pascal said, following her gaze. 'The leg didn't heal as it should, but then nobody expected me to live after the accident.'

Josephine's eyes opened wide in distress. 'I didn't know you'd had an accident.'

Pascal shrugged. 'It happened after you'd finally persuaded me there was no hope for us and, quite honestly, at the time I didn't care whether I lived or died. There seemed little point in telling you about my possible demise.' Pascal regarded her silently before saying, 'It was the worst time of my life.'

Josephine bit her lip as she looked at him mutely and nodded.

It was Pascal who broke the reflective silence that had surrounded them.

'You look wonderful.'

'Thank you.' Josephine smiled. 'You look good too.'

She hesitated before asking the one question she needed to ask.

'Why are you here? The notaire said you would write and he would forward the letter. The last thing I expected was for you to come here unannounced.'

Pascal regarded her steadily for several seconds before saying, 'I was too impatient once I knew you were willing for me to contact you. The thought of involving notaires and having to wait for your reply was impossible for me to do. I needed to see how you were, how you felt about the past. To hear the truth from your own lips, not from written words sent to someone else. I wanted to... to see if, like me, you had any regrets about the past?'

'How can you even ask that knowing what you meant to me?' Josephine whispered, not daring to hope what Pascal's reaction would be to her words.

'Could we talk about that and maybe give ourselves a second chance? Or is it far too late for us?'

Josephine swallowed hard, before slowly moving closer to him. 'I've never forgiven myself for sending you away, Pascal Dupont. Hurting you like that. Hurting myself. The world and people's attitudes have changed so much now. Perhaps the time is finally right for us to put the past behind us and look to the future. Give our love the second chance it deserves.'

Pascal stared at her. 'And Henri? You are willing to stand up to him this time?'

Josephine nodded. 'Henri has changed a lot recently and so have I. This time, if I walk away from anyone, it will be him, not you.'

As Josephine reached up and gently kissed Pascal, he drew her towards him in a tight embrace as if he never intended to let her go ever again.

36

Once everybody had left and Nicola and Odette were on their own in the kitchen clearing up after lunch, Odette began to tell Nicola the complex tale of Josephine and Pascal.

'All Josephine ever wanted to do was to get married and have a family. When she met and married Albert Dupont, she thought she was going to live happily ever after.'

'How did she meet Albert?'

'A friend from school was getting married in Nice and we were both invited to the wedding. Albert was a guest – a friend of the bridegroom's older brother. He appeared to be a successful businessman who took an immediate liking to Josephine. From the beginning, I didn't like him, but Josephine was deaf to any warnings about taking things slowly. She thought she was in love. They were married the same year.' Odette sighed. 'The reality when she moved to Paris was very different. France was going through desperate economic times in the early 1970s and Josephine found Paris to be a turbulent place after here. The student protests of the late sixties had given way to strikes and mass layoffs and general financial hardship all round. Parisians really struggled in those years.'

'A real culture shock for Josephine then,' Nicola said. 'It must have been so difficult.'

'That wasn't the worst of it though.' Odette paused. 'Albert was a few years older than her, set in his ways and, well, let's just say also he liked a drink almost as much as he liked the ladies. After he lost his business, he had his hands in some very dubious get-rich-quick schemes. Josephine quickly realised she'd made the biggest mistake of her life, but in those days, women were still expected to accept that was the way men were and put up with it.' Thoughtfully, Odette put the clean crockery on the dresser. 'Albert was also free with his fists at times.'

Nicola gasped at her words. 'He hit her?'

Odette nodded. 'She didn't tell me or Henri about the violence until it was too late. Thankfully, Pascal realised what was happening and protected her as much as he could. It didn't help matters though when she and Pascal realised how they felt about each other.' She shook her head as she glanced at Nicola. 'Pascal brought her home unexpectedly one weekend. I barely recognised my sister that day, she was in such a terrible state. Thin. Haggard. Nerves in shreds. Two days before, the three of them had been involved in an accident.' Odette gave a deep sigh. 'Albert's drinking was out of control, he was drunk more often than he was sober, and Josephine had learnt staying quiet and out of his way was the best, the only, thing she could do to protect herself.

'The afternoon of the accident, Albert had been drinking with a friend in a local bar and arrived back at the terraced house, where they lived on the top floor, in a drunken state. He'd managed to haul himself up the first flight of steps and was halfway up the second when he met Josephine and Pascal coming down.'

Odette paused as she stood up and moved over to the range.

'I think we could both do with another coffee,' she said, filling the base of the small old-fashioned expresso machine with water, before scooping enough coffee into the top half for the two of them and replacing it on the range and turning the heat up.

'When he saw them together, Albert apparently yelled at Pascal, accusing him of stealing his wife and calling him a "Libertine", in the rudest sense of that word. Josephine told me what happened next was because at that moment she knew things had to change, but she didn't expect the consequences her subsequent action caused.'

Odette's voice broke and she turned away from Nicola to listen for the gurgling water that indicated the liquid was being pushed through the machine.

She was silent for the few moments it took for the coffee to brew. Nicola, realising how upset Odette was even after all these years over what had happened to her twin, stayed quiet too and waited until Odette was ready to carry on with the story. It wasn't until she'd poured them each a cup of coffee and was back sitting at the kitchen table that Odette took a long, deep breath and continued to tell Nicola the chain of events that Albert's words kicked off.

'Josephine saw red. She realised how much she hated him, her life and the way he treated her. But it was the way he taunted Pascal in front of her that brought everything to a head for her. There was simply no way she could stand aside and allow a man she loathed to speak ill of the man she'd realised she loved. In that instant, before Pascal himself could respond, Josephine flew at Albert to punch him on his nose and as he took his hand off the banister to protect himself from Josephine hitting him, in his drunken state he lost his balance and fell down the stairs, banging his head several times on the way. By the time he reached the bottom, he was unconscious.'

Nicola looked at her, horrified. 'What happened next?'

'Pascal told Josephine to run to a nearby café to use their phone to call an ambulance.' Odette gave another sigh. 'Then the gendarmes arrived. A neighbour had heard the argument on the stairs and called them. Josephine found herself being accused of domestic violence against Albert, and the gendarmes called Pascal an accessory to the deed.' Odette shook her head in despair. 'All those years of being the victim of abuse and Josephine ended up being the accused. The only thing left for her to do was to say it had been a crime of passion, even though her punch had never landed, and hope for the best. And in the end the gendarmes did drop the case against both of them.'

'What happened to Albert?' Nicola asked.

'He died two days later from his internal injuries, which was when Pascal brought Josephine home. Pascal didn't stay long on that occasion, he had to return for the funeral, but he'd wanted to make sure that Josephine got home safely and was being taken care of.'

Odette went on to explain how a grateful Henri had thanked Pascal for bringing Josephine home. When Josephine finally told the family about her life in Paris, they were all horrified to hear about how unhappy she'd been with Albert and how he'd treated her. Josephine said she had no intention of returning to Paris and asked if she could stay permanently, help to run the farm. She simply couldn't take any more and needed to get away from the situation. Henri and Bernadette, of course, agreed. It was her home after all.

'It was such a different world in those days. But it was when she told us about her feelings for Pascal, that any friendship between Henri and Pascal was doomed,' Odette said with a shake of her head. 'Henri was grateful to Pascal, of that there is no doubt, but he was also adamant that a relationship between the two of them would be wrong. It all came to a head the next summer when Pascal came back – the summer that Marc wrote about in his diary? He came specifically to ask Josephine to emigrate to another country with him and start a new life there together, married or not.'

'She obviously said no,' Nicola said, 'but why, if she loved him?'

'Henri. He went berserk when he heard their plans and told her there was no way she could entertain a relationship with Pascal, even though the family were grateful to him for protecting her.'

'Why not if she was a widow?' Nicola said.

'In those days, to marry your husband's brother verged on... oh, some form of incest, I suppose,' Odette said. 'In the eyes of the Church – and Henri was still a churchgoer in those days – it was morally wrong.'

'So Henri made her give up Pascal and her dreams and stay here?' Nicola shook her head in disbelief.

'Henri told her it was her own fault she'd married the wrong brother in the first place and it was too late to change things. He convinced her too that if she simply ran away with Pascal, she'd spend her life looking over her shoulder, waiting for what would be considered their illicit relationship, to be discovered. After applying pressure for weeks, in the end he simply said it was her decision but he'd trust her to choose to do the right thing. Which, as far as he was concerned, was to send Pascal away and get on with her life here.' Odette sighed, remembering those traumatic days when her twin struggled with her conscience. 'Josephine, for her part, couldn't get past the guilt she felt over Albert. She once told me she felt that having to give up Pascal was her punishment for her part in Albert's death.'

Nicola shook her head. 'It all sounds like something out of the nineteenth century rather than the twentieth. Poor Josephine.'

'Publicly there was nothing Pascal could say or do. Privately he begged her to change her mind. Not to listen to Henri. In the end, though, he had no choice but to accept her decision and he left.'

'Henri has a certain penchant for interfering in people's lives, doesn't he?' Nicola said ruefully.

'He always thinks he knows best,' Odette agreed. 'Right now, I'm wondering how he's going to receive the news that Pascal is here.' She glanced at Nicola. 'I'm curious too – how did Josephine react when you told her Pascal was here?'

Nicola smiled. 'Shocked initially but so happy. I'd say she was really looking forward to seeing him.'

'Hopefully, Josephine is about to get the happiness she so deserves after all these years.' Odette sighed. 'But I don't suppose for one moment, Henri will be as pleased to see him, and I wish I wasn't the one who has to tell him about our unexpected visitor.'

Nicola was still in the kitchen talking to Odette when Henri and Olivier returned from the co-operative, Henri still unaware that Josephine had a visitor.

As Odette got up to get the lunch she had saved for them both, she looked at Nicola and mouthed the words: 'Here we go.'

'I'm going down to Le Jardin to do some work,' Nicola said quickly. 'Olivier, when you've finished your lunch, come straight down. I'd like you to give me a hand please.'

She mouthed an apologetic 'Sorry' at Odette before she left, but there was no way she wanted to be involved in the rekindling of an old family dispute.

37

The builders were busy working at Le Jardin when Nicola arrived at the cottage, but there was no sign of Josephine and Pascal or his car. As she weeded the flower bed in the shadiest part of the garden, she kept a watchful eye on the farm drive, parts of which were clearly visible from Le Jardin. How would Henri take the news about the arrival of Pascal and his sister's obvious delight at his presence? Fleetingly, Nicola almost wished, like Odette earlier, that she could be a fly on the wall up at the farm when Henri came face to face with Pascal.

Stretching her back after tugging a particularly long rooted nettle out of the ground, she saw Pascal's car slowly travelling up towards the farmhouse. It looked like that face-to-face meeting was about to happen.

Olivier ran into the garden five minutes later and Nicola looked at him expectantly. 'How are things up at the farm? Papa Henri all right?'

Olivier shrugged. 'Same as usual.'

Nicola considered his words. Had Odette postponed telling Henri about their unexpected visitor, wanting to wait until

Olivier had eaten and left before telling Henri about Josephine's old friend arriving? If that was the case, then no doubt he'd had a shock when Josephine walked in with Pascal.

'Mum! What do you want me to give you a hand with this afternoon?'

'I wanted to talk to you about what you want for your birthday next month,' Nicola said, dragging her thoughts away from the scene that would be happening right at this moment up at the farm.

Olivier looked at Nicola uncertainly. 'I don't want a party or anything for my birthday, just Luc and maybe a couple of the other guys to supper.' He paused. 'I'd really like a scooter though.'

'No way,' Nicola said instantly. 'You're far too young.'

'No, I'm not. It's not like it is in England, Mum. You can have a scooter here when you're fourteen. The school even organises the basic training courses. Luc's got one and it would—'

'No,' Nicola said firmly. 'I'm not even going to consider it. The roads around here are far too dangerous. All the boys I've seen riding scooters don't have any road sense. They do the stupidest things – like wheelies down the middle of the main road. And jumping red lights.'

'I wouldn't be that stupid,' Olivier muttered. 'And you let me ride that old bicycle on these "dangerous" roads.'

Nicola was silent. She tormented herself with worry every time Olivier was out on his bike. He didn't go far – just into the village and to Luc's home, a kilometre outside the village – but she was always on tenterhooks when he was out.

'And that's as far as I'm prepared to go because I trust you to be sensible. As soon as you're old enough, you can learn to drive a car.'

'But that's years away,' Olivier grumbled.

'Well, it's all that's on offer,' Nicola said.

She looked at Olivier exasperatedly, disliking the sullen look on his face. Was this the beginning of those dreaded teenage years she'd been warned about? Nicola sighed. Marc had always been so good at handling Olivier when he'd thrown a toddler tantrum. He could usually jolly Olivier out of himself. Would he have been good at handling a stroppy teenager too?

'I'm going to make myself a cold drink,' Nicola said, going into the kitchen. 'Would you like some ice cream?'

'Please.'

Nicola glanced at Olivier as she scooped some chocolate ice-cream, Olivier's favourite, into a bowl.

'When we go back up to La Prouveresse, Josephine's old friend from Paris, Pascal, might be there,' Nicola said in an effort to start Olivier talking to her again. 'You know, the Pascal that your dad mentioned in his diary?'

'D'you think he'll take me sailing like he did Dad?' was Olivier's immediate response.

'Doubt it. He's a lot older now. Besides, I'm not sure how long he'll be staying.' If Henri was true to form, it wouldn't be long.

Thoughtfully, Nicola sipped her drink, wondering how the meeting between Henri and the love of his sister's life had gone.

* * *

An hour later, they walked back up to the farm together: Olivier to make a start on his weekend homework, Nicola to offer Odette a hand preparing supper. There was no sign of Pascal's car in the yard.

The farmhouse was quiet as they walked in and Olivier went straight to his room while Nicola made for the kitchen, where she found Odette sat at the table, a cup of coffee in front of her, a serious look on her face. She glanced up at Nicola and smiled.

'Where is everyone?' Nicola asked.

'Henri's in the barn. And Josephine's gone out for the rest of the afternoon and evening with Pascal.'

'Have Henri and Pascal come face to face yet?'

'Yes. But it's no use asking me what was said,' Odette said. 'They both disappeared into the barn and Henri stayed there when Pascal and Josephine left.'

'Has Josephine told you why Pascal is here?'

Odette nodded. 'He's sixty-five soon and says the biggest regret of his life is his relationship with Josephine. He wanted to see if she had any regrets too, and if maybe there was any chance at this late stage of their lives of her changing her mind and making them both happy...' Odette grinned broadly at Nicola. 'I haven't seen Josephine looking so happy in years,' she added. 'She's promised to tell me everything when she gets back tonight.'

'Is Pascal staying here?' Nicola asked.

'No,' Odette shook her head. 'I did offer, but he didn't think it was a good idea. He's booked himself into the auberge in the village for a few days. He's going back to Paris at the end of the week. I'm not sure what Josephine is going to do then.' She sighed. 'I wish I knew too, how Henri reacted to Pascal.'

'Fingers crossed he behaved. Can I give you a hand preparing supper?' Nicola said in an effort to get Odette thinking about something else. 'Or shall I disappear out to the little garden for a while in case Henri comes in and wants to talk to you in private? The terracotta pots out there could probably do with some attention.'

'Supper's already prepared,' Odette said. 'Disappear indeed! Henri and I have had enough private talk for one day!'

38

Sitting next to Pascal as he drove them down the lane, Josephine struggled to take in what was happening. Staying in the kitchen with Odette while the two men had disappeared to the barn had been hard, but Pascal had said there were things he needed to say to Henri on his own. When he'd joined her and Odette in the kitchen afterwards, he'd given no indication of how their talk had gone.

Glancing across at him now, a large part of her wanted to ask him what Henri had said, how he'd reacted to his presence after all this time, but another, larger part, was indifferent to knowing about Henri's reaction. Pascal wanted to be back in her life and she had no intention of listening to anyone this time who dared to tell her that her love for him was wrong. It was inevitable she'd have to talk to Henri at some point, but she'd wait until she could do it with Pascal by her side and decisions had been made.

'We need to talk about the future, but for tonight we simply enjoy each other's company, yes?' Pascal said, glancing across at her.

Josephine smiled happily. 'I want to hear about everything

you've been up to since...' her voice wavered. 'Since I sent you away. All the places you've been. All your adventures.'

'I became something of a nomad for about twenty years,' Pascal said. 'I went to Canada and just moved from one part to another – the Rockies, the Great Lakes, the Prairies, Newfoundland. I saw bits of them all in the twenty years I was there. I worked as a logger; after the accident, I helped in a restaurant in Vancouver, then I travelled east and became a fisherman in Newfoundland, before returning across country and working on farms in the middle of the Prairies. Such a large country, so many different opportunities.' He sighed. 'But none of them meant anything to me. All I wanted was to forget the reason I was there – alone.' His hands gripped the steering wheel tightly. 'I also took to the drink, which initially helped, but one night in downtown Quebec, I realised I was in danger of following in Albert's footsteps.' Pascal was silent for several seconds. 'That was a wake-up call. These days I only ever drink wine with meals and to be sociable.'

Josephine reached out and placed her hand on his arm.

'Now it is your turn to tell me something about your life too,' Pascal said.

'Not a lot to tell you about that,' Josephine said quietly. She wouldn't, she decided, tell him tonight about her breakdown, about her utter despair that the rest of her life would be meaningless without him in it. There would be time enough to tell him all that. 'I stayed here and helped on the farm. Bernadette and Marc were both here then, of course. Things changed for everybody when Bernadette died, especially Henri, so I helped Odette look after him – which, in a strange way, helped me. Marc refusing to stay and take on the mantle of the farm in the future was another difficult time for Henri. But the farm and family became my refuge and my raison d'être. And that is the story of my life without you.' She smiled as she looked at him. 'We have so much catching up to do.'

'I've booked a table for dinner this evening at the auberge where I'm staying,' Pascal said. 'We'll get more privacy there than in the village restaurant.'

'Sounds perfect,' Josephine said.

After all these years, she and Pascal were having dinner together. She was so happy, she cautiously pinched her arm until it hurt, reassuring herself that she was awake, it wasn't a dream. Pascal Dupont was back in her life. And this time she had no intention of letting him go.

* * *

Later that same evening, Nicola was sitting in the little garden alone, sipping a glass of rosé and deep in thought as she watched the sun set. Olivier had asked Henri and Odette to have a game of boules in the farm yard. Henri had enrolled him in the junior section of the village boules club and he was keen to get in some practice before his first game as a member. Nicola had politely declined the offer to join them – she'd never been very good at ball games. When her phone rang, she picked it up quickly, hoping it might be Gilles, and she pushed a flicker of disappointment away when she saw Andrew's number on the screen.

'How are things going over there?' he asked. 'Building work progressing okay?'

'I'm really pleased so far. We should be able to move back in soon.'

'Henri behaving himself?'

Nicola laughed. 'Henri is Henri. Not only have I discovered he coerced me into moving down here using outright lies, I now hear he made poor Josephine reject the love of her life.'

'What do you mean – downright lies?' Andrew asked, ignoring the remark about Josephine.

'Oh, because of the complexity of French law, Olivier inherits anyway. I'll tell you everything when you get here.'

Nicola heard a sharp intake of breath down the phone before Andrew said, 'So, you didn't have to uproot yourself and Olivier and move to France at all?'

'No, it appears that I didn't *have to* move here,' she said quietly, emphasising the 'have to', 'but I am so glad I did. Not that I'm going to tell Henri that for some time. I love my life here already. I hope you will be happy here too, Andrew, when you get here.'

Fleetingly, she wondered about challenging him over his behaviour at the supper party before deciding against it. Better to let it go and keep focused on the fact that he'd told her he'd accepted the fact that they would only ever be friends.

'Any sign of a date yet for your arrival?'

Her question was enough to change the conversation and Andrew launched into the details of when his new mobile home would be arriving.

'Looks like it's going to be towards the middle, or even the end, of October before I get there, but my mobile home will be arriving in the next few days, which means I have a favour to ask you. Could you please take delivery, make sure they place it in the right place and sign for it please?'

'Of course.'

Nicola was thoughtful as the phone call ended a few moments later. Hopefully, rebuilding his house and preparing the campsite for visitors would keep Andrew busy and happy for the next few months and he'd love living in France as much as she did. She still wasn't entirely convinced that he was doing the right thing by moving to France and she hoped he wouldn't come to regret it.

* * *

It was three days later when Nicola received the phone call to say the mobile home would be arriving within the next ten minutes and she quickly made her way across to the campsite to open the gates.

As she watched the low-loader manoeuvre itself into position and the home was carefully eased on to its concrete pitch, Andrew rang.

'Has it arrived?' he asked anxiously.

'Yes. It's ready and waiting for you. I've got the keys,' Nicola assured him. 'I just have to check that everything is good inside before the truck leaves. Talk later.'

The inside of the mobile home was immaculate, the cushioned settee seats comfortable, the teak table polished. Nicola smiled to herself as she checked out the cupboards; she could do with a few like it in the cottage. The shower and toilet were shiny clean and the double bedroom with its built-in wardrobes was bigger than Olivier's bedroom in the cottage. Andrew would be more than comfortable living here whilst he rebuilt the house.

39

For Josephine, the days sped by like a wonderful dream. Pascal had extended his stay and they'd spent every hour they could together. By an unspoken mutual agreement, most of these hours were spent away from Henri and the farm and it was like their enforced separation had never happened.

Josephine got up extra early, did her usual farm chores before joining Pascal for breakfast in the village, where they decided on the plan for the day. One day they stayed local, another day they drove over the border into Italy, but whatever they did, wherever they went, there was a sense of love and contentment surrounding them both.

Tonight, the two of them had dined at the L'Olivieraie restaurant in the village and Pascal was driving Josephine home. Josephine glanced at Pascal as he turned out of the village onto the moonlit road that led to the farm.

'Please will you stop after the bend?' she asked quietly. 'I would like to visit the shrine with you.' Pascal nodded and slowed the car down before bringing it to a standstill.

'I've come here a lot over the years,' Josephine said, as the two of them stood hand in hand in front of the Virgin Mary and child in her niche a few moments later. 'I talked to her a lot as well as praying for forgiveness and for you, wishing for you to come back.'

'After I lost you, I'm afraid I gave up on praying,' Pascal said. 'But I never gave up wishing things could have been different.'

Josephine squeezed his hand. 'And now they are.'

'So, where do we go from here?' Pascal asked quietly. 'I told Henri the other day what I hoped would happen,' he continued quietly.

Josephine turned to look anxiously at him. 'What did you tell him – and what did he say? We've both been avoiding each other.'

'That you must do what you consider to be best.'

'I can't believe that Henri is being so reticent.' Josephine glanced up at Pascal and gave a wry smile. 'D'you remember what he said all those years ago? *He'd trust me to choose to do the right thing.* What exactly did you tell him?'

'That you and I were not going to lose touch with each other ever again. That the world has moved on and there was no reason why we shouldn't marry. That he was not going to keep me away from the only woman I've loved all my life, ever again.'

Josephine's eyes widened. 'I can imagine Henri's reaction to that.'

'He was surprisingly quiet. I think Henri has mellowed a lot since I last knew him.'

'Marc's death was a terrible blow to him,' Josephine said quietly. 'Deep down, he always hoped Marc would return. The fact that they were estranged when he died is something that Henri has had difficulty coming to terms with. Having Nicola and Olivier living here has made a huge difference to him. Henri dreads the thought of history repeating itself – he adores Olivier.'

'If he takes after Marc, he'll be a good man,' Pascal said. He squeezed her hand gently. 'But you haven't answered my question. Where do we go from here? Now Henri is once again leaving it up to you, shall we do what we should have done years ago and get married? If you still want to marry me after all this time?'

As he gave her an anxious look, Josephine realised Pascal was uncertain of her answer.

'I want to marry you more than anything,' Josephine said instantly. 'I've never stopped wishing for that. This time I definitely know what is best for me and I have no doubt that marrying you is the right thing to do.'

'Then I have something for you,' and Pascal reached into his pocket before holding her hand up in front of him, and slipping a vintage art deco oval diamond ring onto her finger.

'It's beautiful.' Josephine swallowed hard, trying to stop the tears that were threatening as she gazed at the ring. 'I can't believe that, after all this time, you and I are getting a second chance,' she said, shaking her head. 'It's like a dream. Promise me I won't wake up tomorrow and you'll have disappeared.'

'Josie, ma chérie, believe me, this is for real – for the rest of our lives.'

* * *

The others were all in the kitchen when Josephine and Pascal walked in. Odette took one look at her sister and smiled, hoping that Henri was ready for the news she was sure he was about to be given.

'Pascal has asked me to marry him – and this time I've said yes,' Josephine said, holding out her hand for everyone to see her ring while defiantly looking at Henri.

'Congratulations,' Odette said, enveloping her twin in a hug. 'I couldn't be happier for you both.' She turned to Pascal. 'Welcome to the family, Pascal, at long last.'

Nicola too, hugged Josephine and offered the happy pair her congratulations. 'That's a truly beautiful ring.'

A silent Henri had moved across the kitchen and was opening the fridge door. Closing it, he looked at Pascal.

'After our conversation, I prepare for this. Glasses, Odette,' he said, holding a bottle of champagne and carefully twisting the wire. 'We need to toast the happy couple.'

The bottle opened with a gentle pop and Henri filled the glasses with the sparkling liquid.

'Congratulations to you both. I echo Odette's words – welcome to the family, Pascal. I wish you both every happiness.'

Josephine took a sip of her drink before placing it on the table, walking over to Henri and hugging him. 'Thank you, Henri. You have no idea how much your blessing means to me and Pascal.' She kissed his cheek before moving back to stand at Pascal's side, her hand in his.

* * *

Later, when the champagne had been drunk and everyone was making their way to bed, Josephine went outside to the farmyard to say goodnight to Pascal as he prepared to drive down to the auberge. Standing there after kissing him goodnight and watching him get in the car, she sighed, thinking about the logistics of setting up their life together.

'I wish you weren't leaving tomorrow. I'm going to miss you.'

'I've a few loose ends to tie up and I promise I'll be back in less than a week,' Pascal said. 'And then we will have to start to seriously make some decisions. When and where we get married? Where are we going to live? Down here? Paris? Or somewhere completely new to both of us? I have no preference for anywhere so long as we are together.'

'Those two decisions are easy. I would definitely like to have the civil ceremony here at the mairie, followed by a church service. As to where we will live, while I'd love to spend some time in Paris...' Josephine paused. 'Lay the ghosts of the past and see the modern city, I don't think I could live there permanently. I'm a real countrywoman at heart these days. Could we live down here and go for visits – or would you find being so close to Henri a problem?'

Pascal shook his head. 'Non. I think Henri and I will become good friends at this stage of our lives. I've got a small apartment in Paris which I'm happy to sell, so we need to find something down here. While I'm away, you can start to collect some house details from the immobilier and when I get back we can start looking in earnest.'

Watching him drive away, Josephine gave a contented sigh. Her life was going to change so much in the next few months. Leaving the farm, Henri and Odette, for a second time to be married, was a big step but the right one for her. The thought of being called Madame Dupont again filled her with joy because this time she would be Pascal Dupont's wife, something she'd dreamed of forever.

40

True to his word, Pascal was back in less than a week and everyone quickly became accustomed to his presence at the farm. He'd shaken his head when Josephine had suggested he used one of the spare bedrooms. 'Non, ma chérie, it would not be right.' Instead, he'd booked himself into the auberge for an extended stay, leaving Josephine after supper every evening and reappearing after breakfast.

It was the second week of October when Henri announced at supper one evening that the olives were ready for picking.

'I have booked the contractor to come to the farm early tomorrow morning to start the harvesting of the commercial crop. He will take it down to the co-operative at the end of each day for the usual processing.'

His words fell into a stunned silence as both Josephine and Odette looked at him in surprise.

'Can we afford a contractor? You've always insisted we pick them and take them down ourselves, that we didn't need to waste good money,' Josephine said.

Henri looked at her and Pascal sitting together. 'Things

change, as you two know. I can see a future for the family farm now, so I will need to make sure I stay up to date with progress. What we'd take over ten days to pick, the machine will shake from the trees in three days or less. We still have to do the original trees on the old terrace ourselves by hand – there's no way the machine can get close enough. That's a couple of days' work on its own – picking, cleaning, pressing, bottling. We'll still need everyone helping for that. But the olive farm needs to be mechanised and pulled into the twenty-first century.'

The twins shook their heads as they looked at Henri with big smiles on their faces. 'Unbelievable,' they said together.

'What?' Henri asked irritably.

'You, finally coming into the modern world. Who'd ever have thought that would happen?' Josephine said, reaching for Pascal's hand. She knew that Olivier's arrival had started the change in Henri but there was no doubt that Pascal's re-appearance in her life had also contributed to this new attitude of Henri's. Whatever the cause, it was welcome – Henri was clearly a happier man.

When the contractor arrived early the next morning with a huge machine that scraped through the entrance to the farm with barely a centimetre to spare either side, there was an audience waiting to watch it in action. Olivier, in particular, was fascinated by the machine and the way it was manoeuvred to cover the ground beneath each individual tree with a large ridged plastic sheet, before two arms wrapped themselves around the first tree and gently shook the trunk, causing the olives to fall onto the plastic. Once the fruit stopped falling, the plastic sheet and its bounty were rolled up and the olives disappeared into the bowels of the machine. Minutes was all it took and then the machine moved to the next tree.

'Bien, now we go and do the original trees up on the terrace the old-fashioned way,' Henri said.

The olive terrace at the back of the farm was quiet, the noise of the machine busy in the fields below an indistinguishable hum in the air. Henri and the twins swung into methodical action, their years of experience an invaluable asset as they helped Olivier and Nicola to spread the sheets under the trees, before placing the ladders in position ready for the higher branches to be reached.

As they worked, Henri explained how these ancient trees with their gnarled and twisted trunks were the very first ever planted on the farm over two hundred years ago. 'Thankfully, they survived the killer frost back in the 1950s that decimated hectares of olive trees in the area.'

Listening to Henri telling Olivier about the olives, Nicola realised that Henri was surprisingly sentimental about this grove of trees, his love of the farm evident behind his words. At that moment she suddenly understood why it had been so hard for him when Marc had turned his back on the farm, why it had become so personal for him.

Nicola was happy to stay on the ground, reaching up to clear the lower branches of their fruit with a short handled forklike tool, while Olivier was allowed to climb the ladder to reach the top branches with the long-handled version of the tool. Picking the olives and bending down to scoop them off the sheets into containers was hard work but the temperature of the October sun was kinder to work in than the heat of the sun when the vines were picked back in September.

There was something about working amongst these ancient trees that Nicola found soothing. Peace, that down the centuries olive trees had become a symbol of, seemed to envelop her and give her hope that the future would be fine. If one day Olivier wanted to take on the responsibility of running La Prouveresse, Nicola knew it would be something he would do whole-heartedly. He had already learnt so much from Henri and their deepening relationship had already convinced Nicola that she had done the right thing in moving to France. The farming gene might have skipped past Marc, but it appeared to have found a welcome home in his son, although, if in the end, Olivier decided, like Marc, the farming life wasn't for him it would be his choice, no-one else's.

As she stretched up to reach some elusive olives, out of the corner of her eye Nicola saw the two granite memorial stones on the edge of the field. Remembering the day Marc's ashes had been scattered in this part of the farm, Nicola smiled to herself. She would never have guessed on that day, she and Olivier would be living and working here so happily in just a few months.

41

Once the olive harvest was in and the process of extracting the oil was underway in the old barn, Nicola decided to spend the next couple of days starting to sort things at Le Jardin. As much as she loved living at the farm it would be good to be back down in her own home. She knew she'd miss the company and the family atmosphere that had drawn them all together over the last few weeks. And her relationship with Henri had definitely improved, thank goodness. In fact, she was beginning to feel a grudging respect for the man, the way he kept going despite all the tragedy he'd had to endure.

The builders had finished the major structural alterations – even the wooden spiral staircase was in position, giving access to the new bedrooms and bathroom in the attic. Downstairs, a French door had been fitted into the sitting-room wall, which, in time, would lead into the planned conservatory. At the moment, it just led outside to a bare patch of concrete. The builders had already knocked down the adjoining outbuilding and added the rubble to the pile to be removed. Most of the rubble had been removed already and the builders had promised the rest would be gone before they started to plaster the walls. Hopefully it would only be another week at the most before they finished and she and Olivier could move back. Then she could finally start to turn Le Jardin into the cosy home she wanted before the winter nights drew in.

Her phone pinged with a text message from Andrew. Brief and to the point.

Nearing the A8. Eta about 9 o'clock but weather is diabolical.

As Nicola quickly answered,

Drive carefully,

there was a quiet knock on the back door before it opened and Gilles said, 'Bonjour, Nicola.'

She turned, a welcome smile on her face.

'Weather is getting worse,' Gilles said. 'The roads are starting to flood and there's already some minor landslides in the gorge. Still, the meteo say the worst should be gone within twenty-four hours.' He leant forward to kiss Nicola on the cheek and managed to shower her with rain from his wet hair. 'Oh, sorry. It's looking good,' Gilles said, glancing around. 'Made a real difference.'

Nicola nodded. 'Now I've got to start thinking about paint colours and begin looking for some furniture. In the UK, I'd head for the nearest auction or second-hand place. Odette mentioned an Emmaus depot near Nice. I think I might need a visit there.'

'There is also a big dépôt-vente warehouse in Nice, a smaller one in Antibes. I can take you when you're ready, if you like.'

Nicola smiled her thanks.

'Are you and Olivier doing anything next Sunday?' Gilles asked. 'There's a motorbike scramble in the next valley and I wondered if you'd both like to a day out. Give me a chance to get to know Olivier better,' he added quietly. 'Although if this weather keeps up, the event may well be cancelled.'

'Not sure that anything to do with motorbikes is a good idea at the moment,' Nicola answered ruefully. 'I've refused to buy him a scooter for his birthday, so, of course, I'm the world's worst mother! But yes, I'm sure Olivier would enjoy it, if it's not rained off.'

* * *

It was still raining as Nicola made her way back up to La Prouveresse and the gentle breeze of earlier had turned into a fierce wind. Nicola could hear the ominous sound of thunder rumbling away in the distance and the occasional flash of lightning lit up the mountains behind the farm and she was pleased when she reached the sanctuary of La Prouveresse.

Odette and Josephine were in the kitchen preparing supper when Nicola opened the kitchen door and walked in.

'Ah, Nicola, come on in out of the rain,' Odette said. 'Thank goodness we picked the olives when we did. They've just given out a severe weather warning for later this evening and tomorrow.'

'It's bad enough out there already,' Nicola said. 'I can't believe how quickly the weather has changed. Where are Olivier and the men?' she asked, hanging her coat up to dry near the range. 'I'm guessing in the barn with Henri and Pascal, his new friend?'

Josephine laughed. 'Not sure what they are doing, but I guess it will be something manly,' and she laughed. 'They'll be over soon ready to eat, I'm sure.'

A loud clap of thunder overhead made both of them jump and Odette moved across the kitchen to pull the curtains just as a flash of lightning illuminated the figure of Olivier running across the yard followed by Pascal and a slower Henri, trying to reach the sanctuary of the farmhouse kitchen as quickly as they could.

42

Pulling into the toll-booth at the Nice exit on the autoroute, Andrew heaved a sigh of relief. Two more hours and he should be at the campsite.

Torrential rain and wind had made the last hundred kilometres of driving treacherous. His whole body ached from the effort of concentration to keep the van moving safely and he'd be more than relieved when this journey was over. Winding the window down to feed his money into the machine, an icy blast of wind filled the cab. As Andrew took his ticket, a gendarme, his face red with cold, peered in through his window.

'Your destination, monsieur?'

'I'm picking up the N202,' Andrew said, 'and heading up towards Digne for about sixty kilometres.'

'Been a couple of rockfalls on that road. And the weather's not good past Touët-sur-Var.' The gendarme pointed in the direction of a small group of lorries waiting by the side of the road. 'If you really can't wait, I suggest you tag on the end of that convoy – they're making for the N202 as well. Although my advice to all of you is to park up overnight, find a hotel and continue the journey tomorrow.'

Andrew glanced across at the lorries. 'I really want to get there this evening, so I'll join the convoy,' Andrew said.

The gendarme shrugged. 'Take care then – and be prepared for roadblocks and diversions. Bonne chance.'

Andrew wound the window up, rubbed his tired eyes with his knuckles before putting the van into gear and moving off to take his place at the back of the slow-moving line of traffic heading for the main road out into the country.

Thirty kilometres later he saw the lorries turn one by one into the car park of a roadside café. Andrew hesitated before following them into the car park and glancing at his watch: 7.30 p.m.

The conditions hadn't been as bad as he'd feared – the expected roadblocks and diversions the gendarme had warned about hadn't materialised on the stretch he'd driven. And now the rain had eased slightly and there was very little traffic about, driving wasn't so difficult. He'd have a quick cup of coffee, phone Nicola and give her an approximate time he would arrive at the campsite and then set off on the last forty kilometres. With luck, he'd be having supper with Nicola and Olivier up at La Prouveresse by ten o'clock.

Everybody, including Henri, who'd cancelled his supper date with Sylvie because of the bad weather, was in the kitchen enjoying an 'aperitif hour' before supper when Andrew rang.

Nicola answered the phone, with a quick 'Excuse me' to everyone.

'Hi. I've just stopped for a coffee. The weather's eased a bit so it shouldn't take me too long to do the last stretch. Reckon I should be with you in about an hour. Hour and a half at the most.'

'I've put a small gas heater on in the mobile home, so it should be nice and cosy for you. And there's some bedding down there, although the aunts and Henri say you're more than welcome to stay up here tonight.'

'Thanks, but I'm really looking forward to spending my first night down on the campsite.'

'There's a bottle of champagne in the fridge here ready to celebrate your arrival. See you soon.'

Thoughtfully, she replaced the receiver. Andrew had sounded really positive and upbeat. It had been like talking to the old Andrew again and she was surprised to realise just how much she was looking forward to having him around on a daily basis.

A loud clap of thunder made them all jump.

'Sounds as though the storm is hanging around the valley,' Josephine said. 'Hope it doesn't delay Andrew too much.'

'It's not a good night to be travelling,' Pascal said. 'The weather further down might be improving, but up here, nearer the mountains, you never know what can happen.'

* * *

The weather took a turn for the worse soon after Andrew left the café. Sighing to himself, he peered tiredly through the rain-bombarded windscreen. It looked as though this last hour of driving was going to be the most difficult of the whole journey. The rain was so heavy now that the wipers were struggling to cope. Impossible to stop on this narrow section of the road but surely there had to be a layby soon where he'd pull over and wait a while to see if the weather improved.

With the van headlights highlighting the debris littering the road from minor rockfalls, Andrew carefully negotiated his way along the mountain road through the gorge. Large boulders and smaller rocks were scattered all over the road. In amongst the stones and gravel were rock plants which had been torn by their roots from the precipices above. He passed several of the giant nets placed high above the road to stop any major falls before they hit the ground, but as Andrew drove slowly up through the valley, they seemed hopelessly inadequate.

As he braked for the dangerous bend that would take him on the final homeward stretch, a loud rumble of thunder and a flash of forked lightning across the valley to his right momentarily took his attention to the rock face at the side of the road in front just as the boulders began falling...

43

The wind finally blew the storm away overnight and everything was calm early the next morning as Nicola stumbled down the drive and across the road to the campsite.

Blinded by the tears that were coursing down her cheeks, she struggled for several moments before inserting the key into the door of Andrew's mobile home. The heater she'd plugged in yesterday afternoon to warm the place for Andrew's arrival was still switched on and filling the small space with muggy air. Absently she bent down and switched it off before slowly looking around.

Everything appeared normal. She wandered through into the kitchen area. Provisions she'd bought in the village shop still stood on the small work surface – coffee, tea, biscuits, a packet of pasta, salt, kitchen paper. She knew without looking there was milk, butter, cheese, eggs and vegetables in the small fridge. She'd placed them all there only a day ago – alongside the champagne to toast Andrew's arrival and his new life in France.

Miserably, she opened the door leading to the small bedroom. Was it only two days ago that she and Olivier had brought the boxes with the few clothes and possessions Andrew had left behind and arranged them in his new home?

She took a sweater out of a drawer and hugged it against her.

Hoping to make the place feel a bit more like home, she'd put a framed photograph of the three of them on the shelf by the window. She'd found it in one of Andrew's boxes when she was unpacking his things.

Clutching the sweater and the photo to her, she collapsed onto the settee and stared blindly out of the window. Late last night when the gendarme had knocked on the door of La Prouveresse and everyone, except Olivier, had gathered in the kitchen where the tragic news had been broken, she'd struggled to accept what she was hearing. That morning, in Andrew's deserted mobile home, the truth finally began to sink in.

Andrew was dead. He would have been killed instantly when his van had been hit by boulders before skidding off the road, the police had told her.

Nicola looked at Andrew's happy smiling face staring out at her from the photograph. He'd been so looking forward to starting his new life in France.

A gentle knock on the door started her.

'I thought I'd find you here,' Gilles said. 'May I come in?'

Nicola smiled tremulously at him and nodded. 'You're out and about early.'

'I heard about the accident and wanted to be with you.'

'Thanks,' Nicola said. She glanced at him tearfully. 'I just feel so guilty. All I can think about is the fact that he was coming here because of me. If I hadn't moved here, he would never have thought of moving to France. He would never have bought the campsite, and he wouldn't have been driving on that road last night. He'd still be alive. It's all my fault.'

'Stop right now,' Gilles said, taking her into his arms and

holding her tightly. 'I know from what you've told me that Andrew had finally accepted that you and he would only ever be friends. He was looking forward to building his own new life in France and, given time, I know he would have been happy, would probably even have met someone special to enjoy life with.' Gilles pressed his lips gently against her forehead. 'You are blaming yourself for something you cannot possibly be responsible for. Andrew was the one who decided to move to France and buy the campsite. He was the one who thought that his life here in France would be better. And he was the one who took the decision to continue driving in horrendous conditions on a mountain road he didn't know well.' Gilles paused. 'How's Olivier taken the news?'

'Badly. He's lost his father and now a man he regarded almost as a substitute father, all in a short space of time.' Nicola remembered Olivier's tear stained face and the way he'd fallen into her arms that morning when she and the aunts had told him the terrible news. 'I've left him with Henri and the twins for a little while in the hope,' she paused and shrugged. 'I don't know what I hope really, but I had to get out for a while. I'm sure though, the hot drinks and sympathy they will be showering him with, will help.'

Gilles continued to hold her tightly for several silent moments. 'Well, we'll just have to make sure he knows we're here for him. I remember when my sister died, I just couldn't cope. My poor parents were beside themselves with grief and worry.' He looked thoughtfully at Nicola. 'The next few weeks are going to be hard for both of you, but promise me you'll let me help in any way I can.'

As Nicola mutely nodded her thanks, Gilles took her by the hand.

'Now come on, let's lock up and get you out of here.'

* * *

Andrew's funeral was held in the tiny village church. Gilles had helped Nicola with the funeral arrangements, help she had accepted gratefully. Without any relatives back in the UK, it seemed pointless to send Andrew's body back there. Far better to lay him to rest somewhere he'd loved and near people who had cared for him.

Nicola was amazed at the number of people who came to pay their last respects to this Englishman they'd barely known, including a tearful Agnes and her mother. Wreaths and bunches of flowers covered the ground as Andrew was laid to rest in the small cemetery west of the village. Standing listening to the priest intoning the words of the service, Nicola found thoughts of Marc, as well as Andrew, filling her mind. Now, as the priest said a benediction for Andrew, Nicola included Marc in her prayers. A final goodbye to two men who had both played large but different parts in her life.

Nicola found the only way to stop brooding about Andrew and the accident was to immerse herself in work.

Olivier had been surprisingly willing to return to school when Nicola suggested it after the funeral.

'Moping around here isn't going to help either of us,' Nicola had told him gently. 'I know it's hard, but we both do need to keep our lives as normal as possible.'

Two days after the funeral, Nicola was down at Le Jardin to see the builders off. Wandering around, assessing the cleaning and decorating she had to do before moving back, Nicola felt nothing but tiredness. The pleasure she'd been expecting to feel in her newly finished home simply wasn't there.

Standing in the new enlarged open-plan downstairs room, looking out over the garden, she sighed. There was more work to be done out there. Next door she could see Gilles' car parked beside the Taste of the Countryside building. Briefly, she thought about wandering over to see him.

'Nicola?' Claudine's voice floated into her. 'Ah, there you are,' she said. 'Great transformation. I expect you can't wait to start decorating now.'

Nicola smiled ruefully. 'I'm not sure I've got the enthusiasm right now,' she said. 'Anyway, how are you?'

'I'm fine. I wonder whether you'd like to come to Nice with me tomorrow?'

'I should really make a start here, but another day won't make much difference – maybe if I can find some paint for the sitting room it will inspire me to start. Plus, I need some inspiration for Olivier's birthday next week, so yes, a couple of hours shopping in town would be great.'

'How is Olivier?' Claudine asked as they made their way outside.

'He spends all his spare time practising the same mournful tune on his saxophone over and over. Henri's spending a lot time in the barn with him – although I'm not sure that's a good idea.' Nicola sighed. 'I'm hoping next week's birthday tea will be the beginning of getting Olivier back into doing other things. At the moment he doesn't even want to see Luc or play boules with the village lads.'

Organising his birthday treat was proving difficult. Olivier had simply shrugged when asked what he wanted to do on the day. When Nicola pressed him on what present he would like, he pulled a face.

'You know what I want. If I can't have a scooter or a motorbike, I don't want anything.'

Nicola had refrained from telling him off for his rudeness – she could only hope that he'd slowly start to work through his grief soon. Nobody should have to cope with so much tragedy in their life at such an early age.

* * *

Henri was in the kitchen at La Prouveresse, talking to Josephine and Odette, when Nicola returned from Nice the next day. Opening the kitchen door, Nicola heard Josephine's happy voice.

'Pascal and I have made a rendezvous to see the priest about arranging our wedding after the civil ceremony. We were thinking near Christmas. I'm hoping you will walk me down the aisle,' she added quietly to Henri. She smiled at the short nod he gave her. Josephine turned to Nicola. 'D'you think Olivier would like to be a witness?'

'Congratulations,' Nicola said, hugging her. 'I'm so glad everything is finally working out for you. And yes, I'm sure Olivier would love to be a witness.'

'Nicola, I want a word with you,' Henri said. 'About Olivier.'

'Is he all right?' Nicola asked quickly. 'Where is he?'

'In the barn, practising as usual,' Henri answered shortly. 'But I am worried about him. He's not a happy boy.'

'I know that,' Nicola said. 'Unfortunately, there's nothing I can do to alter recent events.'

Henri looked at her sternly. 'I want to get him a bike for his birthday.'

'No,' Nicola snapped.

'The lad really needs something good to happen in his life.'

'Oh, and you call buying him something dangerous like a motorbike good?'

'Non. But I thought we could get him a trials bike. That way, he could ride it on the farm and have lots of fun, but it wouldn't be legal for him to take it on the road.'

'We?' Nicola gazed at Henri in surprise. He was actually talking to her before doing something that might upset her.

'I thought it could be a joint present from us both.'

Nicola looked at him in surprise. 'Yes, an off-road bike he can ride around the farm could be the answer. And yes, a joint present from us both is a good idea. But where will you find one so close to his birthday?'

'I've already got it,' Henri said sheepishly. 'It's hidden in the storeroom.'

Nicola looked at him in disbelief before laughing. 'Oh Henri. Trust you to do things the wrong way round!'

44

Nicola woke early on the morning of Olivier's birthday and lay for a few moments listening to the sounds of the farm and thinking about the future. Living up at La Prouveresse was so easy. Over the last week or two since Andrew's accident, the aunts had comforted her and taken charge of everyday things, insisting she stayed up there for longer. It would be all too easy to stay here and let Josephine and Odette carry on spoiling her.

Nicola ran her hands through her hair. The time was coming when she simply had to return to her own home and get on with her life once again. A few more days and she would definitely summon the energy to move back down to Le Jardin. She and Olivier both needed to get back into their own routines.

Pulling on her jeans, she resolved that next week she'd get to grips with the decorating and start to move things back into Le Jardin. Hearing Olivier and Henri's voices as they came out of the storeroom, Nicola crossed to the window and watched Olivier pushing his new trials bike across the farmyard. Damn. She'd thought she and Henri would give the bike to Olivier after breakfast, instead Henri had done it alone. She smothered a sigh. No point in making an issue of it and spoiling the day before it had even begun properly.

Henri opened the gate into the field and, once inside, Olivier kick-started the machine. Nicola watched anxiously as he began to rev the motor before jumping on the saddle and attempting to steer the bike across the rough terrain.

Henri somehow managed to run alongside him for the first thirty metres or so, shouting instructions, before stopping and watching as Olivier wobbled his way across the field and back again.

Opening the window, Nicola leaned out and called to him. 'Well done, Olivier – and happy birthday!' As Henri glanced up at her, she mouthed a silent, 'Thank you,' at him, which he returned with a smile and a short nod.

* * *

By the time everybody had gathered for his birthday tea later in the day, Olivier was confident enough to demonstrate his skills up and down the farm drive. Later, watching him chase Luc with a paint-balling gun – Gilles' birthday present – Nicola began to feel optimistic that perhaps the healing process over Andrew was starting.

'It's so good to hear Olivier laughing again,' she said to Gilles, who was standing at her side.

'Yes,' he agreed, glancing at her. 'But how are you coping, Nicola? I was talking to Ann-Marie earlier and she mentioned you hadn't signed up yet to be a producer for Le Goût de la Campagne. The opening ceremony isn't all that far off, and I know she wants to invite all the registered producers.'

'It's on my "things to do" list,' Nicola said. 'I've promised myself that this week I will start to get my life back on track.' She smiled wanly at Gilles. 'I've really neglected the garden recently. The weeds are unbelievable. Still, spending time sorting out both the cottage and the garden will be good for me.'

'I can give you a hand a couple of evenings if you like,' Gilles said. 'But only on the condition that you let me take you and Olivier out to supper afterwards.'

'Thanks,' Nicola said. 'Josephine has already offered her and Odette's services for decorating, but I might need you to help us move the furniture.'

'You know you only have to ask,' Gilles said.

As they stood companionably side by side, watching Olivier and Luc playing around, Gilles' hand sought hers and held it tightly. Strangely comforted by the gesture, Nicola happily entwined her fingers with his.

* * *

The next morning, after Olivier had left for school, Nicola, determined to make a start on getting things back to normal, walked down to Le Jardin. Both Josephine and Odette had promised to join her mid-morning to help start decorating, so Nicola made a beeline for the neglected garden.

Two hours later, she was pleased with her efforts. The weeds in the vegetable plot had been banished and she had a small basket full of baby carrots, lettuce and some freshly dug potatoes.

The aunts arrived as she was walking towards the cottage to put the produce in the kitchen.

'We've brought a flask of coffee and some sandwiches for lunch,' Josephine said.

'And we met La Poste,' Odette said, handing Nicola an official-looking letter.

Nicola frowned when she saw the English postmark. It was

from Andrew's solicitors. She'd been in constant touch with them over the funeral arrangements and costs and she was sure she'd done everything that was necessary for them. Slowly she opened the letter.

'Nicola – whatever's the matter?' Josephine asked. 'You've gone very pale.'

Nicola looked up from the letter. 'Apparently I'm Andrew's sole beneficiary. He's left me everything – including the campsite.'

There was silence as the sisters regarded her.

'I don't know what to do,' Nicola said. 'I knew he didn't have any close relatives, but I didn't expect this.' She shook the letter. 'I've got more than enough with Le Jardin. I really don't want to run a campsite as well.' She sighed. 'But it seems so unfeeling just to give up on it. Andrew had such dreams for the place. I feel guilty enough over things already without—'

'Nicola, you've got to stop blaming yourself for Andrew's death,' Odette interrupted sternly. 'I'm sure it's the last thing he'd want you to do. He'd want you to get on with your life and be happy.'

'There's no rush for a decision, is there?' Josephine asked. 'These things always take time to sort out. It will be the New Year before all the paperwork is sorted.'

'You're both right,' Nicola said. 'I'll put off making a decision until next year. See how I feel then.'

'En fait!' Josephine said. 'I have an idea,' she said, touching Nicola's arm. 'Would you rent it to Pascal and me? You know we've been looking for somewhere to live down here, which is turning out to be impossible. Places are either too big, too small, or too far away from here. The campsite would make an ideal base for us. It's close enough to everybody, and yet private too. In fact, rather than rent it – I'll suggest to Pascal we buy it from you.'

45

'Are you sure you want this place?' Nicola asked, looking anxiously at Josephine and Pascal. 'You're taking a lot on. I'll understand totally if you've changed your minds.'

Late afternoon and the three of them were standing outside the mobile home on the campsite. Pascal, Josephine and Odette were off to Paris on an evening flight from Nice later but had wanted to see the place and decide whether they wanted to buy it before they left.

'It's perfect for us,' Pascal said. 'Close enough to family but far enough away to let us lead our own life. The mobile home is comfortable and cosy and organising the rebuilding of the house will give me something to do – a challenge for my retirement.'

'The lawyer in the UK dealing with Andrew's things knows you want to buy the place and he's starting to get all the legal stuff together for the transfer,' Nicola said. 'But I'm quite happy if you want to make a start before it becomes official in the New Year. And Gilles said if you want any help with doing the plans and getting planning permission, for change of use to a private residence, just ask.'

'Appreciate that,' Pascal said. 'It would be convenient for me to use the mobile home as my base from now until our wedding, if that's all right.'

'Have you finalised the date yet?'

'The twenty-third of December – 5 o'clock at the mairie and 5.30 at St Josephs,' Josephine answered. 'And supper afterwards at the hotel in the village. I still can't quite believe it,' she added, smiling happily at Pascal, who returned her smile warmly.

'How is Gilles?' Pascal asked, turning back to Nicola.

'Fine. I've left him and Olivier putting the finishing touches to the sitting room in the cottage. I promised them both a special supper, so I'd better get back. Look, take the keys and treat the place as yours from now on,' and she held the keys out to Pascal. 'Good luck.'

Pensively, Nicola made her way up the drive to the main road. It was such a short time since Andrew had excitedly cajoled her into looking at the campsite, full of plans for it and his future. And now, here she was getting rid of it as quickly as she could without a qualm because it didn't fit in with the life she was building for herself in France. At least it was going to be Josephine's home, a woman whom Andrew had known and liked, not to a complete stranger.

Tiredly, she pulled the wooden gate closed behind her. Andrew's death had not only shocked her, it had left a surprisingly deep, grief filled hole within her, leaving her devastated at yet another loss. Her own grief was one thing but how to help Olivier come to terms with it was her biggest worry.

He'd become very fit over the last few months with all the physical work he was doing on the farm, a growing spurt had seen him gain a few inches, height wise, and he'd also started to broaden out, becoming more and more like Marc as the weeks passed. The combination of grief at Andrew's accident and the hormones burgeoning as his body started to change had turned him into a grumpy, moody adolescent. Mischief was the only one who could count on being greeted with a hug and gentle words these days. Since the accident Olivier had taken to disappearing to ride around the farm on his bike for hours rather than spend time with her or the aunts. Faithful Mischief would chase after the bike for some time until tiring, then she'd curl up near the hedge, watching and waiting patiently.

Nicola, knowing how Olivier had looked up to Andrew, and realising he was having difficulty in coming to terms with the double blow of losing two important people in his life that fate had dealt him, was loath to tell him off. But the time was rapidly coming when she would have to say something about his behaviour. Particularly if he carried on being so aggressive and rude towards Gilles.

Nicola sighed. Life would be much easier if only Olivier could accept Gilles' increasing presence in their lives. She'd really had to insist he stayed to give Gilles a hand decorating today while she went across to the campsite. Hopefully Oliver hadn't been a handful for Gilles during her short absence. She quickened her pace and hurried up the path towards Le Jardin.

'Hey, it's looking good,' she said, glancing into the sitting room where Gilles was up a ladder painting the ceiling and Olivier was putting the finishing touches to the walls.

'Should be dry enough to put the furniture you already have back in place tomorrow,' Gilles said. 'And then you can move in again.'

Nicola smiled ruefully. 'I was hoping to be down here for the weekend, but with the aunts going to Paris tonight with Pascal for a wedding dress shopping expedition, Olivier and I are staying with Henri for a few more days. But next week we're definitely moving back in,' she said determinedly.

'Are you going to register with Taste of the Countryside now the house is finished to offer, how you say, B & B?' Gilles asked.

Nicola laughed at his accent as she shook her head. 'I'm not sure about the B & B side of things. Maybe Olivier and I will just enjoy the place for a little while on our own.' She glanced at him and smiled. 'It's been good staying up at the farm but now we need to spend some time together in our own space. Get on with our lives.' The thought 'And finally put the past behind us' crossed her mind, but she didn't voice the words.

'Can I go out on my bike now you're back?' Olivier demanded grumpily, banging the lid back on a paint pot.

Nicola gazed at him, exasperated, before saying. 'Supper's at 8.30. Up at La Prouveresse. Don't be late.'

'Will he be there?' Olivier jerked his head in Gilles' direction.

'Olivier, that is extremely rude. Apologise at once.' Nicola stared at her son in disbelief. 'How dare you speak like that? And yes, Gilles will be joining us for supper.'

Sullenly Olivier glanced towards Gilles and said. 'Sorry,' but then, to Nicola's distress, as he left the room, they both heard him mutter, 'Think you should stay away from my mother anyway – all the men she likes die.'

In the silence that followed the slamming of the door, Gilles slowly climbed down the ladder. As the tears began to fall down Nicola's face, he gently took her in his arms and held her tightly as she sobbed against his shoulder.

It was several minutes before she raised her head and looked at him.

'Maybe Olivier has a point. Perhaps you should stay away from me. They say these things come in threes and—'

Gilles silenced her with a kiss. Seconds passed before he quietly said. 'Don't be silly. Nicola, I couldn't stay away from you and Olivier now if I tried. And I don't want to. Since I met you, my life has taken on a whole new meaning. All I want to do is take care of you.'

Nicola, speechless after the delight of the unexpected kiss, gazed at him. Not since those early days with Marc had she been kissed like that. Gently she reached out and stroked his cheek. 'That was lovely.' She couldn't quite bring herself to say 'can we do it again', but seemingly Gilles read her mind because his lips claimed hers again for several seconds before he broke away.

'I promise you Olivier will accept my presence eventually. At the moment though, I think he's not only sad and angry about his father and Andrew, but he's also frightened to make friends with me in case he gets hurt again.'

Nicola sighed. 'He's grown up so much this past year, but deep down he's still a young bewildered boy.'

Gilles nodded. 'Try not to worry. He won't drive me away, I promise. Next time I'm alone with him I'll try to reassure him. Now, how about some food? I'm starving. Don't think I can wait till supper-time.'

'That's something you both have in common anyway,' Nicola laughed, realising that right now she had to put those two kisses out of her mind. 'Olivier is always hungry. Come on then, let's go up to La Prouveresse and I'll make you a sandwich before I start making supper.'

The sisters were preparing to leave for their Parisian trip when Nicola and Gilles walked into the kitchen.

'We'll be gone for three days,' Odette said. 'Josephine should find a dress easily in that time, me – I might have a problem,' and she looked ruefully down at her curvaceous body. 'Haute couture is not known for being available in large sizes and I really want something that little bit special,' she said wistfully.

Nicola smiled sympathetically. 'Do you have any particular colour in mind?'

'Josephine is reckoning on going for something in ivory and she wants me in something similar, although I fancy a bit more colour, but we'll see.'

After waving goodbye to the sisters and Pascal, Nicola made Gilles a sandwich and then started to prepare supper. Gilles gave her a hand setting the table.

'The cheeseboard looks a bit bare,' he said. 'Is there some more somewhere?'

'Josephine said she's left a fresh baguette, a round of Brie and some Bleu d'Auvergne in the pantry,' Nicola said, concentrating on making the sauce for the salmon.

Gilles shook his head. 'Can't see it. Just a small piece of Cantal and some Roquefort. No bread either, just some biscuits.'

'Strange. Josephine is usually so organised. I guess she's had other things on her mind recently. Oh well, we'll just have to make do for tonight. I'll go shopping in the morning.'

Nicola turned as the kitchen door slammed closed, expecting to see Henri and Olivier, but Henri was alone.

'Olivier not with you?' she asked. 'I told him to be back in time for supper and it'll be ready soon.'

'I saw him whizzing around the field on his bike about an hour ago,' Henri answered. 'He'll be here soon – Mischief will see to that. She'll be wanting her own food.'

* * *

Olivier hadn't turned up by the time supper was ready and Nicola went out to the petit jardin to ring the bell that hung there. Once used to summon the farm workers for meals, it could be heard even in the distant fields. Olivier knew its sound and had always been back at the farm within ten minutes of the bell being rung.

But not this evening.

'He wouldn't have gone on the road with his bike, would he?' Nicola asked anxiously.

Henri shook his head. 'Give him another ten minutes and then I'll go and look for him.'

'But where to start looking?' Nicola said.

'I think I might have an idea where he's gone,' Henri admitted quietly.

Nicola glanced at him sharply.

'He's been asking me questions recently about La Chambre du Roi.'

Nicola was puzzled.

'It's a small cave that the locals christened after the more famous one up in the mountains. It's about a kilometre or so the other side of the copse,' Henri paused. 'It was a favourite place of Marc's. He would go there whenever he needed to sort things out in his mind. Said it was a healing place. Wonderful panoramic views. There's also a spring and a small pond...'

'A pond?' Nicola interrupted.

'More of a dew pond, it's only centimetres deep,' Henri said, giving her a reassuring look. 'Olivier has been talking about the place since I told him about it. I promised to take him there but...' he shrugged. 'I've been so busy, I kept telling him later. My guess is he's gone across country to find the place for himself.'

'Can you give me directions?' Nicola asked, reaching for her coat.

'Non, Nicola. I will go. I'll take the tractor and go by road, it will be quicker,' Henri said.

'I'll stay with Nicola,' Gilles said quietly. 'Unless you want me to come with you?'

'Non merci.' Henri shook his head. 'It's best if you stay here.'

Gilles reached into his pocket and handed Henri his mobile

phone. 'Here, take this and ring Nicola when you get there. If he's not there, we'll phone the gendarmerie.'

Nicola bit her lip at the mention of the gendarmerie.

'Olivier will be fine. Try not to worry.' Gilles said.

'I can't not worry. And what if it turns out that bad things really do come in threes and something awful has happened to Olivier?' As Gilles put his arms around her in a tight hug, the tears started to flow down Nicola's cheeks.

46

Sitting in the entrance to the cave, Olivier carefully broke the baguette into pieces and spread the Brie with his pocket knife as Mischief watched him hopefully.

'Here you go, girl. This will have to keep you going until we get back,' and he divided the pieces between them.

As he ate, Olivier looked around him. Just knowing that it was one of his dad's favourite places made him feel good. He'd spent some time exploring La Chambre – even finding the initials MJ carved into the slab of rock near the back of the cave, a discovery which, to his surprise, had made him cry.

He glanced up at the night sky. He should really have left for home before now, it was going to be difficult retracing his steps in the dark. Fleetingly, he felt a twinge of guilt knowing his mother would be worried, but maybe she hadn't missed him yet as she had Gilles for company.

Olivier thought about the ride home – the bike didn't have lights and there was no comforting moon in the sky yet. It would be easier to go home by road, but having promised his mum he wouldn't take his bike on the road, Olivier knew he had no choice but to return cross-country.

Below him, open countryside gave way to olive terraces and then, lower down on the south-facing slopes, were the vineyards with their old derelict single-storey cottages. Beyond that, the distant stone walls and ochre-coloured roofs of the village had disappeared from view as darkness fell. Now, Olivier watched as the occasional headlight from a car driving through a distant village flashed between the buildings.

The rutted track he'd ridden along had merged into the shadows of the fields it skirted. Owls preparing to start out on their nightly supper hunt screeched from the high branches of the overhanging oak trees. Bats flew above his head in and out of the cave.

Standing up, Olivier gave the last piece of baguette to Mischief and looked apprehensively in the direction of home, but before he could kick-start his bike, Mischief cocked an ear and whined softly.

Olivier heard the noise then too and recognised the rhythmic chug of the farm tractor engine. Glancing down towards the track again, he saw headlights slowly coming towards the cave. Papa Henri had guessed where he was.

As Henri stopped the tractor, Mischief finished her bread before dashing off with a frenzy of barking to greet Henri and his dog, Meg.

'Bonsoir, Olivier,' Henri said quietly. 'You all right?'

Olivier nodded and waited as Henri took the mobile phone Gilles had given him out of his pocket and hesitated.

'Know how to use this?' Henri asked, looking at Olivier.

'Of course.'

'Better phone your Maman then,' and Henri handed him the

mobile. 'Tell her you are all right and you'll be home within the hour.'

Olivier could hear the relief in his mother's voice when she answered the phone.

'Thank goodness,' was all she said. 'Gilles and I have been so worried about you.'

'I'm sorry,' Olivier said. 'Papa Henri is giving me a ride home on the tractor. See you soon,' Olivier said, before handing the phone back to Henri and bracing himself for the telling off that was about to happen. Instead, Henri started to wheel the bike towards the tractor.

'Better get this secure,' he said.

As Olivier helped tie the bike onto the tractor, Henri glanced at him.

'Any particular reason for coming out here today?'

Olivier shrugged his shoulders. 'Nope. Just wanted to see the place. I didn't mean to worry Mum. Is she very cross? Are you cross? You don't seem to be.' Over the past few months of getting to know his grandfather he'd learnt that, like his dad, Papa Henri didn't always react in the way he'd expected.

Henri shook his head. 'No-one is cross, just concerned. Gilles, he worry too.'

'I wasn't very nice to Gilles earlier,' Olivier said quietly. 'I know Mum thinks I don't like him, but I do. It's just that...' he bit his lip before continuing slowly. 'Dad died and now Andrew, what if something happens to Gilles as well? Mum will be sad again. Why can't we just be us for a while – with you and the aunts of course. We don't need anyone else,' he added, looking at Henri.

Henri sighed before saying, 'Life has been hard for your Maman. She didn't really want to come to France after your Papa died.'

He paused before continuing.

'She told me she needed a life, friends of her own, as well as the Jacques family if she was going to be happy here.'

'But it was her idea to move to France. She said we'd have a better life over here with family around. And she's got the small-holding she's always wanted,' Olivier protested.

Henri shook his head. 'Non, Olivier. It was my idea. I insisted you came.'

He paused, choosing his words carefully.

'I think it's time you know the truth. You see, mon petit fils, one day La Prouveresse will be yours and I wanted you to grow up here, get to know it. I accused your Maman of denying you your birthright if she didn't move to France. I made her believe that if you didn't come I'd disinherit you.' He glanced at Olivier. 'But I was lying. You're my direct descendant and you inherit, whatever I do – or don't do.'

'Does Mum know that you lied to her now?' Olivier demanded.

'Yes.'

Olivier was quiet for several seconds. 'So she could decide to return to the UK?' He glanced anxiously at Henri. 'You don't think Mum is planning on doing that, do you? I don't want to go back. I really like living here.'

'I think your Maman also likes living here now things are settling down. And having Gilles as a special friend is also helping.'

Henri was silent as he pulled the rope securely around the bike and tied the final knot to the tractor framework. When he was happy that the bike was secure, he turned to Olivier and put his arm around his shoulders.

'Talk to your Maman, Olivier – you'll find you're still her number one concern and you always will be but she needs Gilles in her life too. Life has not been easy for her in recent years and I'm sorry to say that I added to her troubles after your dad died, making her sacrifice her life, and home, to bring you here. She is a remarkable woman. If anyone deserves some happiness it is your Maman, and Gilles, I know, is a good man. D'accord?'

Olivier gave Henri a tremulous smile as he nodded. Papa Henri telling him that his mum had said she'd need friends of her own here in France had made him realise that he was lucky to have Luc and his other friends at school. He hated the fact that he'd made his mum sad worrying about him. When they got back to the farm he'd make sure to give his mum a big hug and say sorry to her and Gilles.

'Papa Henri, have you got a torch in the tractor?'

'Oui?'

'May I show you something then before we leave?'

Olivier turned and led his grandfather over to the rock at the back of the cave.

'Look, I found Dad's initials.' And he shone the torch over the weathered MJ carved into the stone. Directly beneath it were two smaller, freshly cut letters – OJ. Olivier glanced anxiously at his grandfather. 'I won't get into trouble for that, will I? I just wanted to be somewhere permanently with Dad.'

'No, you won't get into trouble for that.' Henri put his arm around Olivier and held him tight. 'I miss him too, Olivier, but together we will keep his memory alive.'

47

'I now declare Le Goût de la Campagne officially open,' and the local mayor cut the red ribbon with a flourish and pushed open the door. A smatter of polite applause broke out before everyone moved into the building to sample the wine and other produce on offer.

Nicola, walking around with Gilles, looked at the variety of produce from the surrounding countryside. Seeing it all gathered together in one place was amazing. Honey, olive oil, wine, lavender, apple juice, poultry, cheeses, preserves – the choice seemed endless.

Nicola's own small offerings of fresh herbs and some other plants were quickly snapped up.

'I think next year when you have Le Jardin de Dominic really organised you will have a good outlet for your produce,' Gilles said.

'I hope so,' Nicola said. 'Now the house is finished, I can concentrate on the garden – something I'm really looking forward to.'

Next to the Tourist Information corner with its leaflets and maps, there was also a colourful display of local artists' work, from paintings to bowls and sculptures made from olive wood. The display of photographs Nicola had seen back in August had been enlarged and Nicola spotted another one of Le Jardin de Dominic that she instantly put on her want list.

'Do you think Josephine and Pascal would like one of these?' Nicola said, picking up a large salad bowl complete with olive wood servers and examining it.

Just two days before the wedding and she still had to find a suitable present.

'Good idea,' Gilles answered. 'Will you excuse me for a while? I have to go and talk to Ann-Marie. Shouldn't take long, then we can collect Olivier and join my parents for lunch.'

Nicola was still looking undecidedly at the salad bowl when Odette joined her.

'If you are thinking of buying it for Josephine and Pascal,' Odette said, 'I know Josephine would love it, she was casting covetous looks at the one we have up at the farm, but I told her hands off, it stays at the farm!'

'In that case,' Nicola laughed. 'I'll definitely get it for her – unless you want to?'

Odette shook her head. 'I've already got them something else.'

'Have they decided where they're going after the wedding?' Nicola asked.

'The plan is for them to spend the night at the hotel after the reception, a couple of days over Christmas at La Prouveresse and the campsite – which, by the way, they are going to return to its original name – Moulin du Roc. And then, on the twenty-eighth, they're off on honeymoon proper.'

'And before you ask, not even Josephine knows where they're going. Pascal has simply promised her somewhere exotic!'

'Lucky lady,' Nicola said. She glanced at Odette curiously. 'It's not only Josephine's life that is about to change. How do you feel about living up at the farm without her after all these years?' Nicola smiled. 'Not to mention coping with Henri on your own?'

'You and Sylvie will have to help me keep him in his place.'

Odette laughed at the look on Nicola's face.

'Actually, I've decided to make some changes in my life too,' Odette said quietly. 'Get more involved with things away from the farm for a start.' She looked around before leaning towards Nicola and whispering, 'Some of the villagers feel women should have a bigger say in the running of things. I've been asked to consider standing for maire.'

'Won't you be in competition with Henri?' Nicola asked.

Odette smiled as she shook her head. 'Funnily enough, when I told him I was thinking of standing, he said he'd decided not to stand for maire after all and wished me bonne chance!'

'Well, if it's what you want, I hope you win the election,' Nicola said. 'You'll make a great maire. And don't forget, any time you feel lonely up at the farm, or Henri gets to you, you know where I am. Mind you, the amount of time Olivier spends up at La Prouveresse with you, I suspect you're glad of some peace and quiet when he comes home to me.'

'I adore having him and you around,' Odette said quietly. 'I'm just so pleased that things are finally starting to sort themselves out. Olivier seems a lot happier these days.'

Nicola nodded. 'I think he is. Certainly less moody and he seems to have accepted Gilles too, which is a relief. They were huddled together yesterday in the sitting room making a list or something. Wouldn't tell me what they were up to – just looked very guilty and said it was a secret!'

'Your friendship with Gilles also seems to be flourishing, n'est pas?' Odette said, looking at her quizzically, and Nicola blushed.

But before she could say anything, Gilles himself returned carrying a package. He saw her looking and smiled.

'Time to leave everyone to it,' he said. 'And no, I'm not telling you what this is. You'll find out soon enough.'

48

'Olivier, are you ready? We're going to be late if we don't leave now!' Nicola called.

'Just got to get something from the shed,' Olivier said, running down the stairs and out of the back door. 'Can you give me a hand please, Gilles?'

Nicola sighed exasperatedly as Gilles went to follow Olivier.

'Patience, ma chérie,' Gilles said. 'I'll see you at the car,' and he closed the back door behind him.

Preparing to leave, Nicola glanced around smiling happily. The cottage was, finally, exactly how she'd imagined it could be. Now, with the Christmas tree and the other seasonal decorations in place, the sitting room was ready for her first Christmas in France. A Christmas that promised to be as family-orientated as she'd always dreamt it should be.

Christmas Eve, she and Olivier were joining everyone up at La Prouveresse for the all-important French family celebration evening meal. Odette and Josephine had been planning the menu for weeks – including the traditional thirteen desserts.

'Why thirteen?' Nicola had asked when Odette had roped her in to help make some.

'The idea is you have a small taste of each one and it's supposed to help protect you through the coming months. Thirteen represents Christ and the disciples.'

'Well, it certainly makes our plum pudding look a bit boring,' Nicola had laughed as she prepared some candied fruit under Odette's expert guidance.

Christmas Day, everybody, including Gilles who was spending Christmas Eve with his parents, was coming to Le Jardin for a traditional English lunch. Nicola hugged the secret that Gilles was staying overnight on Christmas Day, ready to celebrate Boxing Day with her and Olivier, to herself. For the first time in years it seemed she was looking forward to Christmas.

Before she turned to leave, she looked at the two framed photographs hanging in pride of place at the side of the fireplace. The sepia one of Le Jardin de Dominic, and the one of Henri and family standing outside the farmhouse – copies of the ones she'd seen in Le Goût de la Campagne which Gilles had ordered and framed for her.

'An early Christmas present,' he'd said.

Smiling happily, she went outside and locked the cottage door behind her.

Watching as Olivier and Gilles appeared from the shed clutching an assortment of tin cans, boots and balloons between them, Nicola laughed out loud.

'So this is what you two have been plotting. I hope Josephine and Pascal are ready for this quaint English custom.' She glanced at her watch. 'They should be at the Hotel de Ville by now. Come on. We don't want to be late for the church ceremony.'

Although Josephine had originally wanted Olivier to be a witness, when she discovered he was too young, she and Pascal decided that just Henri and Odette would witness the legally necessary civil ceremony. Olivier could sign the church registry with them instead.

'It is the church service that is really important for me,' Josephine had said. 'And for that I want all my family there.'

Nicola caught her breath as Gilles drove into the village. The Christmas decorations were all switched on, lending a magical quality to the place in the half-light of the late afternoon. A canopy of small white twinkling lights hung across the square, gently swaying in the breeze. Ropes of fairy lights had been wound around the trunks of the plane trees and up into their bare branches and a large silver star hung between the trees that stood at the entrance to the market.

The words of 'Silent Night' floated on the air from a group of carol singers gathered around an accordion player by the Christmas tree at the head of the square. Villagers were beginning to gather in small crowds waiting for the bride and groom to make their appearance from the Hotel de Ville.

The smell of lilies on the altar of St Joseph's wafted out through the open doors and Father Georges, standing in the porch of his church, smiled benevolently at the gathering crowd.

Nicola, Gilles and Olivier made their way to the steps of St Joseph's to wait with Sylvie, Claudine and Philippe and were soon joined by Raoul, Marie and Luc.

As Raoul kissed Nicola on the cheek in greeting, he said quietly, 'Marie and I are engaged.'

'Oh, I'm so pleased for you,' Nicola said. 'Luc is better then? He accepts you more?'

Raoul shook his head sadly. 'Non. But...' he looked apologetically at Nicola. 'It was really Andrew's accident that brought things home to Marie. She finally saw that we'd wasted too many precious years feeling guilty.'

'Things will work out with Luc, I promise,' Nicola said gently. 'If there is anything I can do to help?'

'Thanks,' Raoul said. 'Olivier seems to be a beneficial influence on Luc, so if you and Gilles can keep up the good work, it should rub off on Luc!'

Nicola glanced across at Olivier who was laughing at something Gilles had said. Looking at her son in the smart suit Pascal had insisted on buying him for the wedding, Nicola felt a surge of pride coupled with hope for the future.

A cheer broke out on the opposite side of the square and Pascal and Josephine appeared hand and hand in the doorway of the Hotel de Ville, with Henri and Odette behind them.

As people clapped and cheered, the accordion player moved across the square towards them, effortlessly playing 'What A Wonderful World' as he walked.

Josephine, radiant in her heavily embroidered medieval-style ivory coat dress with a small round train, held Pascal's hand tightly as she smiled tremulously at the crowd of well-wishers.

The notes of 'What A Wonderful World' faded away, to be replaced by a jazzed-up version of 'The Wedding March' as the musician beckoned the happy couple to follow him in a dance around the square, before slowing the beat down to the more sedate, traditional march, and leading them to St Joseph's for their church dedication service.

Followed by family and friends, Josephine and Pascal mounted the steps and entered the quiet sixteenth-century church where Father Georges welcomed them and began the service.

Nicola, standing between Gilles and Olivier, brushed away a tear of happiness as she watched Josephine finally making her vows to the one man she had always loved.

Gilles looked at Nicola lovingly as he squeezed her hand

entwined with his. He leaned towards her and whispered in her ear.

Nicola held her breath for several seconds, before smiling and leaning in to softly answer to Gilles' question.

It would be several hours before she told anybody her secret – but her acceptance of Gilles' whispered proposal meant that there would be another wedding in St Joseph's sometime in the not-too-distant future.

ACKNOWLEDGMENTS

This book was originally published a few years ago as *Follow Your Star* and editing, tweaking and adding over 23K words has been a real challenge. So, as always, my first thanks have to go to my editor Caroline Ridding, who once again encouraged me to dig that bit deeper to improve the story. Thanks too, go to Nia, Amanda and Claire for all the marketing and the work they do behind the scenes. Team Boldwood rocks! Grateful thanks to copyeditor Jade and to Rose the proofreader.

Thanks to the Boldwood Girls (and Boys) who are all so supportive of their fellow authors.

And finally to all my readers a big Thank You – you are the reason I write.

Love,

Jennie

MORE FROM JENNIFER BOHNET

We hope you enjoyed reading *Falling for a French Dream*. If you did, please leave a review.

If you'd like to gift a copy, this book is also available as an ebook, digital audio download and audiobook CD.

Sign up to Jennifer Bohnet's mailing list for news, competitions and updates on future books.

http://bit.ly/JenniferBohnetNewsletter

Explore more gloriously escapist reads from Jennifer Bohnet.

ABOUT THE AUTHOR

Jennifer Bohnet is the bestselling author of over 10 women's fiction novels, including *Villa of Sun and Secrets* and *The Little Kiosk By The Sea*. She is originally from the West Country but now lives in the wilds of rural Brittany, France.

Visit Jennifer's website: http://www.jenniferbohnet.com/

Follow Jennifer on social media:

facebook.com/Jennifer-Bohnet-170217789709356

twitter.com/jenniewriter

instagram.com/jenniebohnet

bookbub.com/authors/jennifer-bohnet

ABOUT BOLDWOOD BOOKS

Boldwood Books is a fiction publishing company seeking out the best stories from around the world.

Find out more at www.boldwoodbooks.com

Sign up to the Book and Tonic newsletter for news, offers and competitions from Boldwood Books!

http://www.bit.ly/bookandtonic

We'd love to hear from you, follow us on social media:

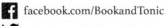 facebook.com/BookandTonic

 twitter.com/BoldwoodBooks

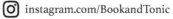 instagram.com/BookandTonic

THURS 15 MAC   12.00   20th FEB
BLOOD TEST.   11.30   ONC.

Printed in Great Britain
by Amazon